HIGH IMPACT

What Reviewers Say About Kim Baldwin's Books

"[Kim] Baldwin and [Xenia] Alexiou have written a barn burner of a thriller. The reader is taken in from the first page to the last. The tension is maintained throughout [*Dying to Live*] with rare exception. Baldwin and Alexiou are defining the genre of romantic suspense within the lesbian genre with this series."—*Lambda Literary*

"With vivid scenes, sexual tension, and gorgeous word pictures, [*Breaking the Ice*] is a book that will glue you to your chair until the last page is turned."—*Just About Write*

"*Missing Lynx* puts the thrill in thriller. A dark, edgy, often grisly tale, *Missing Lynx* has the grit and pacing of a Bourne saga, but with highly engaging and thoroughly challenging female characters. Not for the faint hearted."—*Lambda Literary*

"Fast paced, with dazzling scenes that stir the heart of armchair travelers, *Thief of Always* grabs the reader on the first page and never lets go. [Kim] Baldwin and [Xenia] Alexiou are skilled at fleshing out their characters and in describing the settings…a rich, wonderful read that leaves the reader anxiously awaiting the next book in the series."—*Just About Write*

"With each new book, Kim Baldwin improves her craft and her storytelling. *Flight Risk*…has heated action and vibrant depictions that make the reader feel as though she was right in the middle of the story. …fast moving with crisp dialogue, and effective use of the characters' thoughts and emotions…this reviewer could not put the book down. Baldwin outdid herself with *Flight Risk*. …her best storytelling to date. I highly recommend this thrilling story."
—*Independent Gay Writer*

"A hallmark of great writing is consummate characterization, and *Whitewater Rendezvous* does not disappoint…Captures the reader from the very first page…totally immerses and envelopes the reader in the Arctic experience. Superior chapter endings, stylishly and tightly written sentences, precise pacing, and exquisite narrative all coalesce to produce a novel of first-rate quality, both in concept and expression."—*Midwest Book Review*

"Unexpected twists and turns, deadly action, complex characters and multiple subplots converge to make [*Lethal Affairs*] a gripping page turner."—*Curve Magazine*

"Nature's fury has nothing on the fire of desire and passion that burns in Kim Baldwin's *Force of Nature*! Filled with passion, plenty of laughs, and "yeah, I know how that feels…" moments, *Force of Nature* is a book you simply can't put down. All we have to say is, where's the sequel?!"—*Outlook Press*

"'A riveting novel of suspense' seems to be a very overworked phrase. However, it is extremely apt when discussing…*Hunter's Pursuit*. Look for this excellent novel."—*Mega-Scene Magazine*

"[*Hunter's Pursuit*]…a fierce first novel, an action-packed thriller pitting deadly professional killers against each other. Baldwin's fast-paced plot comes…leavened, as every intelligent adventure novel's excesses ought to be, with some lovin'."—Richard Labonté, *Book marks*

"In a change of pace from her previous novels of suspense, Kim Baldwin has given her fans an intelligent romance, filled with delightful peeks at the lives of the rich and famous…the reader journeys into some of the hot dance clubs in Paris and Rome, and gets a front row seat to some very powerful sex scenes. Baldwin definitely proves that lust has gotten a bad rap. *Focus of Desire* is a great read, with humor, strong dialogue and heat."—*Just About Write*

Visit us at www.boldstrokesbooks.com

By the Author

Hunter's Pursuit

Force of Nature

Whitewater Rendezvous

Flight Risk

Focus of Desire

Breaking the Ice

High Impact

The Elite Operatives Series with Xenia Alexiou

Lethal Affairs

Thief of Always

Missing Lynx

Dying to Live

HIGH IMPACT

by
Kim Baldwin

2011

HIGH IMPACT

ISBN 10: 1-60282-580-7
ISBN 13: 978-1-60282-580-2

THIS TRADE PAPERBACK ORIGINAL IS PUBLISHED BY
BOLD STROKES BOOKS, INC.
P.O. BOX 249
VALLEY FALLS, NY 12185

FIRST EDITION: DECEMBER 2011

CREDITS
EDITOR: SHELLEY THRASHER
PRODUCTION DESIGN: SUSAN RAMUNDO
COVER PHOTO BY NYODA
COVER DESIGN BY SHERI (GRAPHICARTIST2020@HOTMAIL.COM)

Acknowledgments

Most of my readers know I have a passion for writing about Alaska. This is the third book I've set there, after *Whitewater Rendezvous* and *Breaking the Ice*. It's such an extraordinary backdrop for a nature-based adventure, full of plot possibilities and vivid sensory images, and I embraced the chance to revisit some favorite characters from the previous novels as well as introduce a new couple to the landscape. As with my previous books, it's my profound hope *High Impact* not only entertains, but also inspires readers to join in the battle to preserve our greatest national treasure—the Alaskan wilderness—from the threat of oil drilling and other perils.

My deep appreciation to all the women at Bold Strokes Books who contribute so much to making my books the best they can be. Radclyffe, for her leadership and vision, and for taking the chance on a new and inexperienced author. Editor Shelley Thrasher, who inspires and challenges me to always improve my craft, and catches me when I fall short. Graphic artist Sheri, for another amazing cover. Connie Ward, BSB Publicist and first-reader extraordinaire, and all the other support staff who work behind the scenes to make each BSB book an exceptional read.

I'd also like to thank my dear friends Jenny Harmon and author Carsen Taite, for your invaluable feedback and insights. Jenny, you help keep me on track and motivated during the writing of each manuscript more than you'll ever know.

Although all the characters in my books until now have been fictional, two in this book are based on real-life friends, Dita Eidson and Toni Whitaker, who were the top contributors to an auction I held to benefit a woman with cancer. I hope they're pleased with how they're portrayed.

I am blessed to have a circle of close friends who provide unending support. Marty, Xenia, Pattie, Clau & Es, Linda, Felicity, Kat. Near or far, you are always close to my heart. Thank you to my brother Tom, always willing to chauffeur me to the airport.

And especially to all the readers who encourage me by buying my books, showing up for my personal appearances, and for taking the time to e-mail me. Thank you so much.

Dedication

For Mom & Dad

Most people can look back over the years and identify a time and place at which their lives changed significantly. Whether by accident or design, these are the moments when, because of a readiness within us and a collaboration with events occurring around us, we are forced to seriously reappraise ourselves and...make certain choices that will affect the rest of our lives.

—FREDERICK F. FLACK

PROLOGUE

Bettles, Alaska
September 2009

Pasha Dunn pressed her face against the window of the Cessna and gazed at the small settlement coming into view, the first sign of civilization she'd seen since they left Fairbanks two hours earlier. The journey over endless stretches of empty swampland, taiga forest, countless lakes, wide river valleys, and snow-peaked mountain ranges had driven home just how isolated her new home north of the Arctic Circle was.

The village of Bettles didn't look like much from the air, just a scattering of buildings along the Koyukuk River, set in dense green forest. More impressive was its backdrop: the endless Brooks Range, one of North America's most magnificent and desolate stretches of high mountains.

Of all the places she'd lived, this would certainly qualify as the most unique.

Her friends in Minneapolis had been shocked and dismayed when she decided to move to such an isolated, harsh environment, where temperatures during winter could drop to twenty-below or worse and stay there for months. She hadn't hesitated, however, because her keen sense of intuition had led her here.

The power—as she referred to it—had so far proved infallible, though it had taken her years to fully develop and surrender to her gift. She didn't consider herself psychic, exactly. She certainly couldn't produce such feelings at will. But as long as she could remember, she had experienced deep, profound gut feelings about people, places, and circumstances that always panned out. Every job, every major move, everyone she'd ever been close to had prompted that niggling you-can't-pass-this-up sense that seemed to arise when something of importance presented itself. Similarly, she'd sometimes get an impending sense of doom about someone or something, and she'd follow that intuition, often to find later she'd had good reason for her sinking sense of dread.

The power had last manifested itself a month ago, when she'd spotted an advertisement on a job-hunting Web site. It read, very simply,

Do you have what it takes to live the adventure others only dream of? Eidson Eco-Tours, an adventure outfitter in Alaska, is looking for men and women to serve as wilderness guides and support staff. No experience necessary, but related skills desirable. Must be physically fit, reliable, love nature, and play well with others. Contact Dita Eidson to apply.

Pasha was working at a salon, but she'd felt for months that she needed to move on and begin a new chapter in her life. She was waiting only for that boom of recognition, that pivotal knowing her new direction, which had come when the ad caught her eye. She'd immediately picked up the phone and dialed the contact number, and her feeling of rightness had only intensified when she heard Dita Eidson's soft Southern drawl.

Now she was here, anxious and excited to begin her new job as an outfitter's assistant. Dita had explained that her duties initially would involve booking clients, packing for trips, running errands, and in general being her go-to gal. Since the winter months were slow, she'd spend much of her time training with some of the seasoned guides, learning all the skills she'd need to be out in the field with clients—first aid, cooking, safety, survival, and so on.

If she took to the job and did well her first summer season, Dita promised, she'd become a junior guide the next year.

The plane set down on the village's short, single runway and taxied to a stop near what passed as the control tower—a small cabin whose sign read Bettles FAA Station. As the pilot—a middle-aged bearded guy who'd introduced himself as Skeeter—unloaded her bags, she asked directions to the Eidson Eco-Tours office.

"Easy breezy," he said, blowing smoke from the cigarette dangling from the corner of his mouth. "Follow that gravel strip there two blocks, hang a right, and you're there. Can't miss it."

"Thanks."

Pasha hefted her pack onto her back and pulled up the handle of her big rolling suitcase before setting off. She passed an enormous log structure at the edge of the tarmac that looked to be one of the more popular places in the village, judging by the handful of lunchtime patrons. The sign above the door read The Den. She'd have to check it out once she got settled.

The Eidson Eco-Tours office was a two-story wood structure with a wide porch dotted with wicker rockers and massive caribou antlers over the door. When she went inside, a tiny bell above her jangled. She found herself in a cozy waiting area, with couches and chairs, a TV, and walls adorned with framed photographs and native art.

A petite woman in her early fifties, with short-cropped salt-and-pepper hair and wire-rimmed glasses, emerged from a room in the back. She glanced from Pasha to her overstuffed backpack and large suitcase and smiled. "I bet you're Pasha, aren't you?" she asked with a soft Southern drawl as she headed toward her. "Welcome to Bettles."

"I am. And I recognize that voice. Dita, right?"

"None other. Pleased to meet you," Dita said, offering her hand.

"Likewise. I'm excited to be here."

As they shook hands, a faint rainbow-colored aura shimmered briefly around Dita's body. Pasha grinned. Auras were one of her power's most valuable manifestations, because they only appeared around people who would become her cherished friends.

The excellent omen confirmed that she'd made the right decision.

❖

Sofia, Bulgaria
Same day

Emery Lawson raised her first-class seat to its upright position and glanced out the window at the city coming into view. The gilded dome of a cathedral glinted distantly in the noonday sun, golden treasure in a sea of terra-cotta rooftops. Checking her watch, she calculated she'd have roughly ninety minutes after she completed her mission before she had to return to the airport. Better than some jobs, but still never enough to soothe the wanderlust that had been with her since birth and grew exponentially with each passing day. Her career had become a relentless tease, offering her only glimpses of the life she'd always imagined.

As usual, she traveled light, so she was able to bypass baggage claim. Her small backpack contained only a change of clothes, toiletries, a couple of PowerBars, and her iPhone, loaded with dozens of e-books, hundreds of her favorite tunes, and several translation, navigation, and tourism apps. This trip she also carried a hard briefcase, loaded with the confidential documents she'd been contracted to deliver by one p.m. After a brief stop at the currency exchange for some levs, she hailed a taxi and headed to meet her contact.

Sofia resembled many other European cities she'd visited, with its vivid flower stalls, fountains, crowded cafés, Gothic churches, and abundance of bicycles and mopeds. Unique were the distinctive yellow Viennese cobblestone streets in the city center and the completely indecipherable signage. For more than two decades, Emery had spent much of her time in airports and on airplanes listening to language tapes, so she had a reasonable command of basic French, Spanish, German, Dutch, and Italian. And she could get by well enough in a half dozen more dialects, not that she'd had nearly enough opportunities to use all she had studied. But she was lost trying to puzzle out the oddly shaped alphabets of Russia, Greece, Eastern Europe, and Asia. She planned to tackle these next, one by one, so when she finally traveled on her own terms, she'd be reasonably comfortable anywhere.

Emery felt like a voyeur, confined to watching and tasting the life she longed to fully immerse herself in. One day, she promised herself.

All too soon, they'd pulled up before the Arena di Serdica, an upscale hotel in the city center. She'd read online that it was built atop ancient Roman ruins, discovered during construction and now exposed to view on the ground floor. Since she'd arrived well before her deadline, she allowed herself a few minutes to admire them before taking care of business.

The desk clerk rang her client and directed her toward the bank of elevators. Her efficiency in dispensing with the massive paperwork required for international deliveries allowed her to be in and out of the deluxe suite on the top floor within ten minutes. As she did whenever she traveled, she noted the room's view, amenities, and proximity to landmarks. Within her iPhone she kept an ever-expanding database of potential hotels, inns, and guesthouses she might independently utilize one day.

She waited impatiently for the elevator to take her back down. She intended to make use of every minute of her remaining time in Sofia, soaking up as much ambience as possible. She would first stop at the massive Market Hall to glimpse the local handicrafts and sample some local cuisine. The impressive Neo-Renaissance structure would also satisfy her appreciation for the amazing architecture she so admired in Europe's ancient capitals.

When an empty car arrived, she stepped inside and hit the Lobby button. Soothing classical music—a Bach cello suite—wafted around her as she began to descend.

Emery was trying to identify the piece when the car suddenly slammed to a stop and began to buck and sway. *Jesus Christ. Earthquake!* The realization had barely registered when she crashed against the back wall, then tumbled forward and hit the floor face-first. Her nose broke, the wind whooshed out of her, and she nearly bit through her bottom lip, the pain excruciating. The metallic tang of blood filled her mouth as she struggled to breathe. Alarms blared, mingled with the sound of distant screams. Time slowed, and her senses came fully alert as adrenaline poured through her. The car banged against the shaft, shaking her in a bone-jarring vibration as she tried to get to her knees.

Just as she spotted the silver door above the elevator buttons that likely contained an emergency phone or something, the lights in the car blinked out and the music stopped. Over the clanging of the alarms, she heard running footfalls just above the doors ahead of her, a short cadence of quick thumps.

"Help!" she screamed. "Help! I'm stuck in the elevator! Someone please help me!" She stilled and listened, holding her breath. A few seconds of silence, then more footsteps ran past, there and gone in a heartbeat. "Help! I'm trapped in the elevator! Someone please help me!"

No response, no further sounds except the alarms as the shaking lessened and finally stopped.

Emery pulled out her cell phone, the display's dim illumination a comforting beacon of light in the claustrophobic, absolute darkness, but heard no signal. She crawled toward the corner and stood, using the cell's light to find the hatch with the emergency phone. She put the receiver to her ear. Dead.

More running footsteps.

"Stop! I need help!" she yelled, and this time the steps faltered. Someone shouted words she didn't understand.

"I'm stuck in the elevator! I need help!"

The shaking and rolling began again, even more powerful. Loosened bricks smashed against the car's steel roof like a trio of gunshots. Metal screeched against metal, very near. A millisecond seemed like an eternity before a whiplash of cable sang in the shaft.

She was falling.

She lost her footing as the elevator plunged, rapidly gaining speed, then crashed to the floor.

Before the world went black she heard bones snapping and her own screams.

CHAPTER ONE

Detroit, Michigan
Sixteen months later, January 2011

Emery Lawson smoothed the butter-soft leather cover of her journal, tracing the outline of the gold-embossed CARPE DIEM she'd had inscribed. Her hands were shaking too much from excitement and exhilaration to make the first entry. She'd wait until she got to Amsterdam, where she would certainly find ample fodder to fill the first blank pages. Closing her eyes, she imagined herself on a terrace overlooking a canal filled with boats, sipping local beer and watching passersby.

She could scarcely believe it was finally happening.

No longer tied in any way to a person, place, or job, she'd cut away all her obligations, like removing the dead tissue around a wound. Painful initially, but necessary for new growth and renewal. She'd sold her home and stored the few possessions too dear to part with. Her friends had expressed both envy and caution. Lisa was still dealing with it all, but Emery knew that one day she, too, would understand and agree that their parting was inevitable.

Everything changed when that elevator fell. During her long recuperation and physical therapy, she'd not only learned to walk again, she'd sprouted wings, and now she was ready to fly. She was heading forth ready to devour life, to savor every experience. She'd been reborn as someone convinced that each day could be her last, every sunset and sunrise the final one she might see.

Her bosses at Premier Couriers accepted her resignation with regret. She'd been their top courier, with an impeccable delivery record, so they convinced her to keep in touch; she might be useful where she was going, and she'd agreed. Though she had more frequent-flier miles than she could ever use, and a sizeable bank account from her savings and the sale of her townhouse, she might need a few extra dollars down the road. Also, she'd made a lot of friends during her three decades there that she wanted to keep in contact with.

As a pre-emptive strike, she popped two Percocet with the fresh-squeezed OJ the flight attendant had handed her. The endorphin rush from finally setting off had, for the moment, dulled her seemingly ever-present twinges of pain. But even the comfy reclining chairs of first class wouldn't prevent the discomfort she'd experience from sitting nearly eight hours before they reached Schiphol.

Her around-the-world adventure would begin abroad, though she most wanted to visit Alaska. However, she needed to build her strength to experience all she wanted to do there. The remote and unforgiving environment would test her both physically and mentally, so she would spend some time in Europe first, where getting around was usually a breeze. Most major cities—like Amsterdam, her jumping-off point—had efficient and comfortable public-transit systems. As she gained more flexibility and strength, she'd walk, bike, and undertake other adrenaline-pumping endeavors so she'd be ready for the challenges her body would face in Alaska. She also needed to rebuild confidence in her physical capabilities.

Her itinerary in Europe was loose. She planned to work her way south to the Mediterranean, following her whims but with a few must-see sights along the way, including the Louvre, Prague, the canals of Venice, and the Vatican and ancient Rome. She'd stay in each destination until she got a real feel for it and the people who lived here, then move on. If she didn't hit all the countries she wanted to by the end of May, she'd catch them another time, because Eidson Eco-Tours began their new season of guided Alaskan adventures then, and Emery was going to spend five months experiencing several of them.

An attractive, waifishly built redhead in her mid-thirties paused in the aisle beside her to stow her bulging carryon in the overhead bin. The flight attendant was preoccupied with another passenger, so Emery got up and hefted the bag next to the slender black cane she hoped to soon be rid of.

"Thank you." The stranger flashed Emery a dimpled smile when their eyes met, not in the common elusive glance of strangers, but in a just-a-little-too-long look of mutual interest.

Emery smiled back. "No problem. Traveling alone?"

The redhead nodded, and the smile never left her face.

"Business or pleasure?"

"A bit of both," the woman replied. "A three-day conference in Amsterdam, followed by a week's vacation in Paris. You?"

"Pleasure. All pleasure."

"For how long?"

"Indefinitely."

The redhead laughed softly. "Sounds intriguing. I hear Amsterdam is the place to find pleasure of all varieties."

Emery chuckled, thinking of the city's infamous red-light district, its gay-friendly ambience, and the "coffee houses" that drew pot-smoking tourists from around the world. "Amsterdam is just the start," she said, "of an around-the-world trip."

The redhead's eyebrows quirked in surprised delight. "Niiice."

The flight attendant paused between them to secure the overheads.

"Is everyone on board?" Emery asked.

"Yes. We'll be closing the door shortly. Do you need something?"

Carpe diem—seize the day—was her new motto. Emery craned her head around the flight attendant so she could see the redhead. "Want to sit over here so we can get to know each other better? Compare itineraries?"

The woman's dimples reappeared and a mischievous twinkle flashed in her eyes. "Most certainly."

❖

Bettles, Alaska
May 28, Four months later

Pasha hung her coat over the tip of a massive moose antler mounted just inside the main entrance of the Den and paused next to the huge stuffed grizzly bear that greeted patrons with a recorded snarl. She unconsciously rocked on her heels, scanning the faces in the room and seeking an answer to her growing anticipation. Something big was about to happen, she was sure, but she had no idea where or when. She wasn't even sure whether it would be good or bad. She only knew it would somehow change her life, so she was growing impatient with its reluctance to show itself.

Since nothing suggested that she'd have any answers here tonight, she searched the half-filled roadhouse for dinner companionship. Many of Bettles's thirty-six residents often visited the Den, the village's social center. She'd gotten to know most of them during her twenty months here but didn't see any of her close friends. In fact, the bulk of the crowd was unfamiliar, which wasn't unusual, since Bettles was the jumping-off point for a variety of adventure trips and the Den provided the only rooms in town.

Pasha headed toward the long bar running along one side of the enormous room. A barstool was a great vantage point to observe everything going on while catching up on all the local news, weather, and gossip. Everybody opened up to Jerome "Grizz" Hudson, the bartender/proprietor. He was a reliable source, since he often heard every side of every story and had known all the participants long enough to determine who told the truth. Perhaps he had some tidbit of news that could shed some light on her recent feelings of impending change.

She chose a comfy padded barstool near the center, with a good view of the booths that lined the perimeter and the scattering of mismatched tables and chairs that filled the rest. No one sat near her—the only others at the bar were two oil-rig workers on the far end whom she vaguely recognized. When Grizz finished waiting on them, he headed her way, pausing to pour coffee into a mug. His moniker suited him perfectly. His shoulder-length brown hair and unkempt brown beard streaked with gray framed pale-blue eyes and a grin distinguished by prominent, pointed canines. "Hey hey, baby girl. What's shakin'?" He added a shot of Kahlua to the coffee before he set the mug to her left, indicative of his remarkable attention to detail. Grizz had noted during her first meal that she was a lefty and never failed to adjust her place settings accordingly.

"You tell me." She wrapped her hands around the mug to warm them and swiveled the stool to glance around the room. "Anything interesting to report?"

Grizz absentmindedly wiped down the bar with a frayed towel as he too surveyed the crowd. "Well, let's see. Frank…" he nodded toward the bespectacled bachelor nursing a beer, alone, at a table for two, "was asking if he could use our computer a couple times a week. Wants to join one of those dating Web sites."

"Wonder if he's going to volunteer that he bathes only twice a year."

Grizz laughed. "And Helen's taken a room upstairs, at least for the night," he went on, referencing another familiar local. The Battling Biandos were among the best entertainment around. From their ongoing complaints about each other, it was hard to believe they'd been married for nearly fifty years. "*She* says she's staying put until he starts wearing his hearing aid cause she's tired of shouting. Eddie claims she's here because he cut off their TV service. She'd been buying things on those home-shopping networks again."

"I predict a twenty-four-hour standoff, max." She sipped her coffee, remembering the way Eddie always seemed to have one steadying hand on Helen's elbow or back.

"So, what's new over at the office?" Grizz asked. "From the bookings here, looks like you all are gonna have a real busy season."

"Yup, it's shaping up to be a great year. We're already almost solidly booked through the fall. Dita's bringing in some guides from her other offices and talking about adding some more trips."

"Speaking of, where is she?"

"Working late. A big group from Michigan just called and wanted to set up a custom trip for next week. Guess I'm solo for dinner." Dita was much more to Pasha than just her employer. She'd become a dear friend, as the power had predicted when they first met, and they often shared meals at the roadhouse.

"Not so fast," said a familiar voice from behind her.

Pasha turned as Karla Edwards shed her coat over the back of the stool beside her and eased onto the padded seat. She wore green surgical scrubs and had her black medical bag with her. "Heading out or coming back?" Pasha asked.

Karla was the only RN for hundreds of miles, and the nearest doctor was in Fairbanks, so she handled all the priority medical calls for a large region. "Coming back." She arched her back in a long stretch and groaned. "Bryson's due in from a run in an hour or so. Can you wait a while for dinner so she can join us?"

"Of course." Karla and her partner Bryson had become like sisters to Pasha. She had a lot in common with Karla—both were relative newcomers to the state, still adjusting to the isolation of their little village after years of living in metropolitan areas. And she worked with Bryson, a bush pilot who ferried clients and supplies for Eidson Eco-Tours.

"The usual?" Grizz said perfunctorily, already reaching for a Black Fang from the cooler. He waited until he got the nod from Karla to open the bottle and set it before her. Then he excused himself to see to the oil-rig workers farther down the bar.

Karla exhaled loudly as she reached for the beer and took a long tug at the bottle.

"Long day?" Pasha massaged Karla's shoulder, which elicited a soft groan of appreciation.

"A day lasts only twenty-four hours," Karla said tiredly as she closed her eyes and leaned into Pasha's probing fingers.

Without ceasing to manipulate the pronounced knot in Karla's shoulder, Pasha rose and stood behind her, where she could use her other hand as well and do a more thorough job. Karla groaned again, louder, and leaned forward so Karla could have better access to her back.

"Everything okay? Pasha asked.

"Good outcome." Karla sighed. "I delivered a healthy baby girl to a couple in Arctic Village. But the poor mom was in labor for nearly thirty hours so I'm horribly sleep-deprived."

"We'll call it an early night so Bryson can get you home and in bed."

"I like the sound of that," Karla murmured in a husky voice that suddenly seemed not quite so tired.

"Get your mind out of the gutter." Pasha softly slapped her shoulder and returned to her barstool. "No massages for those who remind the deprived how deprived they are." Winter had been very long, and Pasha had discussed with Karla on several occasions how tired she was of celibacy.

"Aww." Karla complained half-heartedly as she sat upright and reached for her beer. "That did help, though. Thanks. So how're you? Ready for the start of the season?"

The tingling sense of anticipation returned, like liquid fire in her veins. "I'm okay. Restless," Pasha replied. "Have you ever had a feeling that something big is about to happen, like a long wait will be over and you just want to…I don't know…*push* it somehow to get it here faster?"

CHAPTER TWO

Bettles, Alaska
One week later, June first

Pasha stared at the neon green numerals—five a.m.—and studied her watch. The sunlight peeking past the edge of her closed curtains often deceived her. On June first the sun rose at two thirty after only a one-hour dip below the horizon, and in another few days, it wouldn't set. Normally she needed at least eight hours and several cups of caffeine to feel this alert and energized. And last night, she and Dita had stayed up until midnight finishing their preparation for the first clients.

The restless anticipation that had consumed her the last several days had exploded tenfold while she slept, until she could barely breathe. She hoped to hell relief would arrive, some answer to the strongest premonitory rush she'd ever experienced. Surely her first day as a junior guide hadn't caused such a reaction, but something much more.

Too wired to sleep, she padded to the kitchen to make coffee. She lived in a sparsely furnished apartment above the Eidson Eco-Tours offices, Dita in the other. Pasha had learned long ago to minimize her personal possessions for maximum mobility. In the thirteen years since she'd graduated college, she'd already lived in six states, moving to a new location and new job every couple of years when her intuition insisted.

After she showered, dressed, and answered her e-mail she wandered to the Den for breakfast. Spotting Bryson and Karla in the corner booth, she headed their way after pouring herself another cup of coffee. Bryson waved, and Karla, who'd been resting her head on Bryson's shoulder, sat upright and sleepily rubbed her eyes.

"Good morning. I know you're headed to Fairbanks to pick up clients," Pasha told Bryson before turning her attention to Karla. "But why are you up this early?"

"Have to check on a couple of patients in town this afternoon." Karla opened her thick black cardigan to reveal her scrubs beneath. "And I'm kinda reliant on my ride's schedule."

"Believe me, honey, I wasn't any more anxious than you to crawl from under that big warm comforter this morning." Bryson wrapped her arm around Karla's shoulder and squeezed, both smiling. Pasha envied the unmistakable head-over-heels gaze of affection and mutual adoration that passed between them. The honeymoon look, still vivid and constant after two years. They lived more than thirty miles north of Bettles, in a primitive cabin on the Wild River accessible only by air or boat. Karla had no option but to hitch a ride with Bryson. In winter, they lived in a room in the Den so Bryson could continue to fly.

"You oughta talk, by the way." Bryson studied Pasha's face with a curious expression. "What's up? You're all flushed."

"Just woke up like a shot, an hour ago," Pasha replied. "Remember what we were talking about the other day, Karla?"

"The big event that's coming?"

Pasha nodded. "I think it's today. I'm about to come out of my skin."

Bryson leaned forward, her eyes narrowing with interest. "Another premonition?" Pasha had volunteered quite a lot to them about her sixth sense.

"Like nothing I've ever experienced. It's been building for days, and waiting is driving me crazy."

"Something good, though, right?" Bryson asked.

"I think so," Pasha said. "I'm not getting the same kind of vibe I do when I sense disaster, but I'm not sure."

"Think it has to do with the clients I'm picking up?" Bryson asked.

"Could be, I guess, since that's the only thing different about today, but I don't see how. The first trip involves three married couples from California. All friends, on a fly-fishing excursion. I didn't recognize any of their names."

"Well, if they're it, we'll know soon enough." Bryson tied her long brown hair back into a ponytail and donned her trademark ball cap with its embroidered logo, I Can Take You There.

"Better get going. Anxious to check out the new plane." Dita had purchased a used green-and-white Cessna Caravan 208 for ferrying clients in Bettles, and this would be its inaugural flight for the company. Like Bryson's Piper Super Cub, the high-winged Cessna could land on short makeshift runways, making it ideal for bush flying. Versatile, it carried up to nine passengers or twenty-seven hundred pounds of cargo.

"Be careful, honey," Karla said. "I know you're eager to see what it can do, but—"

"No worries." Bryson kissed her on top of her head as she got to her feet and grabbed her coat. "Supposed to be clear and sunny from here to Fairbanks, with light winds." She headed off with a pause at the door to smile and wave to Karla one last time.

When Pasha turned her attention from the doorway back to Karla, she saw Karla, eyes moist, brush an errant tear from her cheek.

Highly regarded as one of the best bush pilots around, Bryson had flown in Alaska for twenty-five years. Her father—also a noted flier—began her lessons when she first reached her teens. But weather conditions in Alaska often changed in a heartbeat, and many well-seasoned pilots had lost their lives in what the media described as fairly routine flights.

"Routine" didn't apply to bush flying, one of the world's most dangerous occupations. Pasha had heard story after story of disasters and near disasters and had come to appreciate the dangers pilots faced every time they flew over such a remote, unforgiving landscape.

"Has to be incredibly difficult to watch her head off," Pasha said gently.

"It never gets easier. Alaska demands the true measure of a pilot. I still don't know how she does it. She's the bravest woman I know."

Pasha smiled. "She told me once *you* were the bravest woman *she* knew."

"Did she?" Karla grinned.

"Yup. Very early on, as a matter of fact." Pasha pictured them in Bryson's Cub. "We ran supplies to a kayak trip right after I got here, and I planned to finally meet you that night—remember?"

"I do. Of course." Karla smiled at the memory, too. "You'd been here, like…a week or two already, but I had gone to Atlanta for a friend's wedding."

"Bryson had told me a lot about you. Honestly, she kind of mooned over you during that time. Said you'd never been separated so long. Adorable."

Karla laughed. "Isn't she though, when she gets that puppy-dog look? We got a good-enough Internet connection a couple of times to cam, and I just melted."

"Anyway, I couldn't wait to meet you. And I remember asking her to describe you in three words. She said "brave" first, for facing adversities, doing your job, and moving to Alaska to be with her."

A pinkish tinge infused Karla's cheeks as she swept a hand lazily through her shoulder-length blond hair. "Well, I'd call the last one a no-brainer. I'd do anything and go anywhere for Bryson. And the other two words?"

"Generous, and sexy."

Karla smiled in delight. "I'd pick…fearless, sweet, and, hmm, maybe resourceful…for her. Hard to choose just three. She's an amazing woman."

"I envy you." Pasha sipped her coffee. "I hope to find the kind of connection you two have with someone."

"You will. Believe me, true love seems to strike when you're not looking." Karla laid a hand on Pasha's. "Maybe your strong feeling means your special someone is headed this way."

"Well, I'll be working bookings today and organizing the trip files. Dita's busy packing. Perhaps I'll peruse the clients' vital statistics and see if anyone seems promising." As she said the words, a sudden warmth infused her, a sensation she instinctively translated as confirmation that she should proceed immediately. She jumped to her feet, her hands shaking. "See you later."

"Pasha?"

She shrugged. "Following a hunch. I'll let you know if it pans out."

Chapter Three

"Miss..." Emery narrowed her eyes to read the gate attendant's nametag. "Spires?"

The attractive blonde looked up from her computer, and as piercing blue eyes met hers, the lips beneath curled into a smile. "Sue. Can I help you?"

Emery detected a hint of innuendo in the offer and decided to play along. If Plan A wasn't to be, a possible very attractive alternative might have just presented itself. "I'm certain you can," she replied, imbuing her tone with a similar subtlety. "I'd like to get to Bettles today, if possible." She paused and rested one arm on the counter casually, maintaining eye contact. "Although I'm in no real rush. Can you recommend something here in Fairbanks I simply must indulge in before I leave?"

Sue's smile broadened. "I'm certain you could find some... irresistible indulgences you haven't tried."

Emery allowed herself a lengthy perusal of the blonde's curvaceous figure, starting with the navy fuck-me heels and working her way up toned calves to her short navy uniform skirt hugging firm thighs. Her matching blazer hugged her hourglass waist and ample breasts. The airline uniform was nicer than most, but she'd have much preferred a shirt that displayed a little more cleavage than the formal collared standard. "What's your schedule like, tour guide?"

Sue glanced up at the wall clock beside the gate that read ten thirty a.m. "I don't get off until six." She glanced around, but the gate area was empty except for a native couple sitting too far away to hear them. "I do get an hour break at noon, and I know a place to go."

"Do you now?"

"The staff uses some rooms onsite during weather emergencies." Sue blatantly ogled Emery the same way she had just been assessed and licked her lips. "Soft cots and lockable doors."

"I can feel an emergency coming on."

"Oh, most definitely…uh…" Sue stammered and a grin tugged at her mouth. "Can I have your name?"

"Emery Lawson."

"Emery. Nice." Sue started typing into her computer. She frowned when she read whatever she'd called up, then tried something else. Another frown. "The first couple of flights out are full," she muttered under her breath as she continued to type. After another minute, she grinned. "Mike Sweeney has an open spot this afternoon at four. He's a freelancer, flying a charter for a family of six. Did you want to book one-way or round trip?"

"One-way. And the four o'clock flight is great." She laid her credit card and ID on the counter.

Sue started transferring the information into her computer. "Can't say as I'm not a little disappointed you won't be coming back this way."

"Oh, I didn't say that."

Sue stopped typing and looked up expectantly.

"I like to keep my options open, so when I find something worth revisiting, I can act on that impulse," she said.

"In that case," Sue printed out the boarding pass and handed it to Emery, along with her credit card, "meet me back here at noon, and I'll see what I can do to stir up those…impulses."

❖

"No. Not at all obvious what you've been doing," Emery mumbled to herself as she tried to hand-comb her hair. She wished she hadn't already checked her bag so she could change clothes and fix her tousled hair. Her jeans were fine, but her frenzied encounter with Sue had wrinkled her high-collared, blue cotton shirt and left an obvious hickey just below her ear. She zipped up her black leather jacket to cover the worst and headed to the gate area.

Sue had at least thrown her clothes over a chair while they fucked, so her uniform had survived better, but the afterglow of orgasm shone on her face, all the more obvious as she cast hungry eyes in Emery's direction when she spotted her.

Five dark-skinned natives waited to one side in folding chairs—an older man and woman, and three children, from about ten to late teens. Clearly the family who had chartered her flight. They glanced Sue's way when she spoke on the gate intercom.

"The Bettles charter is ready to depart, ladies and gentlemen. I'll take your boarding passes if you'll step this way."

Emery lingered to be last in line so she could say a few parting words, but Sue spoke up first.

"You have my number. I hope you'll use it if you get back this way."

"I have good reason to. We'll see what the fates hold." Emery put her hand over Sue's as she swiped the boarding pass over the gate scanner. "Thanks for an unforgettable…" She sought the right word and chuckled at the one that came into her head. "Layover."

Sue laughed, too. "I won't forget you, either. Have a safe and fun trip."

Five minutes later, Emery sat strapped into the tail seat of a six-passenger Cessna 180, a bright-orange floatplane with a red tail. The pilot, a brawny man with a flaming red beard and black wool cap, turned slightly in his seat to address them. "Name is Mike Sweeney," he said. "But I go by Skeeter. It's about a two-hour flight to Bettles. Wind's pretty low today, so we should have a smooth trip. Relax and enjoy the view, and let me know if you have any questions. Everybody buckled up?"

He responded to the chorus of affirmative replies with a nod and, after running through the usual safety spiel, started the plane. They took off from one of the two water runways at the edge of the airport and soon soared over a vast landscape of tundra and mountains, with no visible sign of civilization.

"Do you know if the Den's fully booked?" Emery asked the pilot.

"You know the Den?" he replied. "Been to Bettles?"

"No. I'm booked there, but I'm arriving a couple days early."

"Shouldn't be a problem midweek early in the season. In another couple of weeks, may be a different matter. Look for Grizz, the big guy behind the bar. He runs the place."

"Great, thanks." She remembered the name from her e-mailed reservations. Grizz seemed a perfect moniker for an Alaskan man, just like "Skeeter." Relaxing against the seatback, she stared out the tiny window at the rugged terrain. She'd had great fun so far in her travels and had regained her strength, barely a trace of a limp except when she overdid it. She was ready to face the ultimate test of Alaska.

She could easily parallel this lonely, desolate environment to the accident that set her on this course. Both had their own set of rules, life-changing rules. Both placed you in a situation where all that you knew, all the once-important things, didn't matter anymore. You had to assess what really affected your well-being. Most people ran from such forced, world-shaking self-examination, but Emery embraced it. How else would you ever realize your strength and your capabilities?

Her musings shortened the journey. Before she knew it, the pilot was announcing his approach to Bettles and requesting clearance to land. In the far distance, she saw a small settlement, a cluster of buildings surrounded by forest. Her home for the next few months.

Emery pulled out her journal, already nearly filled with impressions of the places she'd visited and how they'd affected her, small sketches, photos of people she'd met, ticket stubs. She'd have to buy another soon. No doubt, her time in Alaska would give her much to ponder and indelible memories to savor when she moved on.

❖

Pasha looked longingly at Dita's well-used backpack, stuffed with supplies for her fly-fishing trip. Being out in the field would certainly help her work off her relentless restlessness. But Dita always took out the first trip of the season, and she'd tapped Lars Rasmussen as the second guide because of his extensive knowledge of the best stretches of river. Pasha would debut as the junior guide of a three-day women-only wildlife-viewing/photography trip, due to set out when Dita got back.

Dita stood checking the large pile of food and other supplies they'd assembled on a large folding table in the back room. She'd just been named one of Alaska's rising young entrepreneurs, whose upstart company was worth—according to the magazine article—four million dollars. Dita, an unpretentious, down-to-earth environmentalist, favored flannel shirts and jeans, and considered doing right by her employees more important than the bottom line.

When building her empire, she'd made some seemingly unwise financial choices by acquiring several failing small companies, including Orion Outfitters in Winterwolf and a freelance group in Bettles, Arctic Independent Outfitters, which Bryson and Lars had helped found. The benefits and wages she offered quickly lured the guides and pilots to work for Eidson Eco-Tours instead. They appreciated her business savvy, as well as her commitment to the environment and emphasis on safety.

Bettles provided an ideal starting point for trips to the nearby Arctic National Wildlife Refuge and Gates of the Arctic National Park, an area of more than thirty-two-thousand square miles. But the tiny village outpost had quickly become more to Dita than just another branch of her business. After overseeing the renovation of the Arctic Independent Outfitter offices and hiring the necessary staff, she'd decided to make it her primary base of operation and moved there permanently. By then, she said, she'd simply made too many good friends to leave.

Last season, the company had barely managed to break even, though it had become the state's largest outfitter. The struggling economy had forced most Americans to forego their vacation plans altogether or choose low-cost options closer to home, and they made up the bulk of their business. But this year Dita had planned for forty trips during their peak May-through-October period, all filling up so fast she had begun plotting out a handful more.

"Wish I was going," Pasha said wistfully.

Dita checked off another item on the yellow pad she held and smiled up at Pasha. "Patience, honey. You'll likely have more fun on your trip than I'll have on mine. You get a buncha young women." Dita's soft twang held a note of regret. "I get three married couples, and if past history holds out, that means at least one of the wives will whine from the get-go."

On every couples' trip, they usually had to coerce at least one woman to go along, a spoiled princess who bemoaned the primitive conditions and complained at every opportunity. She and Dita had discussed ways to deal with the issue when it arose, ways to keep all the clients happy to ensure repeat business. But changing small-minded individuals who preferred hair dryers, makeup, and consistent cell-phone contact with their friends presented a challenge. She could never understand how someone could cling to such petty concerns amidst the grandeur all around them.

"Hope you're right." Pasha had sorted through the client files all morning, seeking some sense of whether one might relate to her premonition. Unfortunately, so far none had triggered a clue. Now she was poring over the files of the clients on the photography trip, and Dita might be right. The five women all seemed to be experienced outdoorswomen, not high-maintenance Barbie dolls. She reached for the last file, wishing for photographs to supplement the extensive questionnaire Dita required. In addition to detailing their previous outdoor experience and health status, guests had to read and sign waivers that stated the risks involved in an Alaskan trip and absolved the outfitter of responsibility.

As soon as she touched the folder, she involuntarily jumped back from the tiny electrical shock that ran up her fingertips. *What the hell?* She stared at it several seconds then reached for it again. No shock this time as she pulled it across the table, but the paper felt slightly warm to the touch. She flipped it open. Emery Lawson. Pasha's vision blurred and she couldn't discern any more for several seconds. When the neat handwriting finally materialized again, she began reading with interest. Emery was forty-five, ten years older than she was, and at five feet seven, a few inches taller. Brown hair and brown eyes. She described her build as athletic. *Nice.* She skipped over the disclaimer portion and flipped the page to find, under the section marked marital status, that Emery was single. *Very nice.*

She had left the section for home address blank, though she'd included her cell-phone number and an e-mail address for updated trip information. Did Emery Lawson have no permanent residence or wish to hide that fact? Oftentimes, a client's home base told her a lot about their frame of reference: their lifestyle and their priorities. Was Emery a big-city workaholic? Or a self-sufficient loner, maybe, who lived somewhere in the wide-open spaces of the West?

At the bottom of the form, Dita had scrawled Emery's date of arrival—three days from now. She would have to stew in this cauldron of bundled nerves and excess energy for another seventy-two hours or so, but at least she had a clue that her feelings related somehow to this Emery Lawson. For the moment, she'd keep her hunch to herself, see if it panned out.

"Pash? You coming?"

"Huh?" She swiveled in her chair. Dita stood by the door looking at her expectantly.

"I said, you coming? It's dinnertime, and Bryson should get back any minute."

"Oh, right." Pasha sprang to her feet and followed Dita toward the Den. She needed a night with her buds to keep from going crazy waiting for Emery to arrive.

Chapter Four

S he didn't say what happened?" Pasha asked.
"No clue at all?" Dita chimed in a second later.

"Nope." Karla tapped the table and stared at the doorway expectantly. Bryson had called the bar a little while ago and said she'd been delayed, but that the wait would be worth it. She had "a great surprise for everyone."

Pasha immediately suspected this surprise could be connected to her premonition of change, since it was rapidly growing stronger.

"I bet it's something to eat," Dita said, "if it's for everyone. Remember when we all talked last week about stuff we craved but couldn't get? I said I'd kill for some fresh collard greens and ham hocks. Maybe she found some."

"No offense, Dita," Pasha said drolly, "but I wouldn't consider that a great surprise."

"Unlikely, I think." Karla chewed the corner of her lip, her gaze still fixed on the entryway. "She rarely goes shopping without asking what I need. And I wouldn't have thought she'd have time." After Bryson delivered the fly-fishing clients to Bettles that morning, she had taken right off again in the Cessna, ferrying equipment and supplies to the Eidson offices in Kotzebue, on the west coast, and Winterwolf, on the North Slope.

"Can't be something for the office," Pasha told Karla. "That really wouldn't benefit you."

"Maybe it's a new board game," Dita said. "I'm getting tired of Monopoly and Scrabble." During the endless winter months, the four of them often played marathon games long into the night at this very booth.

Karla shook her head. "She sounded too excited. It has to—" A big grin spread across her face when she spotted Bryson. "Here she comes. We'll know soon enough."

Pasha turned to look. Two attractive strangers followed Bryson: a tall, buff, androgynous woman with a dark-chestnut shag, and a shorter companion with shoulder-length, medium-brown hair streaked with blond highlights. Both looked to be in their late thirties or early forties and wore clothes typical of native Alaskans—well-used hiking boots, faded jeans, fleece pullovers, and heavy jackets that had seen more than a few winters.

Neither woman triggered any physical or other response—they clearly had nothing to do with Pasha's building sense of anticipation. She opened her mouth to ask who they were, but Karla and Dita had already met the newcomers halfway in enthusiastic embraces. She followed quickly.

"Why didn't you tell me you were coming in?" Dita asked the taller woman as they grinned at each other.

"Wanted it to be a surprise," the stranger replied. "We were getting kinda antsy for some female company, so we figured we'd come down early."

"You must be Pasha," the other newcomer said she as extricated herself from Karla's bear hug and stuck out her hand. "I'm Megan Maxwell, and she's Chaz Herrick, my partner. We've heard a lot about you." She had vivid green eyes and the confident air of an extrovert.

"I am. It's great to finally meet you, too." Pasha placed the couple immediately because Dita had spoken frequently of both. Chaz Herrick, a biology professor at the University of Fairbanks, spent her summers and Christmas breaks working as a guide for Eidson Eco-Tours, usually out of the Winterwolf office. Because the Bettles office was so heavily booked for the next couple of months, she planned to spend the summer here, but she wasn't supposed to arrive for another few days. And no one had known whether Megan would accompany her.

"Oh, I'm sorry," Dita said, as Pasha shook hands with Megan and Chaz. "Where are my manners? Come on, y'all, let's sit and get some dinner."

"Are you staying here at the Den?" Pasha asked, once they'd all crowded into the circular corner booth.

Chaz shook her head. "Grizz needs all the rooms he's got this summer, but he found us a place to stay. We're renting a cabin at the edge of town that's been up for sale a long while."

"Feel kinda bad now that he's given us a room for the next three months." Bryson frowned. "Asked him about it back in November, when it looked like we'd have another slow season. He always had a couple empties last summer, so he said sure. And 'course he's giving us a big discount. So he's losing money."

"And we won't even be in it all the time," Karla added. "We'll probably go home now and then. We're just here so much in the summer, me on medical calls and Bryson getting in late from runs, we wanted to be sure we always had a place to sleep and store a few things."

Pasha had visited them several times for dinner. Bryson had built the log structure with her own hands, in an isolated Brooks Range river valley thirty miles north of Bettles. They seemed content despite the lack of running water and other things most people took for granted.

Megan turned to Chaz and whispered something. Chaz nodded. "That's easy to solve," Megan announced. "Our cabin's got two bedrooms. Why don't you both bunk with us?"

Karla and Bryson looked at each other and grinned. "Done!" Karla said.

"Hey! Whassup, gals?" Grizz's baritone boomed from across the room as he headed toward them. "Didn't know you two were coming in tonight," he said as he reached across the table to wrap first Chaz's hand, then Megan's, in his beefy paws.

"Kind of an impulse," Chaz said. "We were just talking about you, as a matter of fact. Bryson and Karla decided to share our cabin, so you can rent their room."

Grizz grinned, exposing his fangs. "Cool beans. I can use it. How 'bout I say thanks with a free round on the house?" Not long after, they all sat sipping beer or wine and munching a big plate of nachos he'd thrown in.

"It's gonna be a right fine summer with all of us here," Dita said as she flicked a stray crumb of tortilla chip from her lap.

"We've got quite a growing little community of lesbians, don't we?" Karla observed. "Seven now—the six of us, and Geneva." Geneva De Luca, one of two waitresses at the Den, stood nearby busily cleaning a table. "We should form a club."

"That's a great idea," Megan said. "Back in Chicago, my friends and I formed a group called Broads in Broadcasting. We'd meet regularly for drinks and girl time. If any of us are in town at say, six p.m. or so, we could converge here for dinner."

The rest of them nodded enthusiastically.

"We need a name. How about…Arctic Amazons?" Pasha suggested. "No, wait a minute, strike that. I just got an image of us in weird leather outfits and tasseled headbands."

They all laughed.

"Bent in Bettles?" Dita offered. More laughs.

They bandied more ideas around as the evening wore on, their suggestions more ridiculous with each round of drinks. Pasha enjoyed herself but couldn't completely ignore her niggling premonition. After dinner, as they waited for their desserts, the feeling suddenly intensified. She tried to ignore it, focusing instead on the notepad in front of her, which contained some of their less ludicrous options. "So, where were we?"

"You just shot down my latest fine suggestion," Megan said. "Though I don't see what's possibly wrong with The Far-North Fairies."

"Fairies? Really, hon? You see me with wings, do you?" Chaz chuckled, and Pasha had to agree. Chaz epitomized the rugged outdoorswoman, all lean, muscled athleticism. She resembled Peter Pan more than Tinkerbell. "How about…" she grinned at Megan, "the Royal Ice Bitches?"

Megan scowled, but clearly in good fun, and Bryson and Karla joined Chaz in laughter.

Pasha looked over at Dita, also clearly clueless. "Obviously we're missing something."

"What a few of my writers and editors used to call me behind my back," Megan said drolly. "When I was a news VP. Let's just say I had a reputation for demanding excellence, and no one likes for someone to tell them they have to work the three a.m. weekend shift."

Chaz smiled sweetly at her. "You have such a soft, mushy interior. I never see this Ice Bitch person." Glancing conspiratorially at the others, she whispered, "Except, of course, when I forget to pick up after myself, or when I eat more than half of anything with chocolate in it."

"I've trained you well." Megan relaxed into the padded seatback of the booth with a smug smile. "So…we still don't have a name. *Think,* girls."

"Sapphic…something," Karla mused aloud. "Or, um…Bettles Belles? Bettles Babes?"

Bryson grumbled. "I want something with some power, something that respects us living up here. With all due respect, sweetheart, those sound like pink cheerleading teams."

"How about an acronym?" Dita suggested. "Like…" she thought a moment. "ADLIB. Adventurous Dykes Living In Bettles?"

"Hey, not bad," Bryson said.

Karla agreed. "Best so far."

Pasha opened her mouth to voice her assent, but no words emerged. In a flash, all the air in the room vanished. Her heart boomed, and the room spun. She squeezed her eyes shut and tried to catch her breath and calm her raging heart. What was happening?

She forced her eyes open. No one had noticed her, but she heard her friends laughing at something only distantly. She *had* to discover what had caused this sick feeling and weird distortion of perception. She half-turned in her chair, slowly scanning the faces in the room, and as she swept her gaze over them, the booming in her chest intensified and her breathing quickened.

A family stood in the doorway: a native father, mother, and three children. The feeling strengthened, but somehow still not quite *there*. Unsettled, she continued to sweep the room, but when she turned away from the entrance, the sensation lessened. She felt like a child, playing the old game of warm, warmer, hot…no, colder. She looked back toward the doorway. The boom of certainty in her chest resumed. The family had moved into the restaurant and a stranger stood there now. A woman. Their eyes met.

Pasha's world stood still. All grew deadly silent, and she went eerily calm, the raging furor that had boiled up inside her stilled in that instant of connection. The world around the woman blurred, and she became more vividly contrasted against it, cutting a lean and splendid figure in fitted black jeans, black leather jacket, and vivid blue shirt. Her boots made her appear taller than five-seven, and for some reason Pasha had envisioned the brown hair shorter than collar length, but this had to be Emery Lawson.

She had high cheekbones, a straight nose slightly upturned at the end, and rosy full lips pursed in thought. Because of the distance, Pasha couldn't discern what emotion her dark-brown eyes conveyed.

Her stance—legs slightly apart, black leather boots firmly planted—projected an air of powerful self-confidence, She had two backpacks, which rested on the floor on either side of her. Pasha frowned. Was she traveling with someone? Maybe not so single, after all?

She blinked, and the world flashed back to normal. The Den was its usual bustling self, the sound of her friends returned, still debating what they would call their little group. Her seemingly lengthy assessment of Emery Lawson had occurred in only a second or two in real time—their prolonged eye contact an illusion. The stranger had merely scanned the room, her gaze passing over Pasha and moving to the bar. Emery picked up both packs and headed toward Grizz without another glance in her direction.

Clearly, her overwhelming connection to this handsome newcomer wasn't mutual. Her buoyant mood deflated. *I can't be that wrong. Can I?*

Before she could move, Geneva swooped in, sidling up to Emery at the bar with her best flirtatious smile. And damn if she didn't look particularly appealing, tight jeans accentuating her well-proportioned curves and a low-cut V-neck sweater hugging her breasts and displaying ample cleavage. Geneva's long dark hair, flawless olive skin, and smoky-gray eyes had enticed more than a few tourists. Apparently, women who chose Alaska as a vacation destination often enjoyed all sorts of new experiences, because the summer before, Geneva had seemed to snag as many heterosexual women as lesbians for quick encounters after her shift.

Now, she'd obviously set her sights on Emery, who just might bite. She listened with interest to whatever Geneva proposed, and her smile grew bigger by the second.

"Pasha?" Dita's voice penetrated her narrow focus.

She turned back to face the booth and found all her friends staring at her with perplexed expressions.

"Everything okay?" Dita asked. "You kind of spaced out there for a bit."

She considered telling them what she was feeling, relaying this unusual and profound sensation of attraction, but Emery obviously didn't share her fascination. So she kept quiet, feeling foolish that she'd built all this up so much. Perhaps her infallible instinct had gone haywire and wasn't as reliable as she'd always believed.

"Sorry. I'm fine," she lied, feeling anything but.

"Looks like Geneva might have found an end to her dry streak." Bryson's gaze had drifted toward the bar. "Nice newcomer. Anyone know her?"

Bryson felt protective toward Geneva. They had been involved for a few months before Karla came to town, but Bryson broke it off when it became clear Geneva wanted more than she could give. So she couldn't fault Bryson's happiness that Gen had found some company, though it only added to her despair.

"Nope," Karla said, and the rest of the group shook their heads or mumbled agreement. Pasha returned her gaze to the pair. Geneva was still parked next to Emery, doing her best to engage her complete attention. She even suggestively caressed her empty drink tray now, but Emery's focus had shifted at least in part to Grizz, who had joined them.

After a couple of minutes of conversation, Grizz reached for one of the room keys in back of the bar and led Emery toward the back stairs, carrying one of her backpacks. Geneva said something after their retreating figures that Pasha couldn't hear, but Emery stopped at the doorway. She turned and gave Geneva a smile and small nod before disappearing.

As soon as she left, Geneva made a beeline for their booth and planted herself on the edge of one side, next to Dita. "Oh, my God." She dramatically fanned herself with her empty drink tray. "Did you get a load of tall, dark, and gorgeous? Her name's Emery, and she's going to be around for the next few months. Months! She's definitely playing for our side."

"I know that name," Dita said. "She's spending the summer here and going on a bunch of trips with us. But she wasn't due today, I don't think. Pasha, do you recollect seeing her file?"

"Yes, I remember." Pasha tried not to convey her torrent of emotions—confusion, jealousy, and who knew what else—or reveal how she'd practically memorized the file after it prompted such a profound physical reaction. She felt suddenly too vulnerable, and almost ashamed for getting so worked up about something apparently not to be. "She wasn't due for another few days. She's going on the photography trip."

"Hey, since you're already in town," Dita turned toward Chaz, "you up for taking that one out with Pash? It's only a three-dayer. The guy I have scheduled asked for some time off for personal reasons."

"Sure. It'll be a breeze if the rest of the clients are like that one—she certainly seems low-maintenance," Chaz observed. "Fit. Well-used outdoor gear. Obviously a seasoned traveler. And if you're right about her," she told Geneva, "should be fun company."

"Uh…fun company?" Megan scowled, but with obvious mirth in her eyes. "Do I need to play chaperone, honey?"

"You know I just mean it's always more relaxed on these trips when you have some like-minded women along," Chaz said.

"Instead of some urban Muffy who can't stop talking about the mall, and her boyfriend problems, and—"

"I was kidding, honey." Megan stroked her arm. "I know exactly what you mean and how devoted you are."

"Anyway, I intend to keep Emery far too busy for her to even look at another woman while she's here, married or single," Geneva declared. "I thought my hormones had gone into permanent hibernation, but they perked up immensely when she walked in."

Everyone else laughed, but Pasha couldn't even feign a smile. Though she wanted to feel angry with Geneva for treading on her territory, she knew better. She wanted Geneva to be happy, as she wished well for all her friends. And her suddenly unreliable intuition hadn't given her any claim whatsoever over Emery. But no matter how hard she tried, she couldn't help but feel it all a cruel, cruel injustice.

CHAPTER FIVE

Next day, June 2

"Okay, I think this is the last." Dita shouldered her pack as Pasha reached for the remaining food duffel earmarked for the fly-fishing trip. Bryson conducted her preflight checklist while the three couples and Lars boarded the plane. "Hold down the fort, and I'll see you in a few days." Though the guides carried satellite phones, the mountainous terrain, distance, and weather made the connections with the backcountry capricious.

"No problem." Pasha followed Dita out the door and toward the runway two blocks away. The Den had the village's best real estate. The wide windows in its rooms and restaurant overlooked the airport, an unremarkable clearing at the north edge of town with the small FAA station, a trio of hangars, a single gravel runway, and the wide Koyukuk river just beyond, which served floatplane traffic. However, behind the runway stood the magnificent Brooks Range, a seven-hundred-mile long, one-hundred-fifty-mile wide swath of peaks that stretched across Alaska and into Canada's Yukon.

Only a handful of settlements dotted the entire range, so everyone who lived in this isolated wilderness used small bush planes. In most of the state, they provided the only way in and out. Pasha had flown in them so many times she'd long ago lost count, comfortable enough with the experience. She still had a deep respect for the weather's unpredictability, though, and the risks involved in every flight. She'd had one scary trip with Bryson the previous summer, when they searched for a father and son who failed to show at the pickup point for their river-raft trip.

The weather had started fine but suddenly went lousy, with intermittent rain and a low cloud ceiling. Bryson found most of the passes obscured, so she had to make lengthy detours that ran them dangerously low on fuel. Upon their return to Bettles, she had to coast the last several hundred yards on empty tanks, Pasha gripping the handhold above her head so hard she lost all circulation in her fingers.

Because of that experience and the many stories she'd heard, Pasha worried every time one of her friends went into the sky because it might be the last time she would see them. Dita confessed she often thought the same, so every send-off always included a hug. "Have a wonderful trip," she told Dita as they embraced at the doorway. "And take care."

"I'll bring us back something special for dinner."

Bryson, dashing in her aviator sunglasses and ball cap, sheepskin-lined leather coat and jeans, came around to Pasha's side and removed the chock from the right front tire. "I'll come find you when I get back." She routinely stopped at the office when she returned from a trip drop-off run to share impressions of the clients and the location over a cup of coffee.

"Look forward to it. Have a great flight."

Bryson glanced up at the sky, an amazing shade of azure Pasha thought had to be unique to the clear air of the Far North. "Beautiful day for flying. The clients will get some great views." Contentment spread across her face. She clearly had found her true calling, perfect home, and ideal mate. Pasha wished for the same.

Once the plane vanished from view, she returned to the office. Booking calls wouldn't start for another hour, so she poured a second mug of coffee and settled into the back room, where she could be comfortable but hear if someone stopped in. Pasha didn't expect anyone, but Karla or Geneva often dropped by seeking company for breakfast when they rose early.

Dita had remodeled the office when she took over so it would have a more comfortable but rough-hewn look, with dark, rough-paneled walls, hardwood floors, and log beams spanning the high ceiling. Inuit art and photographs taken on recent trips of wildlife, breathtaking views, and happy clients having fun provided tasteful décor.

Before every trip, the guides also used the outer reception area to brief clients on what to expect. The briefings included extensive instruction on the leave-no-trace dictums of camping and hiking through the protected and fragile backcountry environment.

At the rear of the outer room stood the business counter and, beyond that, two doors: one to Dita's office and the other to the employees-only area. A lounge took up half the spacious back room—a tiny kitchen, trio of comfy stuffed armchairs, couch, and coffee table—and long tables, where they packed food and equipment for the trips, occupied the rest.

Pasha pulled her MP3 player from her pocket and stuck the headphones in her ears. She kept forgetting to ask Bryson to pick up some cheap portable speakers in the Fairbanks Walmart. Pasha missed the lack of immediate access to most goods and services. The tiny store in Bettles had a very limited inventory—a couple of aisles of food and bare essentials, so even mundane things had to be flown in on special order. The Internet was a godsend for shopping, but shipping costs were dear and didn't make sense for things like groceries. Fortunately, Bryson generally went to Fairbanks at least a couple of times a week this time of year and was always happy to pick something up for her when she had time to shop. She charged others a gas stipend, but not friends.

As Sara Bareilles's soulful voice filled her ears, Pasha settled into one of the armchairs with her coffee and a stack of client files. After sorting them by trips, she'd check to see if she needed to follow up with anyone. Maybe staying busy would keep her from imagining whether Emery and Geneva were enjoying each other's company, which she'd done half the night.

"One Sweet Love," one of her favorite tunes, came on, and she sang along as she often did. Thank God, Dita didn't seem to mind, but her friends always said she could carry a tune better than most. The song made her think of Emery, and the lyrics hit home. *Could I be wrong?*

Just then the familiar tingling feeling roared back, and she sensed someone was watching her. She quit singing mid-sentence and turned to find Emery Lawson framed in the doorway, wearing a bemused expression.

Pasha leapt to her feet, spilling her coffee and dumping files on the floor. Her earphones popped out as she rose, and a warm blush of embarrassment crept up her neck. As their eyes met she felt almost starstruck, in the worst possible way. Close-up, Emery mesmerized her, and she immediately memorized her every feature and nuance.

Her dark-brown eyes, warm and intelligent, shone with an inexplicable depth of maturity. A scar at the corner of Emery's lips emphasized her smile, and her glossy, medium-brown, collar-length hair, lighter on top, badly needed a trim. Combined with her deep tan, the natural highlights indicated Emery had spent a lot of time outdoors recently in a warm climate. A lot of Floridians visited Bettles, but she didn't look like the typical Miami Beach sun worshipper.

She didn't have the trappings of the typical businesswoman-on-holiday either, though Emery had a rather cosmopolitan look. Her clothes looked expensive and well-tailored, though also well-used. She had style and knew what suited her. But she wore no jewelry or makeup, her luggage more sturdy utilitarian than designer label. And her relaxed air and mischievously twinkling eyes didn't belong to the urban workaholics Pasha knew.

She tried to sort Emery into one of the categories the guides had come up with for types of clients, a half-serious, half-joking endeavor they fine-tuned after every trip. The categories for women, so far, included Barbie dolls and party girls, workaholics, athletes and outdoor-sports buffs, environmentalists and nature lovers, naïve small-towners, scientists, and chatterboxes.

Some of their clients could certainly fit in more than one category, and Emery might be one of them. Since she'd signed up for several trips, she might qualify as an outdoor-sports buff and/or environmentalist.

A sound registered vaguely in her consciousness.

"I'm s...sorry?" She had focused so compulsively on Emery she apparently hadn't been able to spare the brain cells necessary to register that Emery had asked her something. But, from her expectant expression, surely she had. God, she must look like an idiot.

Emery stooped to gather the files Pasha had dropped. "I said, I didn't mean to startle you. Are you all right?"

Pasha knelt and helped, trying to stem the hammering in her heart. She could feel her blush deepen. "I startle easily," she blurted. *Your first words to her, and that's what you come up with? I startle easily? Are you insane?* Usually calm, she had anticipated Emery's arrival so fervently she had frazzled her nerves, and to see the woman she'd thought so obsessively about turn up so unexpectedly turned her topsy-turvy.

"I wouldn't consider that an asset when you live in a state filled with grizzly bears and wolves," Emery remarked in a neutral tone. She handed Pasha the files she'd collected and they stood.

Mortified, Pasha was glad Dita hadn't been here to witness her humiliation. How ridiculous she must seem. She had to correct this impression before she told Emery she was one of her guides. "I didn't really mean to say that." She took a deep breath. "I guess you did make me jump a little, but that's completely uncharacteristic. I'm neither timid nor clumsy. Most of the time, anyway." Now she rambled, defending herself like a desperate realtor trying to sell a fixer-upper.

"I was kidding." Emery's eyes twinkled with mirth. "Obviously you didn't expect company and had your earphones on. I'm sorry. I imagine I gave you quite a fright. Can't say as I regret it, though. You sing beautifully."

Pasha began to reply, but her mind shut down again when Emery casually unbuttoned her leather coat. The burgundy turtleneck beneath tightly hugged her high round breasts. A large silver buckle centered on her low-cut jeans drew Pasha's eyes downward, to the flat plane of stomach and long legs. Dear God, try as she might, she couldn't help envisioning stripping off those clothes, one by one, to reveal the flesh beneath.

"I'm Emery Lawson, by the way."

Pasha tried desperately to find her voice, to respond with at least some humor or intelligence, but Emery had reduced her to a mumbling, stammering clod capable of only speechless adoration. She had to be making the worst possible impression.

"I'm looking for Dita Eidson. Is she around?" Emery asked.

A simple, impersonal, straightforward question. Easy, even for someone in Pasha's apparently compromised mental state. But it still took her longer to form a cohesive reply than it should have. Long enough for Emery to decide she wasn't the brightest bulb in the pack. "Sorry. She just left. Three-day fly-fishing trip."

"Ah. Well, not important. Got to town a few days early and just wanted to check in with her. I'll come back next week." She started to leave, but paused at the doorway. "Again, sorry I startled you." She disappeared before Pasha could find the words to stop her.

Pasha stared at the empty doorway long after she heard the outer door open and close. She replayed every excruciating moment, trying to come up with more clever, witty responses. She hadn't even had the presence of mind to introduce herself.

She wanted to cry, or hit something. Normally she had no trouble making a good impression, and she thought she'd perfected the art of warmly welcoming new clients to town.

Pasha needed to regroup and come up with a strategy for correcting her blunder. She had to gain Emery's confidence, since Emery had booked several trips with Eidson Eco-Tours that she'd guide. Definitely a challenge, because she seemed unable to relax around the woman or be her usual fairly eloquent self.

She hoped to eventually impress Emery with more than just her backcountry skills, because she didn't yet plan to concede that her intuition had misfired, or that destiny could so cruelly point her this forcefully toward someone she would have no opportunity to become intimate with.

CHAPTER SIX

Emery stood at the edge of the runway, admiring how the low sun painted the distant Brooks Range in golden hues. Alaska surprised her, exceeding her expectations in more ways than one, and she'd been here less than a full day.

She breathed in the crisp, clear air. Though she'd seen the splendor of the state in countless movies, documentaries, TV shows, and books, to actually soak in this experience firsthand, to see for herself the endless desolation of the landscape and stark beauty of the unspoiled wild, thrilled her. She couldn't wait to start exploring more of this magnificent place.

And then to discover that her Alaskan base apparently provided a backcountry haven for lesbians. Stumbling upon the lovely Sue Spires in Fairbanks had already surprised her, but to find so many lesbians in this remote hamlet had astounded her. The attractive waitress, Geneva, came on to her less than two minutes after she walked in the door, and certainly at least a few of the women in the corner booth—all attractive and fit outdoorswomen about her age—were "family" as well. Her gaydar pinged loudly as she swept her gaze over them, noting their haircuts, clothes, eye contact, and especially their body language. The brunette with the ball cap had her arm around the woman beside her, and they couldn't stop looking adoringly at each other and smiling.

She'd considered joining them and introducing herself, but, dog-tired, she'd just wanted to hit the sheets. She'd even had to politely decline Geneva's not-so-subtle invitation to join her for a drink after her shift. Despite her first-class naps during the long transatlantic flights, Emery still seemed sleep-deprived and felt the effects of the prolonged journey. She'd spent any reserve energy getting to know Sue Spires.

After a good eight hours' rest and a huge breakfast, however, she wanted to discover all Alaska could offer. She'd hoped Dita Eidson could schedule a custom trip to fill the next few days until her photography expedition. Ordinarily she loved taking off by herself, but she'd read enough about Alaska to know newcomers shouldn't strike off alone.

Right now, she'd check out Bettles and the nearby native village of Evansville, though that should take only a couple of hours. From the air, the two adjacent settlements looked miniscule, merely some clustered buildings and the mountains looming beyond. Probably totaled less than two square miles. But this area would serve as her home between trips, so she wanted to see what was available and perhaps meet some locals.

She'd thought about querying the woman at the outfitter's office, maybe ask some questions about her upcoming trips. But her odd reception made her wary of lingering.

Since her accident, little escaped Emery's attention. In the past, she'd certainly experienced moments of increased awareness of her surroundings, but only when she traveled to a new foreign locale. And she focused only on details that interested her—architectural marvels, unusual landscapes, eclectic costumes and food, a striking or unusual passerby.

But months of forced rehabilitative confinement had changed all that. She'd had long hours to memorize every sight, sound, and smell of her hospital room, the rehab area, and the staff who attended her. Even in a half-sleep, she could tell from the cadence of the mop in the hall which custodian was working. She knew the perfumes each nurse favored, could distinguish the gait and squeak of each pair of rubber-soled shoes, and even had gleaned some knowledge of her doctors' favorite foods. Her surgeon ate a lot of garlic and onions, her Korean orthopedist frequently reeked of kimchi, and one of the young interns who made evening rounds lived on pepperoni pizza.

Now she noted everything. As she slowly traversed the streets of Bettles, she studied the people she met, initiating a greeting of some sort if someone didn't immediately offer one—and they usually did. Often just a wave or good morning, but a few lingered when she slowed and exchanged a few words, introducing themselves or welcoming her to town and asking where she was from. To the latter, she always replied, "I'm from here, for now," which usually elicited a grin. It took a special kind of person to live in Alaska—one who possessed daring, a sense of adventure, and a rugged individualism. She suspected they could easily appreciate her vagabond reply.

After seeing all sorts of people the world over in a different light, with increased awareness, she possessed new tools when reflecting on strangers who crossed her path: assessing their body language, odor, subtle expressions, tone of voice, vocabulary, and more. Recently, she could frequently detect a lie or a false front.

Doubtless she'd badly flustered the woman in the outfitter's office, and she hadn't merely been surprised. She'd looked like she'd seen a ghost. Her hands trembled, she breathed rapidly, and her eyes remained wide in stunned shock too long. The woman seemed almost to recognize her, but she would swear they'd never formally met.

She *did* look familiar, but it was because she'd been among the women in the corner booth at the Den last night. Come to think of it, she'd looked Emery's way longer than normal. *Did she think even then that she knew me? If so, why didn't she say something?*

And the woman had ogled her so blatantly, even though startled, her gaze appreciative. Emery had certainly received similar scrutiny before, from both men and women. But this time the woman hadn't offered her number or even her name. She hadn't seemed anxious for Emery to stick around.

Something simmered in that woman, a lot more happening beneath the surface than she let on. Intrigued, Emery wondered what type of reaction she would get the next time they met.

The average tourist probably would have covered Bettles in a two-hour stroll, but Emery took longer. She paused often, studying the handful of small stores in addition to the Den, the post office, school, Alaska Power building, dozens of small houses, a ranger post and new National Park Service station, and, a quarter-mile distant, a fuel depot. Most handmade, all had thick, double-paned windows. Smoke poured from nearly every chimney, scenting the air with the fragrance of burning hardwoods.

The yard clutter often contained dogsleds, broken generators, and snowmobiles—not the typical fare of her suburban Detroit. She saw very few cars, presumably because people could reach Bettles only by air most of the year. In winter, when the boggy tundra and lakes froze solid, a road plowed over them connected to the Dalton Highway—a desolate, dangerous stretch of snow and ice.

Before she set off on the short hike to Evansville, she stood on the far edge of Bettles, staring toward the mountains and longing to be among them, dwarfed to nothingness in their shadows. Then she detected movement in the sky, and a low buzz flirted at the edge of her hearing. The small plane grew larger as it descended toward the airstrip.

Emery turned and jogged slowly back toward the Den. If she pushed too hard she'd end up limping at day's end. Many bush planes functioned as air taxis, operating for hire when not previously booked. Perhaps she *could* reach the mountains today.

Bryson Faulkner taxied the Cessna Caravan to the Eidson Eco-Tours hangar, a massive structure Dita had erected the summer before, and cut the engine. The hangar housed the 208, Skeeter's floatplane, and her Red Piper Super Cub, with ample room for another small bush plane, if needed, from one of the other Eidson outposts. She'd grab a sandwich to go from the Den and eat it in the office while briefing Pasha on the drop-off. She wanted to get back in the air as quickly as possible, this time in her own plane.

Actually, she could kill two birds with one stone and do some work. Dita had asked her to fly by the outlying areas where they'd drop off clients in the coming weeks and assess the gravel bars that served as her backcountry runways. Too much debris would necessitate finding a nearby alternate.

However, she lived for flying and always loved to take advantage of the days when she had less to worry about. A bush pilot could never say she had no worries at all, not in Alaska. Even during the best months, on perfect days, something could happen—freak winds, sudden turbulence, engine trouble miles from nowhere, fog, you name it. But this calm, sunny spell should remain, the weather fine all over the state.

As she jogged toward the Den, Bryson glanced at her watch. Almost noon. A Christmas gift from Karla, the heavy-duty, waterproof timepiece had both a GPS and an altimeter, a reassuring backup to the plane's equipment. "Forever yours, Karla" adorned its back.

"Hey, Grizz." She hailed him as she crossed through the next-to-empty Den to the bar, glancing at the village's six chronic alcoholics. "Can you get Ellie to make me a sandwich? Anything you got a lot of is fine. To go."

"You got it." He headed toward the kitchen.

As Bryson reached over the bar and poured herself a ginger ale, the mechanical growl of the grizzly at the door announced someone had come in. She turned to look as she settled on a barstool and saw the woman who'd arrived in town the night before and caught Geneva's eye. Emery something. Before Bryson could speak, the woman approached and hailed her with a nod. "You the pilot of that Cessna?"

"I am. Bryson Faulkner." She extended her hand.

"Emery Lawson," the stranger said as they shook. She took the next barstool and shed her coat over the back, slightly out of breath, as if she'd been running. "What are you doing this afternoon?"

"All depends," Bryson answered. "Whatcha got in mind?"

Chapter Seven

Emery recognized the pilot from her ball cap—Bryson Faulkner had sat in the corner booth the night before, beside the woman from the outfitter's office. Small place indeed, this little village. "I'd like to hire you for an hour or two. More, if you can recommend some must-see destination that takes longer and you've got the time."

"You haven't asked what I charge."

"I don't have to. I've done my research, and I expect your fare's reasonable."

"You have a particular errand or a destination you want to visit?" Bryson sipped from her glass. "Or is this just a flightseeing charter?"

"You're based here, right?"

"Yeah."

"So you know this area well?"

"Pretty well." Bryson's tone and the grin tugging at the edge of her mouth indicated a supreme understatement.

Emery didn't need reassurance, though most visitors in her position would appreciate it. "Then please take me to some of your favorite places."

Bryson did smile then, full and genuine. "You looking for awesome views or an adrenaline rush?"

Emery smiled back. "I'd welcome some of both."

"Eaten recently?"

"Not for a few hours."

"Grizz!" Bryson hollered toward the back. "Make it two! And throw in a couple apples." She turned toward Emery as Grizz shouted, "You got it," from the kitchen. "You're going on a bunch of Eidson Eco-Tours trips, right?"

Curious, Emery didn't try to hide her surprise. "Does everybody in town know everybody's business?" She'd found similar overfamiliarity and curiosity about strangers in some of the isolated European villages she'd visited.

She hadn't expected it in Bettles, though. The area attracted so many adventure-seekers she'd have thought strangers in town no longer raised eyebrows or interest. But apparently the long, dark winters made locals long for some gossip about or interaction with new faces. Probably few tourists visited in winter and spring. Eidson offered only a handful of dogsled and northern-lights-watching expeditions then, the reason obvious. Here in early June, temperatures still climbed only into the low fifties.

Bryson laughed. "Maybe that's true, but I'm one of Dita's pilots. I'll likely transport you a lot of the time. When you arrived last night, Dita recognized you. We intended to say hello but you didn't come back down."

"I noticed your group, but the long trip here exhausted me."

"Well, welcome to Bettles. Hope you'll enjoy your stay. Dita does an awesome job arranging trips. Experienced guides. Great destinations and good food. Safety first, always." Bryson gulped her ginger ale when she spotted Grizz coming from the kitchen holding a large paper bag.

"Throw in a couple sodas," Bryson told him as she fished out her wallet. "Diet Coke for me. Emery?"

"Same."

Bryson stuck the sodas into the food bag. "You mind if we take my Cub instead of the Cessna? I can give you a better deal 'cause it sucks less gas, and it's better for what you want and what I need to do."

"Fine by me."

"I charge three hundred an hour, but if we follow my itinerary, I'll cut that in half. Expect you might be repeat business."

"Appreciate it. And yes, I'd like to hire you between trips to see as much as possible."

"Your timing's actually great. I intended to visit some of the places I'll be taking clients the next few months, to check landing possibilities, so you'll get to preview where you'll be. Along the way I'll detour to a couple of my favorite stretches." Bryson zipped her leather coat and rose.

"Sounds great."

"I have to make a quick stop at the outfitter's office," Bryson said. "Need to grab anything from your room?"

"Yes. Camera and binoculars, and maybe another layer."

"Meet you out at the Eidson hangar, then. The big one. Logo on the side. Ten minutes?"

"Sounds good." Excited, Emery headed upstairs to grab her stuff as Bryson left the bar. She'd always wanted to fly low into the Alaskan wilderness with an experienced bush pilot. Bryson projected confidence and maturity, without braggadocio. Emery looked forward to getting to know her because she seemed a kindred spirit. And perhaps spending time with her might give Emery insights into more trips in Alaska and information about the Eidson tours. Maybe she'd even ask what was up with the woman in the outfitter's office, since they worked together and looked to be friends.

"Eidson Eco-Tours, Pasha speaking. How can I help you?" Pasha grabbed a sip of coffee while she waited for the caller to state his business. Her mug had gone cold as she handled both the booking calls and the administrative issues Dita usually dealt with. Dita had briefed her well so Pasha knew how to handle most questions from vendors, clients, and other Eidson offices, and could isolate what to defer until Dita's return.

Soon, when the trips began in earnest, a local high-school girl would man the phone when she was out in the field and Dita had other duties.

She hadn't expected to be so busy after the few phone calls last week. The clock read just after noon as the client finished his long inquiry, and she realized why her stomach was rumbling. "I'm sorry, but we've booked that trip solid and already have six people on the waiting list. I can add your names, but I doubt we'll get that many cancellations. Maybe I can offer you an alternative."

She called up the revised schedule Dita had sketched out. "We're adding an additional fly-fishing trip two weeks later, July 23rd through the 31st, if we have enough interest. Same cost. Would that time period be possible?" When he replied in the affirmative, she continued. "Your party of four should guarantee that we'll add the trip. I'll confirm that in a couple days and e-mail you an update then, if you'll give me your name and e-mail address." She jotted down the information. He told her he'd call back once he got her note. "Great. Talk to you then."

She reached for her coffee, but the front door chimed as she raised the mug to her lips. Pasha started to curse under her breath until she saw Bryson. Praying for a temporary reprieve from the phone, she started to drool when she spotted the familiar Den take-out bag tucked under Bryson's arm. "Please tell me that's lunch."

Bryson winced. "Uh…I'd have gotten you something if I'd known you've been tied up here. Should've called ahead. Sorry."

"It's okay. Wishful thinking. I'll get over there soon, I hope. If not, I can scrounge an energy bar from the trip supplies."

"I'd go get you something, but I'm meeting a flightseeing client. I'll check out some of our trip destinations while I'm up there."

"I thought you had the afternoon free."

"Last-minute gig. Emery Lawson. Just wanted to stop in and tell you the group got off fine. No problems. Looks like a beautiful spot. Dita was in heaven." Bryson shifted the bag under her arm. "Going out in the Cub. Call me if you need me. Should be back in two, three hours."

"Will do. Have fun, and be safe."

"Always." As Bryson headed out the door and toward the runway, leaving behind the aroma of corned beef and fresh-baked bread, the phone rang.

Pasha's stomach protested as she reached for the headset. She'd hoped to perhaps run into Emery at the Den and make a better second impression. But that wouldn't happen today.

At least Emery wasn't with Geneva, though her chances with Emery looked a lot better than her own right now. Not only would Pasha probably miss her lunch break the next couple of days, she'd be lucky if she got out by dinnertime.

She'd likely get some alone time with Emery on the photography trip, still days away. But anything could happen in the interim; Geneva moved fast when she wanted something. The thought depressed her. She'd thought her course was certain, but she'd never experienced an intuitive episode like this unreliable one.

The restless, constant pressure in her gut had calmed since pointing her decidedly in Emery's direction, which confused her, too. Would it flare up again the next time they met? She caught the phone on the sixth ring and tried to sound perky and welcoming. "Eidson Eco-Tours, Pasha speaking. How can I help you?"

CHAPTER EIGHT

Emery didn't view the interior of the magnificent Super Cub as cramped, only cozy. She'd thrown on a heavy sweater because the heaters in some small planes didn't work well, but Bryson had installed a custom one that functioned effectively. Bryson had evidently modified the plane's exterior, too. Its dual landing apparatus allowed it to put down on either skis or huge tundra tires, and the springs and axles looked heavy-duty.

The seating arrangement—hers directly behind the pilot's, with big windows on either side—gave her a panoramic view better than any aircraft she'd ridden in previously. And Bryson, at one with this particular plane, apparently had a lot of experience. She inspected the Cub's exterior slowly and methodically, caressing the red fuselage like a lover while viewing it with a practiced eye. She took the same unhurried approach with her preflight checklist in the cockpit.

"Ever flown in a bush plane before?" Bryson asked as the engine warmed.

"Not like this. Just the orange Cessna that brought me from Fairbanks."

"Skeeter's plane. Well, my safety speech resembles his. I see you're belted in, expect you know how the buckle works." They started taxiing toward the end of the runway after Bryson got clearance on her radio. "We won't fly high enough to need oxygen. In the unlikely event we have to ditch in water, you can use the cushion you're sitting on as a floatation device. A fire extinguisher's strapped under my seat, and we have a first-aid kit in the back. I also carry a survival duffel with blankets, tent, food, water, gun, and stove in it."

"Ever had to use that stuff?"

"Oh, sure. Every commercial pilot up here will run into something unexpected occasionally, usually weather-related. And I've flown more than twenty-five years. We all abide by VFR—visual flight rules. If you can't see at least a mile, or if the ceiling's under 500 feet, you can't fly. If a bad storm or fog moves in when you're still a couple hundred miles from a settlement, sometimes you have to set down and wait it out."

Despite the admission, Emery felt no fear. Bush pilots had to take bigger risks than most of their aviator counterparts, but she loved the risks involved because taking them made her feel fully alive. And even before they lifted off, she felt safe with Bryson, with her extraordinary quarter-century of bush flying and her relaxed, matter-of-fact manner.

When she'd finished with her communications with the FAA station, Bryson half-turned in her seat. "Want to fly low? Better view, but makes some people nervous."

"By all means."

"You got it." The Cub, following a river, quickly closed in on the Brooks Range.

They flew low enough Emery could see a lot of detail in the flat landscape. Small ponds, created by the melting frozen tundra, reflected the azure sky and fluffy clouds in their still, placid water. Bryson banked sharply right over the lumpy green-and-brown mattress, the trees sparse. "Moose," she called over her shoulder as she pointed right.

Emery spotted movement in a bog thick with willow shoots. A dark patch of brown emerged from the edge and ambled toward another, similar thicket. The hulking brute didn't move very fast, either impervious to the circling plane or impeded by the difficult terrain. "Awesome."

They banked away toward their original heading and soon reached a wide river valley with high mountains on either side—their way into the Brooks Range. Bryson kept the Cub low enough Emery could see the crests of whitewater rapids as the wide, serpentine tributary raged over rock falls. "What's that?" she asked.

"The Wild River. We'll pass over my cabin soon."

"Great. Point it out. And anything else of interest." Emery stared mostly ahead, looking over Bryson's shoulder as the valley narrowed. She'd seen no sign of anything manmade since they left Bettles.

The steep cliff faces grew closer on either side until they seemingly roared down a long hallway. The rush of exhilaration made her dizzy. "Unbelievable," she told Bryson. "Exactly what I wanted."

"Tip of the iceberg," Bryson replied as the plane descended another few feet, almost skimming the top of the trees that crowded the narrow strips of land on either side of the river. "Where we're going, we might glimpse the Porcupine Caribou Herd. And I know a couple of valleys where the spring flowers should be at their peak."

Emery pulled out her camera and began to snap pictures. She already had a few thousand photos on her portable hard drive, but she'd easily double that number during her time in the Far North. The automatic-stabilization feature ensured that nearly every shot was postcard beautiful.

The river valley widened again, the mountains retreating a half mile on either side, as the strip of trees lining the water grew into a thick, impenetrable forest.

"My cabin's coming up on the left," Bryson said. "Right at the fork of the river. Built it myself."

Emery could see the rooftop in a small clearing a short hike from the water. Set on a rise with mountains all around it, the log structure had to have a magnificent view. "Looks like a nice bit of handiwork. But where the heck do you land?"

"That gravel bar in the river. I like about three hundred feet at least." The spit of sand she pointed to seemed impossibly short.

Emery looked in all directions, but saw no other sign of civilization. "Hard to get accustomed to the isolation up here?"

Bryson chuckled. "Lived in Alaska all my life, so I'm more accustomed to it than most. But yeah, used to get to me now and then. Not anymore. I have a partner."

"Kind of thought as much when I saw you all last night."

Bryson glanced at her rearview mirror. "Pretty observant."

"I notice things, yes. You're lucky. She's beautiful."

Bryson chuckled. "Yeah. Amazing in a lot of other ways, too. Karla's an RN."

"I imagine a very valuable resource up here."

"Nearest doctor's in Fairbanks. Karla was an ER nurse in Atlanta, so she can handle most emergencies."

"Mind if I ask…were all the women with you gay?"

"Don't mind. And yeah. We kinda pegged you, too. Well, Geneva sure did."

"The waitress?"

"Gen's a good friend. You can imagine up here, opportunities are kind of limited, so she might have been a bit…overly anxious… but you shouldn't hold that against her. She's really down-to-earth. Not a player. Just falls hard and fast, if you know what I mean."

Emery detected concern in Bryson's tone, like she was trying to ensure Geneva didn't get hurt. "Duly noted."

"We're a close-knit group. We look out for each other."

"It's great to be around people you understand, and who understand you. That you can be completely yourself with. I envy you that."

"You'll get to know most of 'em in the next few weeks. For sure Dita, and two of the guides you'll be going out with—Chaz and Pasha."

"I look forward to it. I went over to the Eidson office this morning and sort of met one of your friends there—but I didn't get her name."

"That'd have been Pasha, I expect. She mans the office when Dita's away."

"What's she like?" Perhaps Bryson could give Emery some insight about why this Pasha had been so flustered during their interaction, and why the woman seemed almost to recognize her.

"Pash?" The inquiry seemed to surprise Bryson. "Very capable. Bright. Funny. Why you asking?"

"Just curious about her. We had an odd…chat."

"We'll likely most all be back at the Den having dinner tonight. Around six. You're welcome to join us and I'll introduce you around."

"I'd like that."

They soared over a massive lake, and Bryson dropped low over a cabin on the shoreline and dipped her wings right and left as if in greeting. As she banked around in a circle, Emery saw a woman holding a child emerge onto the porch to wave back. "Maggie Rasmussen and her baby, Karson," Bryson explained as she wagged her wings again and continued north. "You'll meet her husband Lars for sure—he's an Eidson guide, too. Out right now with Dita on a trip. They're my extended family, you could say. Maggie is Karla's sister, and they're our nearest neighbors."

Beyond the lake the valley narrowed again and the river forked. Bryson turned the Cub sharply left, following the smaller tributary, and shot through a canyon where the cliffs seemed mere feet from their wingtips. The adrenaline pouring through Emery's veins intoxicated her so much she could barely keep her camera steady. "I love this."

"Gonna dump out in a wide valley soon," Bryson told her. "Keep an eye on the hillside to your right for Dall sheep."

As predicted, Emery spotted a dozen of the beasts dotting the rocky slope, their white coats starkly contrasted against the brown-and-green backdrop. She could make out the distinctive circular horns on the rams and the game trails snaking through the area. With her telephoto lens and a fast aperture, she could take great close-ups. "Very cool. Think I'll see any grizzlies while I'm here?"

"Might see one in the next couple hours where we're going." Bryson negotiated her way through another maze of river valleys until Emery lost all sense of direction. "Coming up on our main drop-off point for river-rafting trips." The plane descended over another wide, whitewater river and slowed. "You signed up for any of those?"

"Yes. The first ten-day trip."

"Got some debris on my strip, I see. But not too bad. Hang on."

Almost before Emery realized it, they landed on a short gravel bar dotted with logs and other detritus. Bryson artfully maneuvered through the obstacle course, the high wings of the Cub scooting over some of the larger pieces, until the plane stopped just a few feet shy of the water. "Ready for lunch?" Bryson asked as she cut the engine.

Emery's heart hammered from the abrupt and exhilarating touchdown, but she tried to keep her voice steady. "Sure thing."

They found a large rock a few feet from the water's edge to serve as their bench and picnic table, the surface smooth and warm from the sun. Emery snapped photos in between bites of her sandwich. In every direction, majestic peaks, most still tipped with snow, dominated the landscape. "They all look so much alike. And so endless," she said as she adjusted her settings to take a panoramic shot of the vast range. "I haven't seen you consult a map or even use your GPS. How do you keep from losing your way?"

"We're still in my backyard. Very little around here I don't know, I've crisscrossed it so long."

"You said you'd been flying for more than twenty-five years? You don't seem old enough."

Bryson grinned. "Learned to fly before I learned to drive. Dad taught me—never a better pilot or teacher than him."

"Is he glad you're following in his footsteps or does he worry about you?"

Bryson's smile faded as she stared off to the north. "He worried," she finally said in a soft voice. "But he was proud I shared his passion for flying."

"I'm sorry if I hit a nerve."

"All good. Miss him, that's all. We were close."

"Sorry for your loss. I empathize. Both my folks are gone."

Bryson picked up a smooth stone and tried to skip it across the river, but it hopped only twice before a rogue wave snagged it and dragged it under. "So, you got some of my story and a bit about my friends. Why don't you tell me about yourself? Not many outsiders come up for so long."

"Well, I'm here for a few months because I've always wanted to visit Alaska, and I like to spend time really getting to know a place. What else do you want to know?"

"Whatever you want to share. Where you from?"

"That's not starting with an easy one." Emery chewed her sandwich as she thought about her answer. The pat one she'd been giving seemed too flippant for Bryson. "Some months ago, I'd have said Detroit. But I'm in a kind of vagabond place right now. I sold my place, put my few things in storage, and hit the road. I have no idea where I'll finally end up."

"No ties anywhere?"

"None to speak of, no."

"What do you do?"

"Nothing right now. I made a good living as an international courier and got around the world a good bit, but never with time to see much of anything." She ate more of her sandwich, marveling at how simple corned beef could taste so wonderful in such a setting. "You know the deal. Working hard, saving up, always living for the future. One day I decided to just quit and start living the life I'd always wanted to."

"Lot of folks, especially after they come up here and get some time to put things in perspective, vow to do that, but most never will. Why, do you think?"

"Too afraid of the unknown, maybe. It's hard to chuck a job that pays well and isn't half-bad to chase a dream, especially with the way the economy's been the last few years. Or responsibilities to their loved ones tie them where they are."

"You didn't have that?" Bryson asked. When Emery didn't immediately answer, she added, "Or is that too personal a question?"

"No, it's all right." She still felt a deep sense of guilt about breaking it off with Lisa, because Lisa hadn't yet moved on. Every now and then, Emery called to check up on her and tell her she was well and safe. But that might only prolong Lisa's period of healing. Did Emery make the hurt all raw and fresh again every time they connected? "I was involved and living with someone," she told Bryson.

She'd made a lot of friends in her journey, but had opened up to none of them about her relationship. Easy to talk to, Bryson emitted such a trustworthy air Emery knew she'd be a good sounding board. Though she knew in her heart she'd made the right decisions about her life, she always valued an objective opinion. "We were very compatible. Lisa's sweet and down-to-earth, and has such a dry sense of humor she made me laugh several times a day. The sex was still great, after three years. But I always knew she was more, well, you know…she really loved me a lot. And I couldn't return the intensity." She glanced at Bryson, gauging her reaction by her facial expressions and body language. "Finally I realized I was holding her back from finding the kind of deep, mutual commitment she wanted, and needed. So I broke it off. I hurt her pretty badly."

Bryson nodded thoughtfully. "Tough thing to do, when you care about someone." She looked over at Emery. "Pretty much the same story with Geneva and me. I couldn't return her feelings. But we only dated three months or so."

"That explains why you sound protective about her."

Bryson grinned shyly in acknowledgment.

"Sometimes I think I should have walked away from Lisa early on," Emery said. "As soon as I realized it was off-balance and always would be."

"Don't beat yourself up about it. You were true to yourself, which everyone has to be. And you took her long-term well-being into account, even if it maybe happened later than it should've." Bryson's tone held no judgment or criticism. "We move on. It took Geneva a while, but she's in a good place now, open to the right person coming along."

"I really hope Lisa is able to, soon. She deserves to be happy."

Bryson got to her feet and brushed crumbs from her jeans. "Everyone deserves to be happy. Ready to see more?"

"Absolutely."

She helped Bryson clear some of the lighter debris from her gravel-bar runway, then they were on their way again.

For the next ninety minutes, they flew through canyons and over mountain passes in the Gates of the Arctic National Park, which, Bryson informed her, was roughly the size of Switzerland. They landed briefly in the places where her trips would commence, and each and every spot seemed more breathtaking than the last. She took hundreds of photos, grateful for her 16GB memory card and extra batteries.

They spotted two grizzlies, a small herd of caribou, and several more moose. For these, she set the adjustment to the camera's HDVideo setting, and shot moving footage as Bryson swooped low. She was having the time of her life, and she liked and admired Bryson more by the minute, but the experience ended too soon.

"We need to head back." Bryson banked sharply right over a wide plain of tundra so thick with wildflowers it looked like a colorful patchwork quilt.

"Do we have to?"

Bryson laughed. "Getting low on fuel."

"Well, I've had an amazing day, Bryson. I hope I can hire you again soon. I don't have anything going on until the photography trip."

"Must say, I wish we could stay out, too. Had a real nice day having you along. In fact, since I get to charge Dita for my gas for this trip, I'm going to give you this freebie. My welcome to Bettles. Next time, you can get my special-friend's rate. We can look at my calendar for the next few days if you join us for dinner tonight."

"That's incredibly generous, Bryson. I can't thank you enough. And yes, I'd love to meet your friends and firm up our next outing."

Chapter Nine

Pasha tried to force herself to stop glancing at the clock. Every time she did, her heart sank, and she'd already checked the computer readout to make sure the clock was correct. Barely four. Again. Still. The last half hour had crept, and the surreal time distortion increased. She couldn't wait to put the nonstop calls to voice mail and start on the paperwork that had taunted her all day, but she had another hour before the magic deadline.

At least the demands of the day had prevented her from dwelling on Emery Lawson. Well, she *had* found herself spacing out a few times while a client droned on about some insignificant matter, imagining instead that she was out with Bryson and Emery in the Cub. Of course, in her daydream she acted relaxed and eloquent around Emery, not like the bumbling idiot she'd been that morning.

They must be having a great time, she concluded, because they'd been gone four hours, instead of two or three. Pasha couldn't dwell on the possibility that trouble might have delayed them. She believed that projecting "bad karma" only drew it to you, while staying upbeat helped keep things in a positive balance.

Relieved, she spotted Bryson through the big picture windows jogging toward the office. Pasha glared at the phone, demanding its silence for at least a few minutes so she could ask about the flightseeing excursion. Happily, at least for the moment, it cooperated.

"You're back!" She greeted Bryson as soon as she came through the door. "How'd it go?"

"Great! Perfect day for flying." Bryson shed her jacket over a chair. "Gonna grab a soda. Want anything?"

"Nope, I'm good."

Bryson returned from the backroom fridge with a Diet Coke and settled into a big, comfy chair in the waiting area. "Made it to most all the trip drop-off points," she reported, after taking a long swig of her drink. "Everything looked pretty good. Some debris on the gravel bars from spring breakup, but we got in and cleared away what we needed. Emery helped a lot. Had to bypass the one at the base of Eekayruk Mountain, though. I'll have to borrow Skeeter's floatplane to clean it up."

Happy to learn their summer landing sites had no problems, Pasha especially wanted to hear Bryson's opinion of Emery. But she hesitated to reveal her inexplicable draw toward the newcomer, especially since her power seemed to have short-circuited. And something might have already developed between Emery and Geneva. "That's good news. Dita will be happy to hear it."

"Say, did you add anything to my calendar today?"

"Yup, sure did." Pasha called up the flight schedule on the computer and isolated Bryson's bookings. "Phone's been crazy. Added a big freight delivery in a couple weeks to Prudhoe Bay, a handful of custom air-taxi runs in July and August—"

"Anything the next few days?"

"No. Nothing firm. Though I did get a call from a couple in Evansville asking about your availability this week. The wife's due date is coming up and they want to reach Fairbanks before she goes into labor. I told them I'd pass on their number so you can talk to them directly." She fished through the pink message notes from the day until she found the right one and handed it to Bryson.

"Thanks. Can you print out an updated schedule for me? Emery wants to book another flightseeing trip."

"Sure." Pasha felt herself blushing at the mention of Emery's name. Cursing to herself, she turned away from Bryson to retrieve the document as the printer spit it out. She apparently couldn't control how her body and psyche dealt with this insane but undeniable attraction, and her powerlessness frustrated her.

"She's joining us for dinner," Bryson said. "She should fit in great with the group."

Pasha's spirits lifted at the prospect of seeing Emery, but then she remembered the big stack of bills and client inquiries she still had to sort through. "Hope I can make it. I've got a lot to do here before I can think about leaving."

"Even if you miss eating with us, you should come by. You know we'll all hang around."

"I'll do that."

"Geneva's got the night off so I'll ask her, too. They might have some mutual interest, and I like Emery a lot. She seems very centered. Mature. Got a good head on her shoulders."

"Sounds like she made a deep impression. You can really read people."

Bryson grinned. "Yeah, she's good company. An interesting woman."

"How so?"

"Seen a lot, done a lot. Bit of an adrenaline junkie." Bryson chuckled. "Probably why I like her. But I'll let you judge for yourself." She checked her watch. "Better run. Promised Karla I'd meet her back at the room. We're moving our things to Chaz and Megan's rental cabin."

"I'd offer to help, but—" The phone rang.

At her frown, Bryson shrugged in sympathy. "You're swamped. And we don't have much, anyway." She grabbed her coat and headed for the door. "See you later."

"Hope so." Pasha answered the phone with her standard greeting, but had to repeat it a second and then third time when it became apparent the Japanese caller on the other end couldn't understand, especially with the static-filled connection. Would this tiresome workday never end?

❖

Emery spent an hour in her room with her laptop reviewing the photos she'd taken with Bryson, then transferred them onto her portable hard drive. Most were damn good shots when viewed full screen, a lasting, vivid reminder of a perfect day. She looked forward to spending more time with Bryson and getting to know her friends.

But still adjusting to the time change, she struggled against the urge for a quick nap. She was meeting everyone in less than an hour, so if she allowed herself some shut-eye, she'd only become groggy and less apt to sleep tonight. She chose a shower instead and ordered coffee, hoping the combination would kick-start a second wind. The hot water and a Percocet would also help dispel the nagging aches that had resurfaced from sitting so long in the cramped cockpit and helping Bryson move debris.

Wrapping her body in a large towel while she used another as a turban, she emerged from the steamy bathroom and lingered before the closet, mulling over her clothing choices. A knock at the door told her the coffee had arrived, so she half hid behind the door because she expected to see Grizz.

Instead, the waitress, Geneva, stood armed with a tray holding a carafe, mug, cream, and sugar packets. "Hey, Emery. I'm not actually working tonight, but I heard Grizz say you wanted some coffee, so I volunteered." She smiled coyly as she slipped past Emery and set the tray on the bed.

Before Geneva could turn back around, Emery shot back into the bathroom and closed the door. "Be right out," she hollered as she hurriedly redressed in her discarded clothes. Modesty, per se, didn't propel her to avoid having Geneva see her half-dressed; quite possibly they might become intimate, and she always wanted to prepare her lovers. Her many scars had shocked and distracted those she hadn't, particularly the large rose-shaped knot at the base of her throat where the Bulgarian medic had performed a hasty tracheotomy.

When she emerged in her wrinkled turtleneck and jeans, her hair still wet, she found Geneva perched on the edge of the bed.

"I'm sorry if I made you uncomfortable." Geneva frowned apologetically. "Shouldn't have just invited myself in."

"It's fine." Emery sat on the bed, too, the tray between them, and poured herself a mug of coffee. "Don't misinterpret—I'm not incredibly shy. I just…well, I'll tell you about it some other time, all right?"

"Sure." Geneva got to her feet, obviously interpreting Emery's lack of explanation as a signal to leave. "I didn't mean to disturb you. Just wanted to make sure you'll join us for dinner. I ran into Bryson downstairs."

"You didn't disturb me, Geneva. Really." Emery studied the dark-haired waitress. She'd already noted that Geneva had a beautiful face and well-proportioned curves, but they'd spent so few seconds together last night and she'd been so tired she remembered little else. Now she could let Geneva know she was interested, so she assessed her openly and appreciatively. The natural sunlight streaming through the window put amber highlights in Geneva's long, dark hair and played off her smoky-gray eyes and olive skin. She knew how to showcase her natural beauty and killer smile with minimal makeup and jewelry.

Grinning, Emery said, "And yes. I'm looking forward to it. Maybe afterward, you and I can have that drink together or take a walk or something."

"Or something?" Geneva smiled slyly. "I like the sound of that. I was afraid I came on too strong last night."

"No, not at all. I was just beat from all the traveling. I'd love to get to know you better."

"Great. Me, too. I'll let you finish getting ready and meet you downstairs?"

"See you in a few. Save me a seat."

"Right next to me."

After she'd gone, Emery pondered if she hesitated to pursue Geneva because of what Bryson had said.

Emery intended to let Geneva know up front, as she always did with women, that she was just passing through and wanted only some mutual fun and good company. But from what Bryson had said, Geneva fell in love quickly and had been hurt more than once. She didn't want it happening again, even if Geneva agreed to a brief, no-strings affair. And she didn't want to risk alienating Bryson just as they began to become friends. Perhaps she should rethink the situation.

She hoped tonight would give her some answers, not only concerning Geneva, but also about the woman at the office—Pasha—and the weird way she'd acted.

Emery changed her clothes and dried her hair, marveling again at the surprises lurking at every turn. Checking her reflection a final time, she absentmindedly brushed the hair out of her eyes. Her bangs needed cutting, but she kept forgetting and hadn't seen a salon or barbershop in town. Maybe she could hitch a ride with Bryson the next time she headed to Fairbanks.

Filled with optimism about the evening ahead, she took the stairs down to the restaurant two at a time.

CHAPTER TEN

Bryson, Geneva, and three of the other women who'd been there the night before waited for Emery at the corner booth. Pasha wasn't among them. Emery pushed away her unexpected pang of disappointment. A lot of women ran late, and potential new friends sat right in front of her.

Bryson spotted her the instant she hit the doorway and half stood, waving her over. The others all watched her intently, too, and she was glad she'd given some thought to her clothes. She'd left her coat in her room and wore her usual black jeans, her boots, and a thick, black turtleneck sweater that hugged her. Various women had commented favorably on the ensemble, though she didn't entirely understand the appeal. She crossed the room, grateful the Percocet had kicked in and she had no trace of a limp.

"Hey, Emery. Glad you could join us." Bryson motioned for her to sit at the end next to Geneva.

"Emery." Geneva smiled as she slid into the spacious booth, which could seat seven easily, eight in a squeeze. But Geneva stayed put, so their thighs would touch throughout the meal.

"Hi, Bryson. Geneva," Emery said.

"I'd like you to meet my partner Karla. Karla Edwards."

Karla extended her hand across the table and smiled warmly. They both had to reach a bit to touch. "Really happy to meet you. Bryson's been talking about you since she got back." Emery noted Karla's short, light-brown hair, hazel eyes, and fair complexion.

"I could feel my ears burning. I'm glad to meet you, too, Karla. Bryson told me a lot about you, as well."

"Next up is Chaz Herrick." Bryson indicated the athletic brunette next to Karla with a nod. "She'll be one of your guides. And her wife, Megan Maxwell. She's a TV field producer for World News Central."

"Freelance, now," Megan said as she and Chaz also extended a hand. "Nice to meet you."

"I'll be one of your guides next week on the photography trip," Chaz said. "Bryson says you know your way around the out of doors."

"I've done some primitive camping. Backpacking, kayaking, and such."

"Always great when you have someone with previous experience along," Chaz said. "Though that'll be most important on the kayak trips, which are my specialty. You going on any of those?"

"Yes, the ten-day one in August."

"Feel comfortable in a kayak?"

"Up to class four. I know how to roll."

"Good to know. If we get a lot of newbies, I may have you help watch some of them."

"Be happy to."

Grizz materialized at Emery's elbow with a handful of menus. "What can I get ya, Emery?"

The rest of the table, she noted, drank beer out of a now nearly empty pitcher, except for Megan, who had white wine. "Another pitcher of that and a glass?"

"Coming right up."

She scanned the menu, though she'd nearly memorized it during breakfast. It offered an enormous and unusual array of dishes for such a remote establishment and played up local resources. To start, every table got a basket of freshly baked sourdough bread, served with butter and homemade aioli. Because of the size of their party, or maybe because they all knew Grizz, they'd gotten a whole loaf. The specialties for dinner included reindeer stew, caribou or elk steaks, cod and king crab, and smoked salmon tacos. And for dessert, the Den recommended their baked Alaska or Ellie's wild salmonberry crisp with home-churned vanilla ice cream.

"Anything there is good," Geneva told her. "Usually people order the reindeer stew, the caribou steaks, and the king crab."

Most of the other women never opened their menus, no doubt because they, too, knew every item.

Grizz returned with their beer and poured Emery a glass, then topped off the others'. "What'll it be?"

Megan and Chaz both ordered seafood, Bryson got a caribou steak, and Geneva and Karla got the tacos. The dinners all came with salads, and the women selected several different dressings, but Grizz didn't bother to write down anything. She ordered the crab and asked for ranch dressing before reaching for her beer. She sampled local brews everywhere she traveled, and this one had an orangey-coriander finish, unlike anything she'd tried. "This is very good. What is it?"

A couple of the women giggled, and all of them smiled as Geneva replied. "Panty Peeler."

"You're kidding, right?"

More laughs. "No, I'm not," Geneva said. "It's a microbrew from a place in Anchorage. The Midnight Sun Brewing Company."

Bryson raised her glass. "Here's to welcoming Emery to Bettles and into our little group."

"Hear, hear" and "Welcome!" and "To Emery!" followed as they all touched glasses across the table.

"So, I've met Geneva and Bryson…" Emery said, making brief eye contact with them before turning to Bryson's partner. "Now, I know Karla's a nurse…Bryson flew me over your cabin today, by the way. I can imagine how beautiful the view is."

Karla nodded. "Different every morning, depending on the weather."

"And Bryson said you worked in an ER in Atlanta. How long have you been here?" Emery asked.

"Two years. I came looking for my long-lost sister, whom I'd never met—Maggie Rasmussen. I found her, and love, too." Karla stroked Bryson's arm, and Bryson kissed Karla's forehead.

"We flew over their cabin, too. Not very near, to be your nearest neighbors," Emery said.

"Seven miles," Bryson replied with a sly grin. "Ask Karla to tell you sometime about the first time she tried to do the distance in a boat."

Karla rolled her eyes. "We laugh about it now, but at the time it wasn't pretty. Let's just say newbies should never tackle the wilderness alone. Period. Nearly got my feet frozen off, till Bryson rescued me."

"Have you had difficulty adjusting to the move?" Emery asked. "I mean, Atlanta is sure polar opposite Bettles in almost every way."

"Well, when you're head over heels in love," Karla said, glancing over again at Bryson with a look of pure adoration, "you kind of don't notice the isolation or lack of some of the things you once had." She returned her attention to Emery. "Oh, sure, once in a while I hate that I can't get an immediate fix for a sushi craving, or that I've missed some hot new TV series that everyone who passes through is raving about. And the winters...well, I'm still getting used to seeing the thermometer bottom out at minus fifty. But all in all...I wouldn't do a thing differently. It's home, now."

"Are you both native Alaskans?" Emery asked Chaz and Megan.

"Nearly so, for me," Chaz said. "My family moved here when I was ten, from a commune in Oregon."

"I'm a more recent arrival," Megan replied. "I lived in Chicago and worked as a VP for World News Central. Some friends convinced me to come along on a kayak trip five years ago. Chaz was the guide, and the rest, as they say, is history. We live in Fairbanks during the school year—Chaz is a professor at the University of Alaska."

"What courses do you teach?" Emery asked.

"I'm in the Biology and Wildlife Department," Chaz said. "This fall, I'll have animal behavior and wildlife-population-management classes for undergrads, and foraging ecology for the graduate program."

"I can understand why you make a good guide."

"Guess you'll see for yourself next week. Pasha will be the other," Chaz told her.

Emery glanced up at the clock over Megan's head, which read nearly twenty past six. "I sort of met her earlier today. She isn't joining us?"

"With Dita gone, paperwork swamped her," Bryson relayed. "Told her to come by when she's done for a drink, but that stack was pretty impressive. No idea if she'll make it."

Before she could say anything else, Grizz emerged from the kitchen juggling plates and headed toward them. Emery marveled at the size of her king-crab legs, so big they hung over the edges of her oversized dinner plate, and the choices set before the others looked equally inviting. By the time they all had their food and had happily chowed down, the moment to ask more about Pasha had passed.

"So you've got the 4-11 on all of us." Megan cracked open one of her crab legs and dipped the delicate meat into her tea-candle butter warmer. "Tell us about you. Bryson says you're a woman on the move."

Emery chuckled. "That's a good way to put it, I guess. Yes, I'm on an extended trip around the world. Using the gazillion frequent-flier miles I logged as a courier and living off my savings, to see and do things I've dreamed of all my life."

"How long have you been traveling?" Megan asked.

"A little over four months. I came here from Europe and go on from here to Asia."

"Highlights so far?" Megan asked all the questions; no doubt she felt the most comfortable grilling Emery because of her journalism background. But the others all listened keenly to her answers.

"That's a tough question, because I've had a lot. The canals of Venice, the Vatican. Catching and eating fresh seafood on a boat in the Aegean." Snapshots of her travels until now flashed through her memory. "Hot-air ballooning beside the Pyrenees, bobsledding in Innsbruck, snorkeling off Corsica."

"Bryson said you struck her as an adrenaline junkie," Karla said. "She sure wasn't kidding."

"I believe you've got to live life to the absolute fullest while you can," Emery said. "And you don't know what you're capable of until you push your boundaries."

"Good attitude in Alaska," Bryson remarked. "Think you'll really enjoy your stay."

"In light of my first twenty-four hours here, I'd say that's definitely guaranteed. I'm having an amazing time, and it's such a great bonus to find all of you."

Emery felt Geneva's hand on her thigh.

"We're all looking forward to getting to know you better," Geneva said flirtatiously, "some more than others." The rest of them laughed.

"Down, girl. You'll get your turn," Megan said, which prompted more laughter.

During the next ninety minutes, they continued to grill Emery as they lingered over dessert and coffee. They asked few personal questions. Emery suspected Bryson had already told them she was single, had no ties and no home base. They queried about where she'd been, what she'd done, and where she planned to go next. She volunteered nothing about her accident or recuperation, even when Megan asked whether something had prompted the dramatic change in her lifestyle. She merely said she'd decided to pursue her dreams.

Reliving those awful moments still bothered her, and she loathed the pity in the eyes of a few women she'd been intimate with. To Emery, her scars and metal pins and her struggle to walk again were private.

Despite the interrogation, she was having a wonderful time with her new friends, though she glanced toward the Den's entrance now and then, hoping Pasha would appear. She couldn't fathom why the woman distracted her, particularly since Geneva sat right here at her side, charming and effervescent and beautiful. Perhaps curiosity about why Pasha had behaved so oddly and seemed almost to recognize her.

A little before nine, Geneva whispered something in Bryson's ear, none too subtly, and Bryson announced that she had an early flight so perhaps she should call it a night. Karla, Chaz, and Megan all readily agreed, snatching their coats and bidding Emery good evening, after telling her what fun they'd had getting to know her. Geneva stayed put.

"Whoever's in town at six, we converge here every night for dinner," Chaz told Emery. "Hope to see you again soon."

"Count on it," Emery replied.

"I'll catch up with you," Bryson told Karla and the others as they headed out, before turning to Emery. "Walk me to the door?"

"Sure."

"Had an inspired idea about where to take you when we go out next." Bryson had this I've-got-a-secret, Cheshire-cat grin, and her dark brown eyes, framed beneath the curved bill of her ball cap, narrowed in mischief.

Emery was immediately hooked. "I trust your judgment implicitly after today, believe me. And you've sold me just with your expression. Where we heading?"

"Well, since you say you trust me, I'd like to make it a surprise." Bryson's grin got bigger.

"I guess I never told you that I hate surprises." Bryson would have no idea what an understatement that was. "Usually, anyway. But if I know for sure it'll be a *good* surprise, I can be very patient." One could not go from shattered to walking again without endless patience and focused determination.

"Oh, it's very good," Bryson told her. "A rare opportunity for an outsider. A friend owes me a favor."

What could it be? It involved someone else. One of the others from the group? Someone Bryson did business with? She'd read a couple of biographies of bush pilots on her iPhone during the last couple of weeks, just a taste of the literature she'd devoured in preparation for her long-awaited arrival here. If Bryson had been flying here for a quarter-century, she likely had met an enormous percentage of her territory's population. Everyone flew. She'd probably transported them to homes, hospitals, and morgues. To births, weddings, celebrations, and funerals. Away for vacations, and away for good when the cold and the isolation became too much. She risked her life and was available in emergencies. So if Bryson needed to "collect on a favor," Emery suspected she could call on hundreds, maybe thousands of people.

Bryson probably seldom asked a friend for a favor. Solidly self-reliant, bright, and resourceful, she'd do it herself if she could, or pay to have it done, unless it was horribly expensive, ordinarily. Or perhaps it wasn't for sale. What could it be?

For Bryson to ask such a favor in order to give her a memorable experience told Emery volumes about how much Bryson had already become more her friend than her pilot. "Well, whatever it is, I know I'll love it," Emery said. "Can't wait. And I can't begin to thank you for going out of your way like this."

"No biggie. Checked my schedule and I have a few hours free tomorrow, if that's not too soon. Say, ten o'clock?"

"Awesome. Where'll I meet you?"

"Here is good. We can get some to-go lunch again."

"May not be able to sleep tonight, thinking about it."

"Oh, I bet you'll have other things on your mind tonight." Bryson looked past her, smiling at Geneva back at the booth. "Have fun."

Chapter Eleven

"What would you like to do?" Geneva caressed Emery's arm as soon as she returned and slipped into the booth. "Nightcap? Walk? Something…" She moistened her lips. "More private?"

The sun was still hours away from its brief dip below the horizon, and Emery wanted to tread slowly and carefully with Geneva. "It's still early. How about a walk? Anything interesting nearby?"

"I know just the thing." Geneva slipped out of the booth and Emery followed. "Better grab your coat. And bring your camera." As they headed up the stairs, she added, "Meet you outside in a few." Then they split up to head to their respective rooms.

Emery grabbed her coat and stuffed her daypack with her camera, gloves, a bottle of water, and a hat. Though she imagined they wouldn't go far, she also tossed in her survival kit: matches, water-purification tablets, Swiss army knife and Leatherman tool, mosquito dope, Band-Aids and antibiotic ointment, disposable poncho, and signal mirror, all meticulously packed into a waterproof plastic case the size of a small brick. It didn't weigh much and made her feel more prepared for any emergency, especially when travelling in remote, unpopulated areas.

Geneva had on a similar backpack when they met again, and she carried two khaki hats with mosquito netting bunched up around their wide brims. "Bugs may be bad where we're going," she warned Emery as she handed her one.

"Black flies ate Bryson and me alive today at one of the places we stopped. We didn't linger."

"Ready to go?"

"Lead the way."

Geneva took her to the river, where more than a dozen boats were anchored, most just glorified rowboats with outboard engines. Geneva headed toward one of the newer ones and stepped inside.

"Not that I'm objecting, but I thought we were going for a walk."

"We will. Trust me." Geneva started the outboard and tilted her head toward the middle bench of the boat. "Get in."

They set off downriver at an easy clip, and not long after they'd left the village, Emery spotted a bald eagle perched atop a tall dead spruce on the right bank. She fumbled for her camera and got several good pictures with her zoom as they motored by, the majestic bird seemingly undisturbed.

"I take it this is okay?" Geneva asked.

"More than. It's wonderful."

"I aim to please."

After another few minutes, they stopped at a wide, deep spot, where the Koyukuk River forked and gave birth to a new tributary. The John River, according to Geneva.

Hiking inland a short way through a thicket of trees and dense undergrowth, they came upon the ruins of several structures. One was an old storefront, with the word Bettles carved in big letters above the doorway beneath a massive moose rack bleached white from the sun and elements.

"What is this?" Emery asked.

"Old Bettles. The original town."

"What happened?"

"Well, the original settlement was founded during the gold rush. Gordon Bettles, a friend of Jack London, built a trading post here because it's as far as the big paddleboats could get. Miners and supplies had to go on in horse-drawn barges to the claims, another hundred miles upriver."

As Emery took more pictures, Geneva told her more about the area. "In the '40s, the navy decided to build a runway here, but the best spot was upriver six miles. Wasn't long before the whole town up and moved to be close to the airport, once commercial flights started."

"I can almost see them. The people who lived here then." She envisioned the elements reclaiming these once-vibrant buildings, reducing them to half-walls and collapsed rooftops overrun by dense vegetation. "Trappers, miners, and natives in their fur parkas. Had to be an awfully rough existence."

"Not much easier these days for some," Geneva said. "A lot of the Indians and Eskimos in the area still rely on subsistence—getting most of their food from the land. Moose, caribou, fish, berries."

Emery kept snapping photos, lost in the rich history of the location. Fortunately, a light breeze kept the bugs at bay. When she finished, she found Geneva sitting on a fallen tree, watching her. She sat beside her. "Thank you for bringing me here."

"I'm happy to get you alone."

"Why me?"

"Isn't that obvious?" Geneva gave her a look that said she was crazy for asking the question. "You're sexy, and bright. Funny. Well-traveled. You've got to have women coming on to you all the time."

"I'm sure you do, too."

"Pickings are kind of slim up here."

"Geneva, look…you're an incredibly hot and sweet woman. And I'm flattered and honored that you'd think we'd be good together—"

"I sense a very large *but* coming next." Geneva frowned.

"No…Well, let's say I'm not turning down your offer. I'd love to spend some time with you and get better acquainted. I just don't want to jump into something physical too soon. And first, we have to reach an understanding."

"About?"

"You know from the dinner conversation that I'll move on when my trips end," Emery said gently. "This…this quest I'm on is the most important thing I've ever done."

"I get that," Geneva replied.

"I don't make emotional attachments. It's purely no-strings, mutual fun."

"That's how it is with most people I meet up here, Emery. Here and gone, back to their lives. Never see them again. You're not telling me anything I don't know."

"You strike me as the kind of woman I might hurt easily."

"You don't think I can do brief affairs? Why?"

Emery didn't want to confide that Bryson had shared some of her history. She wasn't sure how Geneva would take that, and she didn't want to risk sharing something Bryson might have intended as confidential. She put her hand on Geneva's cheek. "I don't know if you can or can't. Just a sense I get, and I don't want to hurt you."

"I'm a tough girl. Bring it on." Geneva looked at her with longing and resolve, and Emery melted. She always fell for the just-shut-up-and-kiss-me look women gave her now and then, so she reacted as she usually did. She brought her other hand up to cradle Geneva's face and then, ever so sweetly, kissed her.

❖

Pasha tried not to stare at the clock, and when that didn't work, she shut off the office lights so she couldn't see the huge one on the wall and stuck a Post-it note over the digital one on her computer. She'd get done when she got done, and she only wasted time when she wondered if Emery and the girls would still be at the Den when she finally got there.

At long last, she hit the Save button and exited the program. Holding her breath, she peeled away the Post-it. Nine-forty. Not horribly late, but well after dinner. Certainly worth a trip to see whether they had left. She shut down the PC, locked up, and trotted to the roadhouse.

With every step, she tried to tune in to her sixth sense. Would it tell her Emery was there? But it was still on a low boil. Nothing like when she and Emery had met.

She assessed the Den's inhabitants with a quick glance. Only Grizz, the regulars, and two couples she didn't recognize. No friends, no Emery, and Geneva conspicuously absent. Her heart sank. She nearly turned around to retreat to her apartment, but decided to drown her sorrows with a nightcap first.

As she headed toward the bar, Grizz raised his bushy eyebrows in question. She shook her head, shorthand for "the usual?" and "not tonight." Once in a while, she changed from coffee with Kahlua if she was at the bar. When celebrating, she splurged on champagne. With a meal, she might order wine. And when she was down, she went for the hard stuff. Cognac.

"Rémy?" Grizz asked in his most sympathetic tone as he set a bowl of pretzels in front of her.

Rémy Martin had soothed some of her most troublesome days, but she was asking a lot of it tonight. She usually went for the VSOP, but tonight she'd splurge. "XO."

Grizz let out a low whistle. "That bad, huh?"

"Bitch of a day. The phone drove me batty and I only now finished the paperwork."

"'Nuff said. You eaten?" he asked with a paternal tone as he set her drink to her left.

Pasha picked up the snifter and swirled it to admire the thin reddish-gold wave that climbed the sides, considering his question. As her palm warmed the brandy, she drifted it under her nose to inhale its familiar floral-fruity aroma. She'd barely eaten anything all day, come to think of it. Too busy, and too preoccupied every free second with thoughts of Emery. She should be starving, but food didn't sound appealing. "Not hungry."

"You make sure you take care of yourself."

"All the girls left, I see." She tilted her head toward the big corner booth, now empty.

"A while ago. Maybe a half hour."

Had Emery gone to her room? Alone? If so, maybe Pasha could call and invite her down for a nightcap. Get a chance to apologize for this morning. She needed to see Emery again, to assess if they had any spark between them. Literally, in her case. Would she feel her big rush of premonition again? And would Emery, if they spent some real time together, begin to recognize some weird connection existed between them?

However, Emery could be with Geneva in her room, and if so, Pasha shouldn't even think of interrupting them. But maybe they'd moved the party to the two couples' cabin. "Did you notice if they all left together?" she asked Grizz.

"No, they didn't. Bryson, Karla, Chaz, and Megan left through the front, and Geneva and Emery went upstairs a couple minutes after that."

"And Emery hasn't come back down?"

"Don't think so. I've been in and out of the kitchen, though. Might've missed her. Want me to call her room? Bet she's still up."

"No, never mind." She answered apparently a bit too adamantly, because Grizz gave her a puzzled look. "Not that important. I'll catch her tomorrow."

"Whatever you say. Sure I can't get you some food? Maybe some cobbler?"

She shook her head. After inhaling the cognac again, now warm and bursting with aromatics, she took her first sip and let the complex flavors dance on her tongue.

Grizz laid his large hand over hers. "Want me to get Ellie out here to cover, so we can sit and you can tell me what's bothering you?"

"Stop. I hate it when you do that." Her gentle tone conveyed how much she cherished and appreciated his concern. "I'll be fine. Don't worry."

"Let me know if you change your mind." He drifted down the bar and started washing glasses, leaving her to her thoughts.

Pasha took another sip of the brandy and closed her eyes. She had no trouble conjuring up a perfect picture of Emery, as detailed and vivid as a photograph. Two pictures, really—that first glance of Emery from afar, her silhouette stark against the out-of-focus world beyond, and the close-up she'd memorized in the office. She preferred the latter. She never tired of going to that place in her mind's eye that had captured and memorized Emery's classic features, toned body, and low, sexy voice.

The Rémy was doing an unusually good job tonight warming her from within, probably because she was drinking on an empty stomach. The pleasant warmth quickly escalated, however, into an almost paralyzing pressure. Her nerves and muscles went taut, jangling with anticipation, and her heartbeat intensified until her whole body sang with unrequited need.

"Pasha?"

Emery's voice instantly stilled her inner chaos. The jolt made her reel. She might go mad if this continued. Inhaling a deep breath, she opened her eyes.

Emery leaned on the bar, three feet away, watching her with interest and concern.

Her heart leapt, her brain clouded, and she almost wept in happiness, so moved she felt completely out of control. What the hell? The world had gone topsy-turvy; she couldn't function. She just wanted to stare at Emery, ride this amazing, glorious bliss as long as it lasted.

As Emery neared, the power resembled a fireball, gaining strength and velocity as it pulled them together. Then, face-to-face, she felt a heady, overwhelming bliss, as though to confirm Emery as the answer to her dreams.

If she accepted Emery as *the one* and took steps to pursue her, maybe this crazy, dizzying implosion would stop. She would be lucky to be coherent. Eloquent would be impossible. "Emery, hello," she managed.

"Everything all right?"

"Yup." Deep breath. "I'm sorry if I was abrupt this morning." Pasha formed every sentence in her mind before she spoke it. "I didn't even properly introduce myself." Aware of staring, she couldn't stop herself. Emery didn't break eye contact. That calm bliss enveloped her, lifted her off her feet, almost orgasmic.

Emery waited for more. When Pasha remained speechless, she said. "How about we start from the top. A do-over." She offered her hand and smiled. "I'm Emery Lawson."

Pasha tried to force her brain from its euphoric paralysis long enough to form words and willed herself to move. "Pasha Dunn, I'm—" Mid-sentence, their hands met, and the surge of powerful psychic energy struck her like a lightning bolt.

She lost consciousness.

CHAPTER TWELVE

Emery paced the second-floor hallway of the Den, glancing anxiously at the door to her room with every pass. She'd taken her boots off so she wouldn't disturb the other guests and set them, neatly paired, beside the doorway. What was taking so long?

Grizz had helped get Pasha upstairs after sending a bar patron to get Karla. Armed with her medical bag, she arrived quickly. Pasha had still been out cold fifteen minutes ago.

A door opened farther down the hallway and Geneva stepped out, wearing a white cotton robe, her feet bare. "Anything?"

"Not yet."

"Sure you don't want to wait in my room?"

"No, thanks. I'm good." Emery didn't want to sit down. Geneva was obviously concerned about Pasha, too, and meant nothing flirtatious. Earlier, after the kiss, they'd agreed to get to know each other better before they went any further sexually. She usually avoided getting too familiar, to avoid hurting someone, but it seemed the right course, at the moment, anyway. A way to delay any real decision about their future.

"Keep me posted," Geneva said, before returning to her room.

Emery resumed her pacing. Pasha probably hadn't hurt herself when she blacked out, because Emery had managed to half catch her as she collapsed. Grizz had said he didn't think she'd eaten much, so that might explain the fainting. But why didn't she wake up right away?

The rest puzzled her, too. Pasha's hand, when they shook, had felt uncannily warm when she passed out, but she hadn't felt feverish. In fact, her forehead felt normal within seconds. Emery had never heard of a medical condition that could cause such a reaction.

Most notable, right before Pasha collapsed, during that long, unflinching eye contact, pure joy shone on her face, her pale-green eyes moist with emotion. But Grizz had said she'd barely touched her cognac.

Why, then, had Pasha once again had such an extreme response to seeing her? Apparently, something was affecting her both physically and emotionally. This morning, she seemed tongue-tied and clumsy. Now, she'd blacked out, after looking at Emery as if reuniting with some long-lost loved one.

Emery knew they'd never met, because she would remember Pasha, who was definitely smokin' in the looks and build department. Really, all the women she'd met in the group were pretty damn attractive, one reason she hadn't singled Pasha out. Yet.

But tonight had changed that. Now, the woman thoroughly intrigued her, and she couldn't wait to find out more about these bizarre reactions.

❖

"Can you hear me? Pash?"

Pasha roused, as disoriented and groggy as if coming to after a long binge of drinking. She opened her eyes fuzzily to find Karla leaning over her, perched on the edge of the bed she lay on. An unfamiliar bed. "Where am I?"

"In Emery's room. You fainted downstairs. Don't you remember?"

Emery's name transported her back to the moment before her blackout. As she mentally replayed their brief exchange, it began again—the pressure, the knowing, the heat. Not nearly as intense this time, more a subtle simmering of her intuitive power. An understandable pattern was emerging.

Emery must be nearby.

The pressure and energy infusing her renewed and invigorated her, dispelling the hazy stupor she'd awakened with like a healing tonic. How mortifying, though, to faint in front of a client. Wilderness guides should be resourceful and heroic, unflappable under stress, not swooning, fragile femmes. "I do remember. How long was I out?"

She sat up, but Karla immediately laid a hand on her arm.

"Hey, easy there. Slow movements." Karla watched her very closely, a stethoscope around her neck and a blood-pressure cuff on the bedside table. "You were out about fifteen minutes, probably. How do you feel?"

"Good. Really. You don't need to worry."

"Any idea why you fainted?" Karla pulled a mini-flashlight from her pocket and checked Pasha's pupils with practiced efficiency. "Grizz said he thought you might not have eaten much today."

"I'm sure that's all it was. Just got busy at the office."

Karla fixed the blood-pressure cuff around her arm and took a reading. "Well, your BP's good, and your heart rate's normal." Stuffing her medical supplies back into her bag, she looked at Pasha with narrowed eyes. "I'm concerned, though, about how long you were out. Are you taking any medications?"

"No."

"Anything else going on? Stress? Other health issues?"

She wouldn't use the word *stress*, which was a bad thing. Her bizarre, high-voltage reaction to Emery mystified her, but it wasn't entirely unwelcome. "Karla, I'm sure it's nothing. I…I was just too preoccupied to eat, that's all."

Karla knew her well and apparently sensed something more. "Spill. What aren't you telling me?"

Pasha sighed. She trusted Karla and would confide in her before anyone else, but she couldn't talk about it yet. "I'll fill you in, just not right now. I'm really okay and you don't have to worry. Trust me on this?"

Karla looked skeptical.

"I just need a good night's sleep. I'll eat a big breakfast tomorrow and be good as new. I promise."

"I know when someone's dismissing me, but we're going to make a deal." Karla's tone didn't invite discussion. "I don't want you staying in your apartment tonight with Dita gone. Someone should be nearby if you feel unwell again. We can see if Grizz has a room free—I expect he does, this early in the season—or you can put up with me sleeping on your couch. Your choice."

"Can't talk you out of that, I suppose?"

"Not a chance."

"Well, I don't want to incur Bryson's wrath for keeping you away from her. I'll call Grizz."

He readily offered to give her an empty room for the night at no charge and said he'd be up with a key in a couple of minutes. "I'm all set," she told Karla after hanging up.

"Good. I'll head home. Have someone come get me if you need me." Karla stood and grabbed her medical bag. "The cabin doesn't have a phone."

"I will. But don't hold your breath. I'm really feeling totally okay." She got up too and followed Karla to the door.

Karla hugged her good-bye. "I have to make a run to Coldfoot tomorrow, but I'll stop by the office when I get back to check on you."

Pasha felt a marked increase in the power as Karla reached for the door; Emery was just outside. She steeled herself, praying she didn't black out again.

The wave of warmth and energy enveloped her when the door opened and she saw Emery waiting on the other side. For a moment, she felt light-headed, but the dizziness passed quickly.

Emery's face, initially concerned, relaxed when she saw Pasha on her feet and Karla's medical bag in her hand. She looked from Karla to Pasha. "What's happening? You all right?"

"I'm fine." Feeling less tongue-tied pleasantly surprised Pasha. "Sorry to have created such a fuss. Just got too busy to eat today, that's all." She carefully avoided too much direct eye contact and didn't dare get much closer to Emery, unsure about her reaction.

"Are you sure?" Emery seemed dubious.

"She's got a room here tonight," Karla said. "So she can call someone if she feels unwell again."

"Both of you can relax. I'm perfectly healthy." Pasha was relieved to hear Grizz's heavy footfalls. "Sorry to have inconvenienced you," she told Emery. "You can have your room back, now."

"Oh, no trouble," Emery replied as Grizz joined them. She started to say something more, but Pasha breezed past and took the key Grizz dangled from his fingers.

The power spiked when Pasha brushed against Emery's arm, but she concealed her reaction.

"Twenty-three." Grizz pointed to the room four doors down. "Can I bring you something to eat?"

"No, thanks. I'm just going to hit the sheets. Kind of tired, but otherwise okay. 'Night, everybody." She went directly to her room, but glanced back as she keyed the lock to see the three of them still watching her. "Excitement's over, guys. Move along, now. Go back about your business."

Grizz laughed and Karla smiled, but Emery's face remained tight with concern. And something else—something Pasha couldn't decipher. But Emery clearly wasn't looking past her. She'd taken note of her, finally, seeing her as though for the first time.

Her heart lifted, and she might have gone to bed with optimism if Geneva hadn't broken the spell. She emerged from her room dressed in a bathrobe, legs bare and ample cleavage showing, and smiled when she spotted Pasha and the others. "You okay, Pash?"

"Yup, I'm fine." She escaped into her room, trying to forget her last image of the hallway tableau. Reassured the crisis was over, Karla and Grizz started back downstairs, but Geneva headed right for Emery.

CHAPTER THIRTEEN

Next day, June 3

Emery couldn't get back to sleep and went downstairs for coffee a little after six thirty. The few patrons who beat her to the restaurant were all men, and an older woman stood behind the bar, wearing a faded, long-sleeve T-shirt that read No More War, the *o*'s in both *no* and *more* replaced by peace symbols.

"Good morning," Emery told the woman as she took a barstool. "Can I get some coffee, please?"

"Sure thing." The woman poured a mug full from a carafe and set it before her. "Emery, right?"

"Yes." Odd to have strangers recognize her so readily. Could the locals keep up with all the newcomers once the tour season really got underway and the village teemed with unfamiliar faces?

"I'm Ellie. Grizz's wife."

"Nice to meet you."

"You, too. Can I get you some breakfast?"

"Hmm." She opened the menu and scanned it. "Couple of eggs, poached. And some of your sourdough toast?"

"Coming right up."

As she sipped her coffee, Emery wondered about Pasha. What was she doing? How did she feel? And, most of all, when would they get an opportunity to talk?

Not that she wasn't looking forward to going up again with Bryson, especially because Bryson had promised her she'd love the surprise. Anticipating the outing had certainly contributed to her restless night. But the trip would likely prevent her from satisfying the real root of her sleeplessness: what the hell happened to Pasha when they came face-to-face?

Last night had only piqued her curiosity more. Thank God, Pasha had apparently suffered no ill effects from blacking out. In fact, despite the strange episode, she seemed oddly more relaxed and at ease afterward than in any of their previous encounters.

The memory of the unmistakable voltage that ran up Emery's arm when Pasha brushed by her had oddly disturbed her and kept her awake. Similar to the shock from static electricity, like touching a doorknob in winter after shuffling across a rug in stocking feet, only much more powerful. Not quite up to stun-gun standards, but close. For a few seconds, she couldn't draw a breath and felt unsteady on her feet.

The situation completely mystified her. The humid air and the hallway's wood flooring wouldn't produce simple static electricity.

She had to know what was so unusual about Pasha.

She finished eating at ten after seven, and Pasha's office opened at eight. Emery got a large coffee and freshly baked cranberry muffin to go and carried them up to room twenty-three.

"Pasha? It's Emery. You up?" Despite repeated knocks, she got no answer. She tried the door, which opened. The bed had been slept in, but Pasha had evidently left even before Emery had gone downstairs. Probably back home now, wherever she lived, getting ready for work.

Surprised by her disappointment, Emery headed to her room to shower and dress. She would soon embark on what would surely be another wonderful day in the wilderness, and she might see Pasha at dinner tonight, provided her workload didn't keep her away again.

Pasha unlocked the front door and turned on the office lights promptly at eight, though her day had officially started twenty minutes earlier when the first client called. She could have let that one go to voice mail, but returning the call would only add one more task to the day's potential madness, and Dita would get stuck with the long-distance bill.

At least she'd managed a few hours' rest, but only after she'd snuck out of the Den at one a.m., while Grizz was in the kitchen, to go home to her own bed.

She'd planned all along to leave very early to give herself time to shower and change, and most importantly to avoid running into Emery coming out of Geneva's room—or vice versa.

She left much sooner than expected because Emery's proximity put the power at a medium boil, and the pressure kept her awake and alert better than a quadruple dose of espresso. Only after she put some distance between them and climbed under her own quilted comforter did the sensation subside enough for her to fall asleep.

Pasha awoke five hours later feeling more refreshed than she could have hoped for. She'd set the alarm a little early to make sure she had time to eat a good breakfast and pack a lunch. Her fainting spell had definitely been connected to her gift, not the result of not eating, but she wanted some insurance against a repeat episode.

No matter how she felt, or how damn busy the office got, she planned to find a way to spend some time with Emery later.

After Emery finished dressing, she killed time by chronicling her amazing flight and the unsettling episode with Pasha in her journal. When she got downstairs a little before ten, she found Bryson perched on a barstool, sipping coffee and chatting with Ellie. A large paper bag, presumably containing their lunch, rested on the bar.

"I can't wait to see what you have in store for me," she said.

"Hey! Right on time." Bryson downed her remaining coffee and threw a couple of bills on the bar. "Off we go."

As they exited the roadhouse, Bryson asked, "Have you seen Pasha? Karla filled me in."

"No. She left before I came down for breakfast."

"Well, the office is open, so she must be all right. Saw the light on when I got back from Coldfoot."

"Coldfoot?"

"A small village, not too far. Karla's spending most of the day there. She rotates to a lot of the settlements, once every month or so, to treat non-emergencies and check on patients with ongoing issues."

"What did they do before she moved here?" Emery asked.

"Went untreated, mostly. Or had to fly out to get help. Aren't a lot of clinics in the area, and a CHA usually staffs the ones that exist."

"What's that?"

"Community Health Aide. Basically, people with very basic medical training. They only have 'em in Alaska."

They headed toward the red Super Cub parked at the edge of the runway. "No hints about today?" Emery asked as they neared.

"Well, maybe one," Bryson answered. When she pulled the door open, Emery immediately understood the reference.

Geneva sat in an extra seat in the cargo area, behind Emery's. A larger person would never have fit, because Bryson's survival duffel filled the rest of the tail. "Surprise!" she said mischievously.

"That it is," Emery said as she climbed in and fastened her seat and shoulder belt. Bryson stayed outside to conduct her exterior inspection of the plane. "A very pleasant one. Will *you* tell me what Bryson's cooked up?"

"Nope. But I've done it before and found it a richly rewarding experience. I hope you do, too."

Geneva's enigmatic answer didn't help. She pushed her for more, then tried to put the screws to Bryson again once they were aloft, but each one just smiled and shook her head.

After an hour or so of Bryson-style flying—hugging treetops and darting through canyons and circling anything of interest—they descended toward a semi-permanent encampment near a wide creek. Emery could make out a trio of canvas tents, two smoking campfire pits, a large pile of split logs, and stacks of wooden crates. Two bearded men emerged from a tent as they neared and waved at the plane.

They kept descending, and Bryson started fiddling with the throttle and other controls, but Emery saw no hint of a runway below. The lone gravel bar looked clean but impossibly short, even compared to some of the ones they'd set down on yesterday. She gripped the seat as the plane dropped the final few feet and watched, fascinated, as Bryson artfully worked around her limitations. She precisely skimmed the Cub's tires along the water's surface, slowing enough that when the plane hit the leading edge of the gravel bar thirty feet beyond, she could stop before she reached the end.

"That was impressive," she remarked when Bryson cut the engine. "Where are we?"

"Can't tell you. That's part of the deal," Bryson replied with a smile. "Still haven't figured it out?"

"Not a clue. Are you selling me into white slavery? I mean, I like an adrenaline rush, but…"

Bryson and Geneva both laughed as they piled out of the plane. Before they headed to meet the men on the bank, Bryson dug out a bottle of Jack Daniels she'd stashed under her seat.

"Hi, guys. You remember Geneva." Bryson handed the bottle to the shorter one, a lean wiry guy, as Geneva exchanged hellos with the men. "Emery Lawson," she said. "Emery, meet Spike and Watts."

"I'm Spike." The shorter man, probably in his fifties, screwed off the top of the whiskey and took a healthy pull before handing it to his friend.

The second guy, thirtyish, also took a long drink. He might be darkly brooding handsome if he cleaned up and shaved the black beard. They both looked like derelicts—filthy clothes, long uncombed hair, and, from the smell, dirty bodies.

"Watts doesn't talk much," Spike said.

"Good to meet you." Emery shook hands with them both.

"The guys are going to let us pan for gold here," Bryson said. "You get to keep what you find, unless you get lucky and score a nugget more than an ounce. That's worth a grand or more. Anything bigger, they get half."

"That's very generous," Emery said. It sounded like fun, but she doubted they'd find much of value.

"Ever done it before?" Spike asked as his buddy went into a tent.

"Nope."

"Easy. Just takes patience. I'll show ya how." Spike pointed. "Rubber boots and waders in the crate. Find a pair if you don't want to get your boots wet."

Once they had made their selections, Emery wearing rubber boots a bit too large, Spike led them to where they were working. Watts followed, juggling a trio of pans and a shovel. Bryson and Geneva had obviously panned before. When they got to the creek's edge they immediately started scooping soil into their pans.

Spike explained how much soil to use, where to get it, and what to look for, before demonstrating the proper technique for extracting the gold, which involved swirling the soil with water and tapping it to separate the lighter sand, heavier black soil, and gold, the heaviest of all. Patiently swirling and tapping, he carefully washed the lighter material away, layer by layer, until they could see the gold.

Emery paid respectful attention throughout the long process, though she thought she'd gained the hang of it long before Spike reached the bottom.

She was stunned when, in the end, Spike showed her the myriad of gold flakes shining amidst the remaining few teaspoons of black soil. "Probably worth a hundred dollars or so, I'd guess." He scooped the mixture into a small jar and extended the pan in her direction. "Go on, give her a try."

"Thanks, Spike." Emery headed toward Bryson and Geneva, while the men returned to their campsite. "How's it going?" She scooped up a panful of dirt from an area they'd been working and bent to add some water.

"Bryson's doing better than I am," Geneva said. "But we're both finding something."

"I was excited to try but wasn't expecting to find any gold," Emery said. "Spike had quite a few flakes in his pan, though."

"It's a great spot," Bryson said. "You'd never know from looking at them, but they've gotten a couple hundred thousand dollars from this claim. Some from panning, but most from those sluices." She pointed to a number of metal box-like structures with riffles in them that lay in the shallow water. "They really help speed the process."

"Can you still find a lot of gold in Alaska?" Emery patiently swirled and tapped, swirled and tapped. "I thought the gold rush was something in the history books."

"Oh, it's far from mined out. Big business with all the high-tech methods and equipment they have now. Earth movers, dredges, all that stuff."

"I read somewhere that a billion dollars' worth was mined here last year," Geneva said. "The most in a century."

"I had no idea."

"Gotta be more places like this," Bryson told Emery in a low voice. "No one knows there's gold here. No written history of it. Spike inherited the claim from his great-grandfather, who discovered it. No one in the family believed in it, until Spike."

"What a great story," Emery said.

"Obviously, they want to keep anyone from finding out about it, for now. One reason they haven't brought in heavy equipment and more help." Bryson tipped her pan carefully to capture a bit more water. "So you understand why I couldn't tell you exactly where we are and why I need to ask you not to tell anyone."

"Hey, no problem," Emery said. "I appreciate the trust. Mum's the word. And thanks again for arranging this."

"Glad you're having fun. Just wait."

Intent, they worked in silence for the next few minutes. Staying hunched over the stream hurt her legs and back, so Emery had to stand and stretch more often than the others. And fairly quickly she wished she'd brought her pain meds.

But her discomfort faded when she reached the bottom of her pan. "Yee haa! I got gold!"

CHAPTER FOURTEEN

Pasha barely tasted the tuna-salad sandwich, eating it between phone calls when she also tried to keep up with the paperwork. She'd paid the bills and placed the vendor orders. Now she sat transferring information that clients had mailed—registration forms, mostly—into the computer database. She wanted to leave earlier for dinner tonight.

Others might defer some tasks to the next day, but she couldn't, though tempted. Obsessive, she had to complete every task, large and small, as efficiently as possible. She couldn't leave something half-finished, because she'd think of little else until she wrapped up every loose end. Accomplishing any goal satisfied her.

Pasha's bosses had always praised her meticulous nature, especially when she decided to move to another town and occupation. All her life, she had changed direction erratically but now wondered if she had intuitively followed a psychic master plan designed to help her find her soul mate.

When she'd listened, her sixth sense had always led her to great jobs, destinations, homes, pets, and people she felt preordained to meet, who quickly became her extended family. When she saw them the first time, she detected an aura around them, like with Dita, a thin band of indistinct kaleidoscopic color, as if they carried their own rainbow. The vision never lasted long but didn't need to. Her involuntary feeling of joy and connection demanded she follow up and get to know the individual, and never steered her wrong. She'd seen the aura around Karla and Bryson, too.

The situation with Emery was different, though, and had been that way from the start. Her gift had never acted so haywire and powerful. Its unpredictability frustrated her at times, and she didn't appreciate it completely incapacitating her last night in front of Emery. But it was hitting her over the head with a baseball bat with a message: *Emery is the one. Don't let her get away.*

She knew nothing about Emery yet, except what little Bryson had told her. Though she'd relish some alone-time with her, Pasha also worried how she'd react, since she apparently had little control. So she'd be perfectly content just to finish in time for dinner. At least she could find out more about Emery without having to make brilliant conversation if she got tongue-tied again. And she could put a few feet between them in the big corner booth if her close proximity to Emery impaired her ability to function again.

Every time the bell over the door sounded, Pasha jumped, half-expecting to see Emery, though she never sensed an increase in the power. Not that she had many visitors, but a few locals came by to book charters with Bryson, and she'd had a few deliveries.

This time when the bell sounded, Geneva appeared, one of the last people she expected to see. "Hi, Pasha, how you feeling?"

"I'm great, Gen. What're you up to?"

Geneva seemed in especially good spirits. Her cheeks pink, eyes shining, she couldn't stop smiling. "Bryson asked me to tell you she's headed over to pick up Karla in Coldfoot and will stop in when they get back."

"Bryson?"

"We stayed out longer than we expected, so she had to refuel and go right back up again." Geneva sank wearily into a big comfy chair.

"I didn't know you went up with Bryson today."

"She took Emery and me to a place to pan for gold. We had such a blast we didn't want to leave."

Pasha forced herself to smile. "Sounds like fun. How'd you do? Find anything?"

"We sure did. Enough to make the flight a freebie and more," Geneva replied. "Bryson found probably eight hundred dollars' worth, and Emery and I about half that, each. Bryson's buying everyone dinner tonight."

"I'm doing my best to get out of here. So far, it's looking good."

"Wish I could join you, but I've got the evening shift." Geneva stood, stretched, and headed for the door. "Take care of Emery tonight for me, would you? Especially if the others decide to bag it early again. Keep her entertained?"

"I'll do my best."

What a mess. She *had* seen a different look in Emery's eyes last night. Emery had finally noticed her, but did that notice mean *interest?*

Should she pursue Emery or be a good friend to Geneva and remain silent? Her gift battled for one thing and her strong standard of ethics wanted the other. Either option, she suspected, would hurt someone.

❖

At the airstrip's edge, Emery enviously watched the Super Cub ascend again, headed northeast. Riding in Bryson's little red plane thrilled her like none of her countless flight experiences. They could see almost any feature of this massive landscape, whether a grizzly mom and her two cubs, the deep ice-blue crevasses of a glacier, or a tundra plain lushly painted with wildflowers. Bryson's piloting skill and impressive knowledge of the region created an unparalleled experience.

She remained still until Geneva disappeared, headed toward the Eidson outfitter's office. Emery wanted to see Pasha and for a second considered going along and lingering after Geneva had departed to start her shift. But as soon as she got out of the plane, she nixed that idea. Walking anywhere after sitting uncomfortably in the Cub, plus all the hours of stooping and shoveling, seemed murderous.

Finding gold and constantly moving had kept the pain tolerable. But sitting almost still during the long return flight had nearly crippled her. Her joints locked up and her muscles cramped. Very slowly, she started toward the Den, trying not to limp too much. Emery hated for others to gawk and pity her. She'd had her fill in the hospital and before she shed her cane. But anyone with half a clue could see how badly she was hurting.

Grizz, working the bar when she came in, was occupied, and hopefully, Geneva was upstairs changing. Emery managed to get through the restaurant unnoticed, grateful she didn't run in to anyone during her painful, lengthy ascent to her room. By the time she got inside, she was sweating.

After she downed her pain meds and lingered under a hot shower she could move more comfortably. Dinner was still more than ninety minutes away, so she had time for either a nap or a visit to the Eidson office. A tough choice, but her physical needs won out.

Emery climbed into bed after setting the alarm. Pasha would probably be too busy to talk now, anyway.

The nap helped revitalize her, but her stiffness remained, particularly in the knees. After a few stretches, she took another hot shower, then pulled on dark jeans and a thin, crème-colored turtleneck under a heavy emerald hoodie. No bounding down the stairs this time, though she'd limbered up enough not to limp.

Emery paused before she reached the last steps, closed her eyes, and wished for Pasha to have made it, before continuing through the doorway.

There she sat, sandwiched in the middle of the booth, with Karla and Bryson to her left and Chaz and Megan to her right.

The two couples chatted, but Pasha looked right at her. They smiled at the same instant, and her mood buoyant, Emery headed toward her. The seat open on the end would place her directly across from Pasha.

"Hi, everyone," she said.

Several replies came her way, including a "Good to see you again" from Pasha, which stood out from the rest.

"What'll it be, Emery?" Geneva appeared at her elbow, carrying a drink tray, even before she'd taken a seat.

The women weren't sharing a pitcher tonight. An assortment of beer, wine, and mixed drinks sat before them. "Got a good Alaskan stout on tap?" she asked.

"We've got three of 'em."

"Surprise me, then. I trust your judgment."

"As you should." Geneva laughed as she headed off to get the beer.

Emery slipped into the booth beside Bryson. "What a fabulous day. Can't thank you enough."

"Love to take you out again tomorrow," Bryson said. "I've had a blast, too. Got charters, though, and I have to pick up Dita's fishing group."

"Oh, great. I've been wanting to talk to her. When does she get back?"

"Between five and five thirty tomorrow afternoon." Pasha answered before Bryson had a chance to, giving Emery good reason to do what she most wanted—give Pasha her undivided attention. "Technically, that's after we close, but I'll keep the doors open if you want to come by." Pasha seemed relaxed, but alert and aware. No sign of anything amiss or unusual tonight. At least not yet.

"I'd like that. Thank you."

"And if you want some ideas for tomorrow since Bryson's busy," Pasha said, maintaining eye contact, "I can recommend a couple of things within walking distance."

Emery tried to sound casual. "Maybe we can chat about them later."

"Sure." The reply sounded equally offhand, but didn't match the intensity in Pasha's eyes. They seemed to use their own private code, keeping the weirdness between them from the others, but acknowledging it with their eyes.

Emery hoped she wasn't misinterpreting, but Pasha apparently wanted to talk to her as much as she wanted to.

"Pipeline." Geneva appeared and set a tall glass of black stout with a thick tan froth before her. "Also called Black Gold. From the Moose's Tooth Brewing Company."

Pipeline, incredibly smooth and creamy, was more dessert than aperitif, but Emery loved a good stout. "Wonderful stuff."

"You a beer aficionado?" Pasha asked.

Emery nodded. "Sort of. You missed my full bio last night. They grilled me pretty good." The others smiled.

"That was only the warm-up," Megan warned her with mock seriousness. "We thought we'd give you a day or two before we get to the really personal ones."

Emery played along. "Uh-oh. Should I be worried?"

"Depends. Have you ever played Truth or Dare?"

"Sure."

"Well, we call our variation Probing Questions. On trips we use it as an icebreaker. Fun way to get to know someone," Megan said. "And also appropriate to initiate new members into our club. ADLIB."

"ADLIB?"

"Adventurous Dykes Living In Bettles. You'll be the eighth member."

"Cool. I'm honored."

"We'll do it tomorrow night after Dita gets back. Geneva's working the day shift, so we can all be there," Bryson said.

Grizz came to get their orders, then they started sharing stories, with Emery first relaying her gold-panning experience in great detail. Karla talked about some of her unusual and funny cases, Chaz and Pasha shared information about their upcoming trips, and Bryson volunteered a few of her misadventures. In general, they just got to know each other better, amidst so much laughter their sides hurt.

The women's rapid-fire back-and-forth wisecracks, the kind of teasing familiarity that came from close camaraderie, entertained Emery. She liked them a lot already and more each day. Despite the merriment of the evening, however, she wanted the group to break up early so she could spend some time one-on-one with Pasha. Emery could hardly keep her eyes off her and had to force herself to give equal time to whoever was talking. And every time she looked at Pasha, Pasha was looking her way.

Pasha also frequently found ways to slip questions to Emery into the conversation, without being too obvious. Not the usual *where are you from, what do you do,* and *what are your favorite food* types of questions, like she'd received the night before. But queries that went deeper, more thoughtful ones that could reveal quite a lot. The latest, slipped into an exchange between Megan and Karla about their fear of small planes, provided a prime example.

"Are you afraid of anything, Emery?"

The question took her by surprise, and her first potential light replies included "Beanie Babies," maybe, or "tapioca pudding," or "mayonnaise." She usually deflected invasively personal questions by going for a laugh. But Pasha's eyes locked with hers, and she couldn't lie. "I don't like elevators."

CHAPTER FIFTEEN

Pasha decided to pursue Emery's answer further when they were alone. She sensed Emery considered not answering and didn't want to elaborate. But the power had verified that she'd answered truthfully and provided a significant answer.

Pasha's gift had so far succeeded in getting her attention, and possibly Emery's, in spades. Now, it had become a guide.

Pasha had sensed when Emery left her room and headed downstairs, because the power increased exponentially with each step she took. By the time Emery hit the bottom step, Pasha's whole body vibrated.

When Emery appeared in the doorway, the vibrations stilled again, leaving Pasha totally calm, like she'd just had a massage. And for the first time, the special aura shimmered around Emery, as with every other significant person in her life, though not a rainbow.

Emery's aura shimmered gold.

Ecstasy filled Pasha, Emery's reaction amplifying her bliss. She'd entered with an anxious, expectant expression and immediately sought the corner booth and, in particular, *her*. Once she'd spotted Pasha, she never looked away, their smiles triggering simultaneously as Emery hurried toward her. Had she begun to feel something, too?

Emery sat just a few feet away. Her aura had faded, though Pasha sensed the power remained nearby, content to let her behave normally but ready to flare up if necessary. Relaxed and serene, she became her old self again, but with enhanced alertness, her senses heightened to fully absorb the moment.

For most of the evening, the power lay in silent wait. But as she asked Emery more serious questions, her gift told her when to pay especially close attention. Another brief aura would shimmer around Emery when she confided something important.

The gang chatted happily, laughing so much no one seemed inclined to leave soon. As the evening wore on, Pasha became increasingly impatient to speak to Emery privately. If everyone was still there at nine thirty—just a couple of minutes away now—she'd create an excuse to get Emery alone. Much later than that, Emery would likely decline.

Pasha waited for the first lull in the conversation to pull out her wallet. "I'm heading out, ladies. Need to stop by the office before I turn in." She dropped enough bills to cover her share of the check. "If you want to walk with me, Emery, I can give you some material on things you might want to do between trips."

"That'd be great. I'll just run upstairs and get my jacket." Emery slid out of the booth. "Thank you all for another wonderful evening, ladies. I had a great time." The others said good night or good-bye as she headed toward the stairs.

Pasha felt a keen sense of loss when Emery left. After only a couple of minutes, the sensation shifted and swelled to her now-familiar anticipation and joy as Emery returned. Very tidal-like, she mused.

"Ready when you are." Emery extended a hand signaling Pasha to lead the way, so she headed for the door. Once they were outside, Emery asked, "No more dizzy episodes today, I take it?"

"No. All good."

"It was…worrying," Emery said softly.

"No need. I'm sure it won't happen again."

"That's comforting."

Pasha froze the images in her memory: Emery's glossy dark hair, tossed by the breeze, bangs obscuring her face; the faint smell of wood smoke; the crunch of their boots over the loose gravel.

They fell into step together at a slow, easy pace, as though neither wanted to rush this opportunity. Walking beside Emery felt so *right.*

"Tell me about this initiation thing you're putting me through tomorrow night," Emery said.

"Honestly, we're playing it by ear. We only named the group a few days ago, and you're our first recruit. We voted to play Probing Questions, but that's about as far as we've gotten."

"How personal do these questions get?"

"Every game varies, because the participants make up the questions. When we play it on trips, they tend to be mild, unless the clients all know each other. Or are all lesbians," she said with a laugh. Emery didn't smile at the comment, and Pasha immediately regretted the levity. "Not that you have to answer anything you don't want to."

She stopped walking. Emery pulled up short, too, and faced her.

"I'm sorry if I made you uncomfortable with a couple of my questions at dinner," Pasha said. "I'm just...very interested in getting to know you."

Emery's dark brown eyes softened. "I didn't mind them, coming from you. But I don't usually volunteer some things about myself."

The *coming from you* warmed Pasha. "If I step over the line, just tell me."

"I'll say the same, since I hope to get to know you better, too."

"Deal. Come on, then." Pasha let them in the office and led Emery to the back lounge. "Have a seat. I can make decaf, if you'd like some."

"Sure."

"How do you take it?"

"Black, please."

As Pasha scooped grounds into a filter, Emery asked, "What brought you to Alaska? You're not from here, are you?"

"No. I've been here less than two years. I saw an ad for this job and it caught my eye." She hit the Brew button and the carafe began to fill. "I like it a lot. The work's fun, the people eclectic, but really down-to-earth. They care about each other. And, of course, you can't beat the view."

"I always dreamed about visiting Alaska," Emery said. "You?"

"No, not really. I mean, I remember seeing movies shot here and thinking about the spectacular scenery." She poured two mugs full. "But I never dreamed I'd be living here."

"Have you always been a guide?" Emery asked as they settled into two of the cushy chairs with their mugs.

Pasha had opted to turn on the lamp beside the microwave instead of the overhead fluorescents, the resulting ambience thankfully more living-room-like than hospital-sterile. "To be absolutely honest, our photography trip will be my first as a guide. I've been training for more than a year."

"I can't wait to get out there. Just think, forty-eight hours from now, we'll be chatting like this beside a campfire."

"Yup. And the spot's breathtaking. I flew supplies to it last year."

"Bryson showed me the landing site. She said the area has an abundance of wildlife." Emery sipped her coffee and looked thoughtfully at Pasha. "Tell me about yourself."

"What do you want to know?"

"Well, you have an advantage. At least you have my questionnaire." Emery nodded toward the pile of client files on the coffee table. "I don't even have your basics."

"Okay. Let's see." Pasha flipped open the nearest folder and scanned the vital statistics required of clients. "To even things up, I was thirty-five on February 13th. Blond hair, green eyes—"

"Wheat-blond. And pale-green eyes, to be precise. The color of limes before they're fully ripe. Very unusual."

Pasha looked up from the file, pleased Emery had noted their precise color. Her cheeks warmed as their eyes met. Ordinarily, she didn't make the first move, but her instinct screamed, "Go for it." Glancing at the paper, she said, "I'm five-five, weigh one-twenty, no health issues, not on any medication, I live in the apartment right above us…"

Prompted by the final blank spaces on the client questionnaire, she jotted down some numbers on a Post-it note, closed the file with a flourish, and handed Emery the note. Pasha couldn't help grinning like an idiot. "Here's my phone number. And I'm single."

Emery laughed and carefully tucked the yellow slip into the thin wallet she'd stuffed into her back pocket.

"Now we're even, so to give *you* the advantage, I'll add that I'm left-handed," Pasha said, "and a bit of an organization freak. I love ethnic food, and I'm not seeing anyone right now." Pasha wasn't nearly ready to divulge anything about the power and its revelations about Emery. She'd learned long ago that many people viewed the idea of premonitions as preposterous or flaky. Some, even when confronted with evidence, remained skeptical. But she would at least let Emery know, if she didn't already, that she was definitely interested.

"Well, as you may know, I plan to see Geneva," Emery said. "It's not serious. We've barely spent any time together, and I don't know where it's going."

"Geneva's a good friend, and I don't want to create an awkward situation. But if it's not serious yet, I just wanted you to know I'd like to go out with you, too."

Emery smiled. "I'd like that very much. And I appreciate how straightforward you're being. I can't tell you how much I value the art of speaking frankly. So many women I've met like games and drama." She sipped her coffee and studied Pasha's face, her expression difficult to read.

Pasha tensed. Was she being duplicitous by not telling Emery about her premonitions? Her gift, a lifelong, integral part of her, was a much more important and vital statistic than her address or phone number, and clearly responsible for her determination to date Emery. Was she doing the right thing by not immediately volunteering it?

"You probably know Geneva better than I do. How do you think she'd react to me dating both of you?"

"I'm not sure, to be honest." Pasha had never known Geneva to be spiteful or bitter over a match that didn't last. Bryson said Gen had been incredibly supportive of her relationship with Karla, though she still carried a torch for her. "She might be fine with it, since she and I are friends and because you two haven't gone out long. But…well, Geneva wears her heart on her sleeve. She can fall pretty fast for someone and take a long time to get over them."

Emery cradled her mug in both hands and looked earnestly at Pasha. "I told her right up front, like I tell every woman I may become intimate with, I'm only interested in fun. No strings, and no emotional involvement. I don't do relationships."

Pasha managed to say only, "I see." The unexpected pronouncement made her fight not to let her disappointment show. How could her gift lead her to an emotionally unavailable woman?

"Are you all right with those terms? Still want to go out?"

"Yup." Pasha didn't hesitate, though her instinct for self-preservation told her to proceed cautiously. The power pulling them together insisted on seeing where this led.

Emery smiled and relaxed against the seat, seeming visibly relieved, like she wasn't sure Pasha would agree to a brief affair. "Geneva needs to know I'm seeing both of you. How should I tell her?"

"I can talk to her, or you. I doubt it matters."

"I will, then," Emery said. "I'll catch her after her shift tonight."

"I promised you some information on things to do around here." Pasha went to the file cabinet to retrieve some stuff they'd put together for clients. "Birch Hill Lake is about a three-mile walk from here. The trail starts in Evansville, behind the medical clinic." She handed several Xeroxed pages to Emery, including a topographic map with the trail clearly marked. "Definitely worth a day hike. Great views, lots of wildflowers. Pretty easy terrain, but boggy in spots, so make sure you have the right footwear."

Emery glanced at her polished leather boots. "No worries. I've got others."

"If you go alone, make sure you take plenty of water and pack a lunch. And…" Pasha returned to the file cabinet and dug through the bottom drawer. "Pepper spray, and a PLB."

"PLB?"

"Personal locator beacon." She gave Emery the cell-phone-sized device, along with a small metal cylinder in a leather case.

"We make sure we have at least one every trip. Needless to say, don't activate it unless you need to. Search-and-rescue here provides them."

"I've got a GPS, as well." Emery stuffed the two items into her jacket pockets. "You think I might run into a bear?" She showed no fear at the prospect, unlike many clients. Some, freaked out, asked about the possibility when they called to inquire about wilderness trips.

"It's always a possibility. Though I haven't heard of any problems around Birch Hill Lake, you'll see some large berry patches up there. Do you know how to act if you encounter a grizzly and he sees you?"

Emery nodded. "Stay calm. Don't run or make eye contact. Speak normally and wave your arms so he can identify you as human. Back up slowly. Climbing a tree may help—if you can get high enough fast enough. Worst case—if he charges, stand your ground and use the spray once he's within twenty feet or so. Ball into a fetal position on your side if that doesn't work, protect your stomach and head. Play dead. That about cover it?"

"You've done your homework." Emery had certainly prepared well. "Also good to make yourself look big when you first see him. Spread your jacket out. Stand tall. And watch out for two situations in particular. Moms with cubs—this is the right time of year for that—and bears protecting their kill sites. If you see a lot of scavenger birds—ravens and such—congregating in an area, for example, get out of there as quickly as possible."

"Got it."

"And make noise while you walk and when you stop. Sing, hum, whatever. The village store sells bear bells you can hang on your belt or pack. Bears don't like surprises and usually will give you a wide berth if they know you're there." Pasha refilled their mugs before she settled back in her chair next to Emery. "Those sheets I gave you contain all that information and discuss some ways to react around black bears. We have them, too, but you're even less likely to meet one. Oh, and you'll find photos identifying some of the local wildflowers and birds."

"Sounds like you'll be a great guide."

"I hope so. I've had incredible teachers, particularly Lars Rasmussen, Karla's brother-in-law. He's guided here for a couple of decades and really knows his stuff. He's also an incredibly sweet guy."

"I look forward to meeting him." Emery paused for another sip. "Will he guide one of my trips?"

"At least one, the fishing excursion, because he knows all the best spots. Maybe others—Dita's still rearranging things a bit to add a few more trips."

"Is she? That, and the fact you've been working your tail off since she left, must mean business is good."

"Yup. Way more people seem to be taking vacations up here this year than the last couple of seasons. Splurging to reward themselves, I think, now that the economy's improving."

"Of course I'm happy for all of you, but I'm hoping you won't be so busy you won't have time for me between trips." Emery set down her mug and looked at Pasha expectantly.

"We'll have part-time help soon, and Dita rarely goes out in the field, except the first trip of the season, so I should have regular hours and weekends off."

"Great. I'm really looking forward to spending time with you on the trip."

"Me, too, Emery."

"Well, knowing I'll be doing that in just a couple days, and since you have to get up early, I'll reluctantly say good night." Emery got to her feet, carefully folding the papers Pasha had given her in half. "I appreciate the info about Birch Hill Lake. I'll head out after breakfast, so I'll be back in plenty of time for the initiation."

Pasha rose. "And remember, you can stop by after closing and talk to Dita, if you like. I'll leave the door open." She led Emery outside.

"Will you be here, too?" Emery asked as she faced her on the porch.

They stood just two feet apart. Pasha trembled with the sudden surge of electrical power that roared through her as their eyes met.

"Are you—" Emery's eyes darkened in worry as she reached for her, obviously able to discern how unsteady she felt on her feet.

Instantly reminded of the humiliation of her previous blackout, Pasha raised her hand and cut Emery off. The day after tomorrow, she would be placing her trust—and her very life—in Pasha's hands, and she didn't want to appear frail or vulnerable. "Don't start that again." She spoke lightly, teasingly, like Emery was acting like a mother hen and imagining things. "I'm just *fine*. Okay, already?"

Emery still looked skeptical, but she nodded. She also took the hint that she shouldn't touch Pasha right now. Pasha's sudden surge of power warned her that she could experience another blackout, and she couldn't risk that. Emery might even say something to Dita out of worry. Dita knew about her gift, but still might pull her from the field until a doctor in Fairbanks cleared her. Unthinkable.

Pasha had to make certain Emery understood, however, that she wasn't pulling away because she'd changed her mind. She had to be giving off conflicting signals. How could she explain her erratic behavior without opening a can of worms she wasn't ready to deal with? "Emery, please don't misunderstand. I really like you. And I know I act kind of…unpredictable around you, I guess it would be fair to say?"

Emery's smile eased some of Pasha's anxiety.

"You'll understand. Soon. I promise." She stepped back and put a hand on the doorknob, pleading with her eyes for Emery to accept the explanation.

"I can be very patient, Pasha. And I understand that some things are difficult to talk about." Emery's aura glowed. "Good night. Sleep well."

"Good night, Emery."

CHAPTER SIXTEEN

Pasha stared out her apartment's big picture window at the lowering sun as it painted the distant mountaintops amber-gold. Later she'd regret staying up so late, but she wouldn't see another sunset for a long while and would miss it. The sun would dip beneath the horizon for about forty minutes and wouldn't set until mid-July. Actually, she wouldn't see another sunset then because she rarely woke for the brief two a.m. transition.

She'd had no problem staying awake tonight, her mind churning with thoughts of Emery. Vacillating from joyous to despondent, whatever image or snatch of conversation she recalled swayed her. Once again, she felt overly sentimental and emotionally polarized, experiencing every high and low so profoundly she almost cried at both ends of the spectrum.

When she recalled Emery's golden aura, bliss infused her once again. And she recalled so many other wonderful moments. She and Emery were definitely mutually attracted. Their intense, prolonged eye contact revealed their chemistry. Emery looked totally enraptured with their conversation, and her eagerness to spend more time together encouraged Pasha.

Though she tried to focus on the positive developments, she had to be realistic. A romantic at heart, she had learned to weigh the negatives before she leapt headlong into anything life-changing. And right now, she couldn't push a huge, glaring problem to the back of her mind for very long.

She seriously risked having her heart badly broken. Emery had made it clear she didn't want anything except a transitory sexual fling, and meant it. In a few months, she would move on, into the arms of another woman, and not look back.

Pasha longed to somehow connect with Emery. She told herself just to treasure each day and enjoy what she offered as long as possible. Her gift apparently couldn't guarantee she'd find the life-long soul mate she'd always imagined and hoped for, but wouldn't it be wrong not to embrace whatever happiness she could, despite the consequences?

❖

Emery struck off toward Birch Hill Lake not long after nine a.m. She wished she could have started even sooner since she was awake at six, but decided to wait until the village store opened so she could pick up a bear bell, fishing license, and portable rod and reel. A spruce-birch forest surrounded Bettles, so thick in spots she was grateful the trail was fairly well delineated. The material Pasha had given her also contained the GPS coordinates for both the lake and Bettles, so she had those as a backup to chart her course.

In addition to her new purchases and GPS, her daypack contained food and water, binoculars, her survival kit, journal, and the PLB. She'd hooked the pepper-spray canister to her belt so she could access it quickly if she ran into problems.

She started off with her camera in the bag, too, but she found so many photo opportunities she had it out and around her neck before she'd traveled a quarter of a mile. Despite the bear bell's constant tinkling as she walked, her presence didn't seem to affect the birds and smaller forest creatures. She took some impressive shots of a porcupine working away at the base of a tree, a rabbit munching on willow twigs, and a pair of red squirrels engaged in a game of chase along the trunk and low branches of a black spruce. Her lens also immortalized chickadees, ravens, woodpeckers, and several birds she didn't recognize, along with some vivid wildflowers near the path. Thanks to Pasha's printouts, she could identify the yellow arctic poppies, pale blue forget-me-nots, and purple lupine and wild sweet pea, but she encountered a number of other varieties that weren't listed.

Time passed quickly and she didn't reach the lake until noon. She stopped frequently, but boggy terrain had also slowed her. In the shadows of the forest, the permafrost remained fairly solid, but the areas hit by direct sunshine had become spongy traps that could trip her up or suck her boots into a quagmire. She saw no one else, either on the trail or at her destination.

A myriad of small streams fed Birch Hill Lake, a scenic, elongated body of water. Emery had good luck casting from the shore with her fishing rod, but released the half dozen or so whitefish and grayling she reeled in. After a quick lunch, she walked the nearest shoreline with her camera and took some more wildlife snapshots: a variety of ducks, loons, and cranes she couldn't identify, and other migratory birds passing through on their way farther north. At one of the creeks, she spotted a weasel-like marten working the shallows for food, but he scampered into the woods before she could focus on him. A moose on the far shore also eluded her—too distant even for her zoom lens.

Emery was having a wonderful time, but she started back at two so she'd reach Bettles by the time Dita Eidson got back. She still wanted to meet the woman she'd corresponded with and review in more detail some of the trips she'd signed up for, but her primary motivation was a few minutes alone with Pasha before the group convened for dinner. Not that she expected any quick explanation to their puzzling good-bye last night.

Pasha had clearly suffered some sort of episode again as they stood on the porch. Her eyes had reflected the same flash of glazed confusion that had immediately preceded her blackout, all the color drained from her face, and she seemed unsteady on her feet. But Pasha had obviously not wanted Emery to know what was going on, at least not yet, and she definitely didn't want to be touched. Considering what had happened on the previous occasions they'd made physical contact, this latest incident only piqued Emery's curiosity all the more.

Most likely, she'd get no answers tonight, but tomorrow, they'd both be in the backcountry, with fewer distractions and hopefully ample time to discuss what was going on.

On the hike back, Emery added a few more photos to the gallery she'd already amassed: a bald eagle soaring overhead, its distinctive white head and tail feathers outlined against the vivid blue sky; a large gray owl perched on a broken birch limb; and paw prints in the mud that might belong to a wolf. She'd have taken more shots, but the bugs were out in force during her return trip, so bad she had to wear the hat with the head-net Geneva had given her. The repellent she'd liberally applied before she set off couldn't keep the biting flies and gnats away from her face.

Her watch read four thirty when she reached the outskirts of Bettles, which gave her enough time to dump her stuff in her room and grab a quick shower. She also took one of her pain meds. The distance and boggy terrain had been hard on her joints, and sitting long hours at dinner would likely exacerbate her discomfort.

A Closed sign hung on the entrance of Eidson Eco-Tours, but Pasha had left the door open as she'd promised, so Emery walked inside. The chime of the bell over the door brought Pasha from the back room, just ahead of a woman with short, salt-and-pepper hair who she presumed was Dita.

"How was your outing?" Pasha asked as Emery neared.

"Awesome. Thanks again for pointing me there, and all the info."

"Emery Lawson, Dita Eidson," Pasha said by way of introductions.

"Pleasure to meet ya, Emery," Dita said as she offered her hand.

"Likewise, Dita. How did your fishing trip go?"

"You can find out for yourself. Ellie's going to cook up the catch I brought back for our table tonight." Dita spoke slowly, with a soft Southern drawl that reminded Emery of something from *Gone With The Wind*. "We caught a mess of lake trout and grayling."

"I had some luck myself up at Birch Hill Lake, but tossed them back."

"Pasha's been saying you're making yourself right at home here, and I understand our little group is officially welcoming you tonight. Sorry I wasn't here to greet you properly."

"Oh, I've been well looked after." She glanced over at Pasha.

Pasha's mouth was turned upward in a smile, but her eyes betrayed an underlying current of unease and her posture couldn't be more unwelcoming. She had her arms crossed over her chest and stood off to one side, four or five feet away. Was she worried Emery would touch her and possibly trigger another fainting episode in front of her boss?

To set her mind at ease, Emery turned her attention back to Dita. "I know you just got back, but do you have a few minutes before dinner to chat about my trips?"

"Sure. Come on back to the lounge." Dita tilted her head toward the back room and headed that way.

Emery followed, steering clear of Pasha. As she drew abreast of her, their eyes met, and she could see that relief had replaced the disquiet.

"I'll see you both at dinner," Pasha called after them.

The time got away from Emery and Dita because they clicked immediately and found ample common ground for conversation. The woman's professionalism and welcoming demeanor in their e-mail correspondence and a couple of quick phone calls had already impressed Emery, but Dita's dry wit, gentle nature, and passion for what she did sealed the deal. Dita put her clients' safety and enjoyment foremost. She aimed, she said, to do all she could to ensure that the people who took her trips came back from them with memories they would cherish the rest of their lives, while gaining a new appreciation for preserving the unspoiled wilderness.

Emery couldn't have chosen a better outfitter than Eidson Eco-Tours. Dita brought out her client file and reviewed all of the trips she'd signed up for, filling in details about the locations, staffing, meals, and so on. She had endless, colorful stories about previous trips, most hysterically funny and a few describing some of the rarer wonders that clients had seen or experienced. Emery felt she was in good hands and especially looked forward to the women-only trips coming up.

"Look at the time," Dita said when she glanced at her watch. "We best go if we don't want to miss the fun. Bet the others are already there."

When they arrived, the Den was busier than Emery had ever seen it. Because Geneva had worked the day shift she was supposed to be off now but was still busy bustling between tables along with the other waitress. The rest of the gang sat in the booth, with Pasha once again sandwiched between the two couples: Karla and Bryson on one side, Chaz and Megan on the other.

Emery suspected Pasha had deliberately chosen the seating to keep them from touching, even accidentally. As they all exchanged greetings, Dita slid in next to Bryson and Emery took the end seat.

Again, Pasha sat almost directly across from her, a prime location for them to make frequent eye contact without drawing the others' attention. They did so throughout dinner, as Dita regaled them with an account of the fishing excursion and the others chimed in with stories of some of their adventures. Just as they finished dessert, Geneva joined them. They all squeezed closer so she could perch on the other end, opposite Emery.

"Finally," Geneva said, drawing the word out as she relaxed against the seat back. "It's been crazy. Sorry I missed dinner."

"Least you could break free in time for our little initiation." Bryson retrieved her baseball cap from a hook on the wall. "Shall we?"

"Where we headed?" Emery asked.

"You'll see, soon enough," Chaz said, rubbing her hands together like a cartoon villain plotting some evil deed. "We've prepared everything." Her declaration drew giggles from most of the others.

What the heck had they planned?

CHAPTER SEVENTEEN

Once they were outside, Megan pulled a long black scarf from her jacket pocket and held it up. "Stand still, Emery."

"What's that for?"

"Blindfold."

"You really are taking this very seriously, I see," Emery remarked as Megan fastened the scarf around her eyes.

"Oh, you bet we are, little missy." Dita sounded an inch away from laughing as they spun Emery around to make her lose her sense of direction.

When they stopped, a hand gripped her left elbow as another took her right. From the left came Bryson's voice. "Straight ahead. Let's go."

They walked her probably a quarter mile, warning her of bad footing ahead or a dip in the terrain. She heard gravel under her boots so she knew they were still somewhere in the village proper, or possibly at the edge of the runway. They could be marching her in circles for all she knew. They kept changing direction, giggling with every twist and turn. Now and then she heard murmured whispers. More plotting, no doubt.

Finally they led her up three stairs and into a building. They didn't remove the blindfold until they'd seated her on a plain metal folding chair, and Megan warned her beforehand to keep her eyes closed.

"Okay, you can open them now." Chaz's voice, from several feet behind her.

When she did, she saw nothing but darkness. Either the room had no windows or they'd effectively blocked them. Before her eyes could adjust, a spotlight clicked on in front of her, aimed at her face. Then a second, a few feet to the left of the first, and a third, a few feet to the right. She couldn't see anything in the room, like being in a bad black-and-white movie—the FBI grilling the suspected spy. The giggling, however, and the fact they'd focused the lights away from her eyes so they wouldn't completely blind her, made the situation more fun than threatening.

"Now, ordinarily in Probing Questions, everyone answers all questions." Megan's voice came from behind the light on the left. "On this special occasion, however, we've altered the rules. You're the only one who has to answer every question, but you can name one other person each time who must also answer. Got it?"

"Yes. Fire away."

"We're going to give you a break because we all like you." Pasha stood right behind her. "So if one of these is too personal, you can get off the hook if your answer is funny or entertaining enough."

"I appreciate the latitude." Had Pasha suggested to the group that they allow her that alternative?

"We'll start off easy," Megan said. "Ever had any nicknames?"

"Mmm. Well, one. As a kid I stayed up late a lot, reading with a flashlight, so my folks used to call me Firefly."

"That's actually kinda cool," Megan replied. "Who do you want to answer that question?"

"Let's say Dita."

"Good pick." Dita chuckled. "I was a fiend for swimming, so Daddy called me Tadpole."

"Next question, Emery," Megan said. "Tell us about your most embarrassing or awkward moment."

Emery didn't want to share the answer that sprang to mind. The leaking-catheter story wouldn't entertain and would require her to explain the circumstances. She tried to come up with a funny alternative and finally remembered a conversation she'd overheard. "One day in Venice at a café," she told the group, "I was flirting with this beautiful local woman, trying to impress her with my Italian. At one point, I thought I was saying I was really discouraged I wasn't making headway with her. 'Discouraged,' in Italian, is *scoraggiata*, but my pronunciation came out *scoreggiata*, which, I subsequently found out, means 'farted.'"

They roared with laughter, and Emery joined them, remembering how the real woman who'd inspired the story crashed into a waiter as she ran from the café in embarrassment. When the laughter died down, Emery said, "All right, now Bryson gets to humiliate herself with her story."

"Mine's from when I first started doing commercial charters," Bryson said. "I was eighteen or so. Hired to fly these three hunters way out in the bush, but weather kept us grounded half of their weeklong trip, so they were really itching to go by the time it cleared. Anyway, we get all the way up there, them razzing me all the while about how young I was, and I unload the cargo only to realize I'd left all their guns back at the hangar. They weren't amused, especially since I'd set them down in prime grizzly country."

After more laughter, Chaz asked a question. "As you know, we call our little group ADLIB: Adventurous Dykes Living in Bettles, which means we need some proof of your qualifications. What's the most daring or dangerous thing you've ever done?"

Getting on that elevator in Sofia qualifies. In retrospect, nothing she could ever do could match the danger of that, but presumably this question referred to risky endeavors she had willingly embraced. "Let's see. That would probably be skiing in a closed avalanche zone in the Swiss Alps." That adventure had been even riskier than it sounded, since she'd strapped on skis long before she was physically up to it and had barely made it back. "Geneva? You get to take this one."

"Most daring or dangerous, I believe the question was, and I'll go with the daring part." Geneva's voice came from her right. "In college, I streaked across campus on a dare. Not a bad decision on my part, by the way. A lot of women asked for my number later."

More laughter.

Bryson had the next query. "Do you play any musical instruments?"

"I dabble on the harmonica some, if that counts."

Her answer drew a chorus of approving comments: "Great," and "Oh, that'll fit right in," and, from Bryson, "We have a little group that jams in the Den now and then, so we may have to recruit you."

"So you play?" Emery asked.

"Yeah. Drums."

The next question came from Karla. "Ever rescued anyone or done anything heroic?"

"I saved my cousin from a sugar overdose every year by stealing most of his Halloween candy. Does that count?" Collective groans answered her for the most part, but a couple of people snickered. "Chaz, how about you on this one?"

"No, I'll take this," Megan said, "since she rescued *me*. I tipped over in some whitewater on the kayak trip where we met and cracked my head against a rock. I'd have drowned if she hadn't gotten to me. She's too damn modest to tell you, but I'm sure not the first client she's gotten out of trouble."

"That's quite a novel way to get the girl, Chaz." Emery brought up one hand to shield her eyes from the lights. "Next question?"

"Who do you think is the most beautiful woman in the world?" Geneva asked.

Emery answered without hesitation. "Michelle Pfeiffer."

"Oh, yeah, I can go there," Bryson remarked, and a few others murmured agreement.

"Who would you say, Karla?" Emery asked.

"Michelle's a great pick, granted, but I'm into brunettes, to no one's surprise." Bryson chuckled. "So, I'd probably say Sandra Bullock."

"Next question, Emery…" Dita's turn to ask, apparently. "What food and drink could you never give up?"

"Definitely coffee," Emery answered. "And as for food, probably fresh-baked bread. It's a major weakness. How about you?"

"Sweet tea and my momma's fried chicken. She made it every Sunday after church when I was growing up. Had this great crispy crust and was so moist inside. Put that with some mashed 'taters and cornbread, and I'm in heaven."

"Oh, man, I'm so glad I'm full," Chaz said, and they all laughed.

"No lie," Emery said. "Who's next?"

"What's the most significant event in your life so far?"

The hardest question had come from Pasha. Emery wiped suddenly sweaty palms on the thighs of her jeans. Sometimes Pasha seemed to know much more about her than she should, almost like she could read her mind. The questions she asked were too damn insightful, always dancing around the secrets she managed to conceal so well from everyone else. That Pasha might have some unusual ability to see inside the "real her" both thrilled and disconcerted Emery.

She couldn't answer honestly, so she took the "out" Pasha had allowed and tried to come up with something witty. When that failed, she shamelessly decided to go for the suck-up approach. "Coming to Bettles, since it allowed me to meet all of you." In a way, that wasn't entirely bogus. She truly enjoyed these women's company; she liked and admired every one of them. And Pasha, in particular, had especially impressed her.

A few groaned, and a couple said, "Awww," and "That's sweet."

"How about you answer that question yourself, Pasha?" Emery asked.

"Turnabout and all that, eh? Okay. Well, sorry to be redundant, but coming to Alaska is mine as well, for the same reasons."

"We're degenerating into a syrupy love fest," Megan proclaimed with feigned irritation, amid more laughter. "Which means it's time to move on to phase two."

"Phase two?" Emery was steeling herself for another round of summer-camp-like shenanigans when the spotlights started clicking off. Someone pulled the curtains back and she had to blink several times to adjust to the sunlight. She sat in the cozy living room of a cabin, no doubt the one the two couples had rented because their things lay scattered here and there.

The furniture—a long couch, two matching armchairs and a coffee table—had been pushed back. She was in the middle of the room, her back to a massive stone fireplace.

"The toasting phase." Bryson ducked through a doorway and returned with two bottles of champagne as the rest of them started to applaud."

"So, I'm in?" Emery stood up. "That's it?"

As everyone started to move the furniture back, Dita slapped her lightly on the shoulder. "Come on, you knew getting in was as easy as sliding off a greasy log backward. They've all been talking my ear off about you since I got back."

Karla and Megan started passing out the limited assortment of drinking vessels that apparently came with the cabin—coffee mugs, a juice glass, and three plastic wineglasses—while Bryson popped the cork on one of the bottles and poured.

"To our new member and friend, Emery. May she always consider Bettles a second home and come back to visit whenever she can." Bryson raised her mug and the others followed.

"To Emery," Pasha and a couple of others echoed enthusiastically.

Emery noted that Pasha seemed relaxed and at ease, but kept her distance until time to clink their glasses together. As soon as they did, she backed off and took one of the solo armchairs.

Emery wedged between Dita and Geneva on the couch. "Well, that was pretty painless. I had no idea what kind of questions you might come up with."

"Got one more surprise." Bryson reached into a shopping bag beside the coffee table, pulled out a stack of baseball caps, and tossed one to each woman. The caps were navy-blue, with ADLIB tastefully embroidered in white across the front. "Place in Fairbanks does 'em."

Everyone put theirs on, amid a chorus of approving remarks and several versions of "Thanks, Bryson."

They chatted for another hour or so as they polished off the champagne, then Dita played the bad guy and suggested they call it a night. Most of them had to get up early to prepare for the photography trip, so few objected. Emery was ready to head back to her room as well. Her joints had stiffened and her muscles were cramping from the long day's hike. She desperately needed more pain meds.

"Walk me back?" Geneva tucked her arm in Emery's as they all gathered on the porch for good-byes.

"Sure." Emery glanced over at Pasha, who was watching them from a few feet away with an unreadable expression.

"See y'all in the morning." Dita put her hand on Pasha's back. "You ready for your first big trip?"

"More than ready." Pasha's eyes never left Emery's. "I can't wait."

"I'm with you there," Emery said. "I'm sure it'll be memorable." They were using their secret language, half words and half body language/eye contact, again, equally anxious to spend some quality time together.

"Sleep well, everyone." Pasha fell into step next to Dita and headed off toward the Eidson building as the rest waved good-bye or replied with similar sentiments.

Emery and Geneva veered left, toward the Den. They walked slowly, Geneva's hand still tucked into the crook of Emery's arm.

"I'll miss you while you're gone," Geneva said. "Can I reserve the first night you're back? Ellie will let me cook something special in the kitchen. Maybe we can do a candlelight supper in my room?"

"I'd like that," Emery replied. "You a good cook?"

"I have many hidden talents." Geneva's tone was flirty and playful.

Emery couldn't help but smile. "I'm sure you do."

"And you'll succumb to them. Wait and see."

Pasha intrigued Emery more, but she couldn't help but like Geneva a lot as well. She was funny, spirited, and a well-versed flirt, not to mention very compelling physically, and Emery had been impressed with how well she seemed to be taking the news that she would also be dating Pasha. She'd knocked on Geneva's door last night after her shift to tell her, and Geneva had reacted with a calm, "That's cool. Pasha's a great gal." Perhaps Geneva *was* capable of a no-strings affair without repercussions, as long as she knew the score upfront.

As they ascended the final stairs to their rooms, Geneva said, "I've been reliving that kiss in Old Bettles. Think I can get a repeat to tide me over until you get back?"

"That can be arranged," she replied as they paused in front of Geneva's door.

Geneva looked up at her expectantly as she wrapped her arms around Emery's neck. "In case I don't see you before you leave, have a fabulous time. Be safe."

"I will. You, too." Emery put her arms around Geneva's waist and kissed her, a soft, sweet kiss of good-bye that Geneva escalated into a more passionate exchange.

"I don't know if that's actually going to help my missing you, or make it worse," Geneva said when Emery gently pulled back.

Emery kissed her forehead as she extricated herself from Geneva's embrace. "Good night. Sleep well."

"You, too. 'Nite."

Emery quickly recorded the day's events in her journal before she retired, to give her pain pill a chance to kick in. As she snuggled under the comforter, she envisioned what would be happening in Geneva's room right now had she allowed their kiss to go on much longer.

The image was certainly inviting.

When she pictured herself becoming intimate with Pasha, however, she had a much stronger visceral reaction. Just thinking about it aroused her.

CHAPTER EIGHTEEN

June 5

Pasha stuffed an extra PowerBar into Emery's client pack, zipped it closed, and stacked it with the others by the door. "That's the last of it," she told Chaz and Dita. Her heart already beat faster than usual in her excitement about this trip. Who knew what would happen once Emery got here.

She'd stayed up late wondering how the power would manifest itself when they interacted constantly in close quarters. Most of all, she hoped she wouldn't faint again. Another blackout would not only jeopardize her burgeoning career as a guide but would endanger her and her clients, Emery in particular.

What if, for example, she slipped going up a narrow trail or scree-strewn hillside, and Emery reached out to help her? Certainly not improbable, as were dozens of other similar scenarios, particularly during the more risky trips later in the summer.

Her gift had always made Pasha feel special and comforted, like having a cosmic guide to help her make the right decisions. So she still had a difficult time imagining that it might steer her so forcefully and so irrevocably toward Emery without the possibility of a happy future together. She wanted to trust her instincts as she always had, whatever the risk to her heart, but her responsibility as a guide necessitated she use caution around Emery.

The weather radio in the corner blared the public-alert tone that indicated a special advisory. A developing storm front would hit the interior with gusty winds and potentially heavy rain the day after tomorrow—the last day of their photography trip.

"Let's hope they're wrong again," Dita said. Dita wasn't slamming the meteorologists. Alaska's terrain, latitude, and vastness meant that every type of possible weather might occur somewhere, all at the same time. And conditions could, and did, change by the minute.

"We're prepared if they're not. Just won't be as much fun for the clients," Chaz replied as she stowed her camera gear into her own pack.

Heavy rain would keep them all inside and make for less-impressive meals. But on the plus side, Pasha might get additional time with Emery to talk and get to know each other.

The bell over the entrance jangled. "Here they are," Dita said.

They headed to the outer office to greet their clients, Pasha sensing that Emery hadn't arrived yet. The six men and women who'd signed up for the photography trip knew to assemble in the outer office at nine a.m., and it was still a few minutes before.

Dita greeted three women who'd come in. "Good morning and welcome to Bettles. "I'm Dita Eidson, and here are Pasha Dunn and Chaz Herrick, your guides."

All three clients wore brand-new hiking clothes and boots that looked barely broken in. Their duffel bags containing their personal gear also appeared right off the rack. Fortunately they planned to set up a base camp and only take short outings from there every day. These clients didn't look like they did a lot of hiking and camping, which wasn't uncommon. They billed the three-day, two-night photography excursion as a "beginner, non-strenuous" trip, which pretty much opened it up to everyone. Dita had more rigid requirements for some of the backpacking and kayaking trips. She always built in contingency plans for injuries or delays due to weather, but plotted the longer trips with a daily mileage quota to their campsites and final pickup point.

The first one who stepped forward and offered her hand, an older white woman with steel-gray hair cut in a soft wave, was petite and wiry and had a quick smile. "Hi, Dita. I'm Ruth Thomas. From Pittsburgh." As they shook hands, Pasha filled in what she could remember from Ruth's client file. At sixty-six, she looked at least a decade younger. A widow with five kids, and recently retired.

"My friends," Ruth said, turning toward her companions. "Toni Whitaker and Alyson Jones."

Toni Whitaker, in her early thirties, cut an imposing figure. A six-foot-three black woman with broad shoulders who looked like she could be playing for the WNBA, she spoke so softly her voice seemed completely at odds with her formidable appearance. "Hello. Nice to meet you."

Alyson, short and stocky, had spiky blond hair and multiple piercings in both ears and eyebrows. Though twenty-four, Pasha recalled, she could have passed as a teenager. "Hey there."

The three women couldn't seem more different from each other, and Pasha wondered how they'd become friends.

"The rest should be here soon," Dita told them. "Why don't y'all take a seat and get comfortable. Just made a pot of coffee if anyone's interested."

Ruth and Toni wanted some, so Pasha went to the back room to fill a couple of mugs. She heard the entry bell again, and by the time she returned to the outer office two more newcomers were introducing themselves. From the look of their clothes and gear, Joe and Mandy Fillmore, a married couple from Seattle, were serious fly-fishing enthusiasts. Both had on worn, multi-pocket vests crammed with flies and other equipment.

As she shook hands with them, Pasha felt a sudden uptick in the power, a warm infusion of strength and a heightening of awareness. Emery.

The sensation built as it had before, gaining ferocity the closer Emery got. By the time she appeared in the doorway, Pasha's nerves were stretched tight and she had to remind herself to breathe, but when their eyes met, she felt calm again, the familiar sense of bliss settling over her like a blanket.

"Sorry, am I late?" Emery asked when she saw the rest already comfortably seated, their gear stacked by the door.

"Nope, right on time," Dita told her. "Why don't you grab a seat and we can get started."

Pasha tensed until Emery selected a chair on the other side of the room from where she stood.

For the next half hour, Chaz detailed all they'd need to know for their three days in the backcountry. To minimize any problems with bears, they would set up their cooking/eating area well away from their sleeping cots and put all food and trash into bear-proof containers and carry it at least two hundred feet away from camp each night. "If you help with the cooking or spill food on yourself, change before you go to bed," she told them. "And don't keep anything with a strong smell—candy, flavored drinks, lotions, toothpaste, and such—where we sleep."

She provided the same instructions Pasha had given Emery about making noise outside of camp, particularly when they made a pit stop alone. Then she explained the importance of the leave-no-trace tenets of camping, designed to minimize their impact on the fragile Arctic landscape. As she spoke, Pasha handed out printouts that included all the information Chaz was imparting as well as guides to the plants, birds, and wildlife they might encounter. As she neared Emery, her euphoric bliss from their connection intensified until her entire body buzzed.

She paused a couple of feet away and extended the handouts in Emery's direction.

Emery smiled, the look in her eyes communicating that she seemed aware of Pasha's current heightened state. "Thanks," she said in a low voice as she accepted the papers.

"Look these over, and let me know if you have any questions," Chaz said. "Now, unless anyone has anything to add, I suggest we head to the plane and get this party started."

Bryson stood waiting by the nine-passenger Cessna, having already made one round-trip to the site to deliver equipment and supplies. Chaz and Pasha helped her load the remaining cargo while the clients boarded, and soon they flew north into a blue sky dotted with high, wispy clouds. Emery, the first aboard, sat in the rear, while Pasha rode in the cockpit beside Bryson.

"Where exactly are we going?" Ruth asked.

"A river valley just outside the Gates of the Arctic National Park," Bryson told them. "My dad used to take me there. Lots of wildlife and wildflowers, great fishing, and spectacular views."

Pasha heard the click of cameras from behind her and turned in her seat. Ruth, Toni, and the Fillmores all busily snapped shots out the windows as they approached the foothills of the Brooks Range. Alyson had her MP3 headphones on. Though rocking to the beat of whatever she listened to, she also focused on the scenery.

Emery, however, was watching *her*.

Flying high above the mountains, Bryson followed a wide river for about an hour, then turned to follow a smaller tributary leading off it and started to descend. "Here we go, everyone. Might be a little bumpy setting down. Nothing to worry about."

They hit some turbulence right before they touched wheels on a long, wide gravel bar, but no one seemed unduly concerned. They quickly unloaded their gear and supplies on the riverbank.

"Have a great time, and I'll see you about four p.m. day after tomorrow," Bryson told Pasha. "If we get that rain and wind they're forecasting and I'm grounded, I'll try to contact you by radio for an alternate pickup."

"Got it." She watched the Cessna take off and took a moment to survey her surroundings. Though she'd helped deliver supplies to this location, she'd never spent any time here and was eager to explore the environs. Wonderful photo opportunities abounded. Majestic mountains surrounded them, no sign of civilization marring the view. Behind the wide, rocky beach where they would erect their tents grew forest, so thick with birdlife she heard a dozen different calls.

"If we can all gather around." Chaz started to pick through the pile of gear. "You're all responsible for setting up your own tents, but Pasha and I will help if you need us. Find a nice level spot somewhere in this area." She tossed a three-man tent to Ruth, Toni, and Alyson, a two-person tent to the Fillmores, and another two-person to Emery. "We'll put the cooking area over there." She pointed to a rocky stretch of beach farther downstream. "Once we set up camp, I'll take you out to take some pictures while Pasha starts lunch. Any questions?"

"I know we'll need help," Ruth said after a brief whispered consultation with her friends. "None of us has ever pitched a tent."

"It's really easy." Pasha headed in their direction. "I'll show you." She got theirs up while Chaz erected the two-person tent they'd share.

Twenty minutes later, they had a tidy campsite. They'd stowed sleeping bags and other personal gear inside the tents, and Pasha had almost put a kitchen area together. Although she would cook everything on a portable gas stove, she set rocks in a circle for a campfire as well. They used this area because they could find ample firewood—driftwood littered the banks on either side of the river—so they didn't exploit limited resources or adversely impact the environment.

Clients loved campfires, even during the summer when the sun didn't set, so the guides always tried to provide one. They considered it worth the trouble of eradicating all evidence of the fire pit before they left—part of the leave-no-trace philosophy—because a campfire in the evening after dinner bonded clients in a spirit of shared camaraderie and fun.

Pasha was leaning over, sorting through the food they'd packed in large bear-proof containers, when a sudden surge in the power told her Emery was behind her and nearing rapidly. She shot upright and pivoted as Emery halted just beyond arm's length. She seemed surprised that Pasha could have heard her approach. "So, you're not coming with us?"

"Afraid not, though I'd sure like to. Chaz knows both photography and this region a lot better than I do. Because I'm the junior guide, I get to do all the cooking, so that'll limit how much I can go out."

The clients were all assembling with Chaz, cameras in hand, back by the tents.

"Lucky you." Emery frowned. "Need an assistant? I can't cook worth a damn, but I can chop vegetables or something. Give us a chance to chat."

"That's incredibly sweet." Deeply touched that Emery wanted her company so much she'd forego Chaz's hike, Pasha wanted to accept the offer. They needed time away from the others so she could see what her gift would put her through this time. But Emery had paid good money to experience this photography excursion. "We'll have time to talk. I want that, too. But you should go. You really don't want to miss wherever Chaz plans to take you. She's camped here a lot and knows the area well. Besides, I want to dazzle you with my culinary skills."

"Whatever you say. I'll look forward to lunch." Emery started off toward the others but paused and turned back before she'd gone three steps. "Tonight. Let's find a way. All right?" she asked in a low voice.

"You got a deal."

Chapter Nineteen

Thoughts of Pasha absorbed Emery so fully she nearly collided with Mandy Fillmore, who stopped abruptly and pointed to the right. The dense spruce forest made it difficult to see what had captured her attention.

"What is that? The big thing up there in the tree? See it?" Mandy, a fifty-something redhead, had surgically enhanced double Ds.

Her husband Joe, a balding corporate type, peered through his binoculars. "Hawk of some kind, maybe."

"A northern hawk owl, I believe." Toni Whitaker spoke from behind her own binoculars. Chaz, no longer in sight, apparently hadn't heard them.

"Are you a birdwatcher?" Mandy asked as the four of them started off again.

"No. I just read a lot," Toni replied. "I borrowed a lot of books from the library about Alaska."

"Good memory, then," Joe said.

Chaz, Ruth, and Alyson had waited for them a short distance farther on.

"We're cutting through a mountain pass," Chaz told them. "Pretty soon we cross over a shallow creek and climb a hill. Over the rise you'll have a great view and a chance to see some wildlife."

As promised, they emerged from the trees a half hour later and found themselves on a high plateau, looking down at an expanse of open tundra cut in half by a wide river and framed by mountains. Everyone quickly brought their camera up. Below them they saw at least a couple of hundred caribou, the massive bulls with their still-velvet-covered antlers and the females and their frisky young. The herd seemed to move as one, grazing slowly, pawing the landscape with broad, flat hooves and stripping the tundra of every lichen, wildflower, tuft of moss, or shoot of cotton grass. Ahead, the vast plain glowed with color, but the route they'd traveled looked like a newly plowed field of brown.

Emery and the others stood mesmerized, awed, the only sound the clicking of shutters.

They stayed there more than an hour, watching and snapping photos, speaking in church-like whispers. Appropriate, Emery thought. This, too, was a sacred experience.

❖

Pasha glanced at her watch. The group should be returning any minute and she was anxious to see what the clients, particularly Emery, thought about the lunch she'd prepared. Dita paid meticulous attention to the menus for her trips, determined to ensure that each meal reflected her commitment to providing clients with a truly first-class wilderness experience. Pasha's previous experience in a kitchen had been a key factor in her beating out a couple of hundred other applicants.

For their first meal, she'd start them off with a mixed greens salad with sliced pear, goat cheese, walnuts, and balsamic vinaigrette. The main course included lobster-shrimp bisque and grilled baguette rounds brushed with herbed butter. Just before serving, she'd finish each bowl with brandy, fresh parsley, and a generous handful of sweet crabmeat. And for dessert, she'd prepared dark-chocolate brownies, laced with orange liqueur and crowned with fresh raspberries.

For dinner, she'd make one of her specialties, Alaska chicken Oscar: grilled chicken breast, topped with asparagus and king crab smothered in Béarnaise sauce. All the meal plans were similarly upscale, with room for some creative alterations if Chaz or the Fillmores got lucky and caught some fish.

Pasha had found it fairly easy to adapt most of her recipes and others they'd found on the Internet to the limitations of cooking outdoors, but a couple had required some fine-tuning, particularly the baked goods. Last fall, after the season ended, she'd cooked a lot of practice dinners for her and Dita on the field equipment, until both were well satisfied with the results. They could afford to feed the clients well. Three-day guided trips in the backcountry cost upwards of fifteen hundred dollars per person.

Cooking so close to the noisy river, she couldn't hear the clients approach and relied on the power and her frequent glances toward the trailhead to alert her. When the power started inching stronger, she knew they were getting close. The first person she spotted emerging from the woods was Chaz, with Emery and the others right behind. Judging by their smiles it had been a productive excursion.

Some of them went to their tents to drop off their packs, but Emery headed toward her.

"We saw the most amazing herd of caribou," Emery called as she neared. "Chaz took us to this great lookout point, where we…" She halted abruptly when she saw the spread of food Pasha had laid out on their folding table. "Whoa. I was expecting grilled-cheese sandwiches and tomato soup or something."

"Not on my watch," Pasha said, and grinned. "Though I do make a mean gouda-apple grilled cheese, and my homemade basil tomato bisque is to die for, you get the real gourmet treatment on these trips."

"You're making my mouth water." Emery glanced back toward the others, who were still busy in their tents or washing up for lunch. "Don't suppose I can nibble on something?"

"Go ahead and get some salad," she said. "No need to wait."

Emery shed her pack and dug in. She was happily munching away as the rest ambled over and started to serve themselves.

Once the clients had all settled into the folding chairs she'd set up around the cook site, Pasha walked around with a carafe, serving fresh-squeezed lemonade.

"This rocks," Alyson said. "I live on takeout pizza."

Other compliments followed, increasing dramatically once they got their soup.

Toni raved. "I can't believe you made this on a gas stove. Amazing job."

"Best I've ever had." Mandy echoed her, and her husband nodded in assent.

"Did you go to cooking school?" Emery asked.

Pasha shook her head. "I worked as a line cook for four years at a restaurant on Cape Cod and picked up stuff. I've had a lot of jobs. You can kind of say I'm one of those jack-of-all-trades, master-of-none types."

"What else have you done?" Ruth asked.

"Well, let's see. I worked for a florist for a while right out of college," Pasha said. "Then I helped out at a fish market. Went from there to the restaurant…did a stint with a landscaping company…a pet-sitting/dog walking service…and finally a salon, before I ended up here."

"Don't suppose you learned how to cut hair at that salon, did you?" Emery threaded her fingers through the long errant bangs that kept getting in her face. "These are bugging the hell out of me. "

Pasha had noticed Emery was long overdue for a trim, and she was certainly capable of doing a more than adequate job. It would be a good excuse to get some alone time together so she could assess what her gift would do when they touched again. She just had to ensure they had some degree of privacy so no one but Emery would know if she got dizzy again. "As it so happens, we've got a good sharp pair of scissors along. I can fix you up after dinner tonight if you like."

"Great." Emery smiled, her dark eyes narrowed in understanding. Another fine example of their secret communication without words.

"What do the rest of you do?" Chaz asked the other clients.

"We're the Geek Squad," Ruth said. "Toni, Alyson, and I are all computer programmers for a firm in Silicon Valley."

"So, is it a relief to be off-line for a few days or is it driving you crazy?" Pasha started passing out the brownies, glad she'd planned for extras when she saw Joe and Mandy Fillmore start with two each.

"It's making me a little nuts," Toni admitted with a frown. "Not to mention the fact that I preordered the new iPhone months ago, and it's going to arrive while I'm gone."

"How many computers does a computer programmer own?" Chaz asked.

"Seven," Ruth answered. "If you only count the ones I have at home."

Alyson chimed in. "Five."

"Okay, I guess that makes me the nerd queen." Toni chuckled. "I have twelve."

"Twelve?" Mandy Fillmore gaped at her.

"I have a weakness for every new high-tech gadget that hits the market," Toni explained. "I don't want to think about how many cell phones, laptops, e-book readers, computers, and iPods I've gone through in the last few years."

"I thought I'd be missing my big flat-screen and soaps more than I am," Mandy said. "This was Joe's idea and I wasn't happy about it at first, but I have to admit I'm having a blast."

"Me, too," Toni quickly added. "Ruth had to do a lot of convincing to get me to come along. I've never been camping, I hate bugs and snakes, and the thought of having to use the bathroom out here…" She glanced around and winced as the others laughed. "But I'm really glad she did. I had no idea I'd enjoy it this much."

"Glad to hear it," Chaz said. "I've got some other great hikes planned, but this afternoon is free time. You can nap, read, take a walk along the river—not too far, please, and don't strike off alone. We can do another hike after dinner if anyone's interested. The later the better, really, in terms of taking pictures. The diffuse light as the sun gets low really makes colors pop."

"I may take you up on that nap, if that's the case." Ruth rose and stretched. "Didn't seem like we walked that far, but I'm beat.

Maybe it's just all this fresh air or my incredibly full stomach, but I think I better catch a few Zs if we may go out again later."

"Well, Mandy and I are going to do some fishing. The licenses up here sure aren't cheap," Joe said as he wiped his chin with the back of his hand. "We've been into it for several years. One of the few things she'll do with me outdoors."

"I actually kind of like all the fuzzy little flies and fake beetles," Mandy said. "And Joe takes the fish off my hook for me."

"Want to walk up the river a ways?" Alyson asked Toni.

"Sure. If you promise to keep an eye out for a rock that resembles a luxury ladies' room."

The rest laughed or smiled as the group broke up and everyone went their separate ways.

Everyone but Emery. She stayed put in her folding chair. "How can I help clean up?"

"There you go again, getting all gallant on me," Pasha replied as she stacked dishes to wash. "You're the client. You're supposed to enjoy yourself and let me do all the work."

"Enjoy myself? Let's see…I'm here with a very intriguing woman, in one of the most beautifully pristine settings on earth. Check. Mission accomplished." She got to her feet but didn't come nearer. "It will in no way diminish that enjoyment if I help you with the dishes or whatever else needs doing."

Emery watched her intently, with such a sweet, playful expression that Pasha melted. How could she bear this kind of attention from Emery, even though she'd longed for it? During moments like this, when Emery seemed to also feel some kind of connection, her insides knotted and a low tremor of anticipation stretched every nerve ending in her body taut. The deliriously wonderful feeling frightened her at the same time. She didn't completely embrace such loss of control. Yet she also knew that when Emery left, she'd miss it very, very much. "Pretty smooth talker, aren't you?"

Emery grinned. "That mean you're convinced?"

"Didn't take much, and not because I mind cleaning up. But if you want to hang out and help, I certainly won't object too strenuously."

"Excellent. Assign me a task."

"Well." Pasha surveyed the cooking area and mentally ran through a list of things she needed to accomplish. "You get your choice. You can police the area and wash dishes, or you can help prep dinner."

"Better put me on the former. Can't mess up there too badly or poison anyone."

"Something tells me you overstate your inabilities. I bet you claim you can't cook so you can get others to cook for you," she teased her, "but you're secretly a whiz with a whisk."

"I plead the fifth on that one." Emery started to gather up the bowls and utensils.

"If there's any uneaten food in those dishes—"

"Nope." Emery seemed delighted to interrupt. "Everyone polished off every bite. Proof of how fabulous everything was."

Pasha's cheeks warmed from embarrassment. "I'm very happy you liked it." She grabbed a squeeze bottle of biodegradable soap from the supplies. "Use these," she said, tossing the bottle, a sponge, and a quick-dry towel to Emery. "As little soap as you need, please."

"Yes, ma'am." Emery walked to the water's edge and stooped to begin. She worked quickly and efficiently on the first load and returned for the pots and pans. Those took more time but came back sparkling clean as well. Then she cleaned up the area, bagging the trash and depositing it into a bear-proof container.

Pasha busily prepped dinner, her back to the river, but the ebb and flow of the simmering tension in her body told her precisely when Emery was near, or far.

"All done," Emery announced.

Pasha turned to find her relaxing in her camp chair, a few feet away. "How about some coffee? Or tea?"

"Coffee sounds great, if it's not too much trouble."

"Not at all. I brought a French press. I'll have some, too." She lit the camp stove and put water on to boil.

"Mind if I ask you some questions?" Emery asked.

"Not at all. How about we swap? One for you, one for me?" Pasha measured out coffee into the press.

"I'm good with that," Emery replied.

"Okay. Shoot."

"Where were you born?"

Pasha handed her a mug and sat in the next chair, a couple of feet away. "I'm from a village in Michigan I'm sure you've never heard of." The humming sensation in her veins intensified with their proximity. The royal blue of Emery's turtleneck seemed suddenly more vivid, and the bird sounds in the adjacent woods amplified. Even the taste of the coffee seemed enhanced.

"Michigan? No kidding. Where, exactly? Emery asked.

"Hey, I thought I got a turn."

"Call it a follow-up. You'll get two in a row," Emery said with a trace of impatience. "The name of the village?"

"Conway. It's in the—"

"I know where it is." Emery's aura glowed briefly, like a camera flash.

Pasha's mouth went dry. She took a sip of her coffee, her hand trembling slightly. Her body thrummed loudly. No one ever recognized the name. Conway was too tiny. The pounding of her heart accelerated. "How do you know it?"

"My family had a summer cottage on Crooked Lake." Emery's voice was full of awe. "I spent summers there when I was a kid." She looked intently at Pasha. "You were born in February, you said, and you're thirty-five—so you were born in…'76?"

Pasha nodded.

"The cottage was sold right around the time you were born. Almost the same month, I think," Emery told her. Her gaze drifted to her feet, and she clenched her coffee mug. She seemed half in shock. "What are the odds of that?"

Pasha let the question go unanswered. This was no far-fetched coincidence, only more proof they were destined to be together. "Where on the lake was it?"

"Closer to Odin than you were," Emery said, referencing another small village on the big lake. But we used to go to the convenience store in Conway a lot to get hot dogs and things."

"Why did your family sell the cottage?"

Emery's expression turned serious and she didn't answer right away. "My parents died in a car accident. I was ten, an only child. That place and our home were sold right after, and I went to live with my grandmother in Detroit."

"How awful. I'm so sorry, Emery." Pasha didn't visit her parents nearly often enough, but they kept in touch frequently by e-mail and tried to webcam at least every month or two. She couldn't imagine losing them now, let alone as a kid when she'd thought them invulnerable. "I'm an only child, too."

"I'm almost afraid to ask another question," Emery said, her tone half-kidding, half-serious. "Besides, you're due a couple."

The Conway connection still floored Pasha so much she took several seconds to answer. "Tell me about your work. Are you on a long sabbatical? Bryson told me you were a courier."

Emery sat back and sipped her coffee. "Yes, I was an international courier for many years. And *were* is the operative word. I doubt I'll ever go back. I delivered documents, diamonds, human organs, you name it. Even a couple of Academy Awards. A great job, for the most part. I got paid well and traveled in style to a ton of places I'd always wanted to visit. But sometimes it exhausted me, and I got to stay in exotic, fabulous places only long enough to get an enticing glimpse. That part became maddening."

"So, you'll be on the road sort of indefinitely, I understand?"

"That's the plan. I'm finally doing and seeing everything I ever dreamed of. As long as my savings and frequent-flier miles last, anyway."

"When did you start, and where have you been so far?"

"I left in late January, and I've been all over Europe. And aren't I due another question or two about now?"

Pasha laughed. "Okay. Go ahead."

"Favorite things to do?"

"Hmm, give me a second." Pasha got up to make more coffee. "Swim. Hike. Read a good book. Listen to music. Dance. Pretty typical things. You?"

"Anything with an adrenaline rush. Not that I've done a lot until this year. But in the last four months, I've been high-altitude

backcountry skiing, scuba diving, hot-air ballooning..." Emery
ticked off the endeavors on her fingers. "Still to come: skydiving,
caving, rock climbing, bungee jumping, hang gliding, cliff diving...
well, you get the idea. If it's an extreme sport, I'm there."

Pasha knew, of course, that Emery had been on adventure trips
even before she reached Alaska. Bryson had filled her in on a few
of the exciting times Emery had shared. But she had no idea Emery
had apparently decided to risk her life in every possible way, at
every opportunity. The idea unsettled her, especially in the context
of building a future together. She couldn't empathize with heedless,
brash disregard for one's safety. It was way outside her comfort
zone. "Have you always been so reckless?"

"I wouldn't call it reckless," Emery said. "Bold, maybe. Or
more daring than a lot of people. I don't want to take the path of
least resistance, you know? Life's too short. You have to chase your
dreams while you can. And I mean really *do* it, not just *say* it." She
stared out at the river. "How can you really know who you are, and
what you're made of, until you face your fears?"

"But you weren't always this way, were you?" Pasha asked.
"Didn't something change you?"

CHAPTER TWENTY

"No. I wasn't always this way." Emery tried not to squirm. How did Pasha so easily come up with such probing questions? "Sometimes you need a wake-up call to realize how quickly time is passing you by. It forces you to assess whether your life is taking the direction you want and motivates you to change things."

Pasha nodded thoughtfully. "A lot of clients say that being in this magnificent vastness, alone with their thoughts, has made them reconsider their lives."

"I can see how," Emery remarked. "You feel so small here, yet so much a part of the earth. Things you considered essential are stripped away yet you don't miss them. Well, I don't, anyway."

"I respect your privacy, Emery," Pasha said softly. "You clearly don't want to talk about some aspects of your past, so I won't push. But I'm a pretty good listener, and trustworthy."

Emery met her eyes. "I don't doubt that." The sentiment came from her heart, though she couldn't explain it. Pasha exuded an air of compassion and loyalty. She'd gained her trust very quickly, which was unusual. "It's difficult to talk about, and now probably isn't the time."

As they chatted, Joe and Mandy had worked their way along the riverbank with their fly rods and were getting near.

"Maybe I'll skip the walk after dinner and have you cut my bangs instead. I'll tell you my story then. But I have a condition."

"Which is?"

"You finally tell me about this weird stuff going on every time we get close. Will you do that?"

All the color drained from Pasha's face. She took so long to answer, Emery wasn't sure she would.

"Yup. Tonight. It's time." Pasha got to her feet. "Why don't you go enjoy yourself while I get some work done?"

Emery rose and faced her. She could discern so much more in Pasha's eyes than with any other woman she'd met. Right now she saw fear and apprehension, but also an underlying excitement. Pasha could read her extraordinarily well, too. "I'm not imagining this, am I?"

"No, Emery." The fear in Pasha's eyes eased, and the excitement grew. "It's very real."

Emery's heart sank when the Fillmores broke their moment.

"Pasha, got some more lemonade?" Joe asked as he propped their fly rods against the folding table and Mandy settled into a camp chair.

"You bet. Coming right up." Pasha's voice had regained its usual chipper quality and she was smiling, but her eyes betrayed how much she, too, regretted the interruption. "I'll see you later," she told Emery before heading to get the drinks.

"Later, then." Emery grabbed her pack and headed toward her tent, mulling over Pasha's words. She was relieved to discover she wasn't imagining something very odd between them. But Pasha's confirmation only confused her more. Emery could find no reasonable explanation for the phenomena, yet Pasha apparently had some reason or rationalization. She couldn't wait to hear it.

❖

Pasha spent a good deal of the afternoon contemplating how much she would tell Emery. Emery's acknowledgement of something extraordinary between them encouraged her, as did the fact she seemed curious, not distressed. She needed to try to explain her gift but wasn't certain she should be entirely frank yet, especially about their destiny.

Preoccupied with her thoughts and cooking chores, she discovered dinner over and the cleanup done. All the clients but Emery eagerly anticipated their evening hike because Chaz had promised to take them to a swampy area where moose frequently congregated.

"You're sure you don't want to go?" Pasha asked, as she and Emery watched the others return to their tents for cameras and jackets. "I feel guilty, you missing what might be a great photo opportunity."

"With all the trips I've signed up for, I'll get other chances to see moose up close. It hasn't been easy to find alone time with you."

"No, it hasn't. Still up for that haircut?"

"Absolutely."

"I'll go get the scissors, and a comb and towel. Be right back."

Pasha lingered in her tent until Chaz and the others had departed. The anticipation building all day made her shaky and anxious. Sometimes a few minutes alone to calm and center herself helped her focus her gift and better read its message. It also might help prevent her from totally losing control again and getting light-headed when she touched Emery.

Emery had a splendid setting to look at, but seemed to have focused on Pasha from the moment she left her tent. With every step nearer she took, the power surged, pulsing through her veins, enhancing her senses.

Emery lounged in a camp chair, her legs stretched out before her, posture relaxed, until Pasha got close. Then she sat up, hands gripping the arm rests, her expression expectant.

Pasha stood behind her. "Just a trim, or do you want it shorter?" Hopefully Emery didn't detect her nervousness. She wanted Emery's reaction, if she had any, to be completely spontaneous, so she didn't tell her what she was about to do. She draped her towel around Emery's neck and fastened it with a clothespin, then held her breath while she lightly placed her hands on Emery's shoulders.

The voltage between them forced the air out of her lungs in an audible sigh as her vision swam, and she fought to keep upright. Emery gasped and her aura glowed brightly, almost blinding Pasha.

The intense electrical charge abated almost immediately, however, ebbing to a dull roar in her ears and a sustained ache of bliss permeating her every fiber.

"Jesus." Emery twisted in her chair to look up at Pasha. "What the hell just happened?"

"What did you feel?" Pasha still had one hand on Emery's shoulder. She didn't want to break the physical contact; it had grounded the current, or that's what it felt like, and she wasn't sure she could remain composed if another big shock occurred.

"When you touched me…I felt a huge hit of static electricity or something. The same thing happened when you brushed by me outside my room at the Den. But that's impossible out here. Conditions aren't right at all. And now…" Emery's gaze focused inward, as though she was assessing the after-effects. "I feel kind of like I'm high. Almost giddy-happy. My senses seem especially sharp."

"Have you ever felt anything like this before?"

"No. Never. You?"

"I think I understand what's happening better than you do."

"Well, fill me in, please, would you?"

Pasha reluctantly removed her hand from Emery's shoulder and pulled a chair over so they could sit facing each other. A profound loss settled in the pit of her stomach from the separation. "Do you believe some people have a sixth sense that enables them to see things others can't?"

"You mean like psychic abilities?"

"Yup."

"Well, I try to keep an open mind, not that I have any first-hand experience. But I've read accounts of premonitions and such, and I've seen a few episodes of *Medium*." Emery's eyes narrowed. "Are you…like that?"

"Sort of. I mean, I don't see dead people, and I don't consider myself psychic because I can't predict someone's future or read something by handling an article of clothing…those sorts of things." She licked her lips. "But all my life, I've had this crazy kind of intuition that kicks in now and then. A gut feeling, if you will, about people or events. Both good and bad. I can't control it, and I can't predict when it'll surface. It's completely involuntary but pretty infallibly reliable."

"What sort of things does this intuition tell you?"

"Well, it's guided me away from danger and directed me toward all the jobs I've had. This one, too. And it tells me when a stranger I meet will be important in my life. It's pointed me to all the people who've become my closest friends." Pasha didn't want to reveal that her gift was telling her Emery was *the one*. Not yet. Emery already had a lot to absorb. She needed to reach that conclusion on her own.

"So…this electric shock, when you touch me, is part of all this? You go through this every time you meet someone you're going to be good friends with?" Emery asked.

"I don't get the same reaction with everyone. Most of the time, I just get this weird feeling, and I see an aura around them briefly when we meet."

"An aura?"

"A shimmering ribbon of light that conforms to their silhouette."

"Fascinating. Did you see one around me?"

"Yup."

A look of realization came into Emery's eyes. "Did your blackout have something to do with this?"

"I'm certain it did. Probably kind of an overload when we shook hands. I've been a bit leery, as I think you know, about touching you again. Especially in front of others. I've never fainted before."

"Couldn't something else, like a medical condition, have caused it?"

"I'm very healthy. I had my annual physical a month ago. Dita requires it. My gift sometimes does a number on my body. During my period of waiting and anticipating, I'll feel really hot, or like all my nerve endings are stretched tight. Or my stomach knots." Her mind raced to come up with a clear explanation. "Like a boxer must feel right before the big bout, or a ballerina about to go onstage. A bundle of nerves and restless energy. Somehow, touching you releases that energy as a very real spark."

"So if you touch me right now, it'll happen again?" Emery asked.

"I honestly don't know. My intuition's been acting screwy recently. I'm not sure what'll happen."

Emery held out her hands, palms up. "Try it and let's see."

Pasha was excited. Emery accepted everything she'd told her and wanted to discover more. They were so close Pasha didn't even have to move her chair to reach her. She held her hands out flat, palms down, but before she touched Emery, she said, "Indulge me, will you? Close your eyes. Tell me what you feel."

"All right."

This time when they touched, another spark leapt between them, but much less intense. Pasha also felt another surge in the euphoric bliss and pulled her hands away.

"Static electricity again, but not nearly as strong," Emery reported.

"Okay. Now look at me and let's try it again."

Emery gazed so intently into her eyes that Pasha felt the power increase even before they touched, and when they did, the bliss crested again and swept her up in another emotional tsunami. She could almost weep from the joy infusing her. However, she could barely discern the static-electric spark that had caught Emery's attention.

She felt almost disappointed until she recognized the pattern and understood why. Their first real touch in the Den, when they shook hands, had affected them the strongest; after all her days of anticipation, the release of the pent-up energy had overwhelmed her and she'd blacked out. Since then, the voltage of their encounters had varied and seemed related to how long they'd been apart.

At least she knew she could touch Emery without passing out. She just had to be careful if a long time elapsed between occasions. She almost laughed out loud. The more she touched Emery, the less chance she would faint. *Cool.*

At some point while Pasha had been absorbed in her thoughts, their hands had relaxed and entwined. She wasn't certain which, if either, of them had initiated it.

"Hardly felt any electricity that time." Emery's eyes locked with hers. "But…that sense of feeling almost giddy-happy has come back. Difficult to describe, but it's…it's very nice. And very strong right now."

"I think I know exactly what you're feeling."

"It's…well, it's very *different,* isn't it?" Emery smiled.

Pasha had to laugh. This was going better than she could have hoped. "Yup. It is that."

"I'll need a while to understand."

"I think we've got a good bit. You're scheduled for the big rafting trip right after this one, as I recall."

"Yes. You, too?"

Pasha nodded. "And Chaz again as well. All women, and ten days in the wilderness."

"Excellent."

Pasha reluctantly removed her hands from Emery's. "We'd better get going on your haircut, if you still want one before the others get back."

"I do."

"I can do a better job if we wet your head." She got to her feet and hefted the pot she heated coffee water in. Quite a bit was left, and when she poured some over her hand she found it still warm. "This'll do." She set it behind Emery's chair and almost automatically reached for Emery's turtleneck collar to fold it down and tuck it into the towel. She wanted to gain access to the nape of her neck and keep the cut hairs from getting all over her clothes.

But as soon as Emery felt her hands there, she brought her own up abruptly. "Stop. I don't like my neck exposed."

"All right." The sudden chill in Emery's tone and especially the faint flickering of her aura surprised Pasha. "I'm sorry, I didn't mean—"

"No, Pasha. I'm the one who should apologize. I didn't mean to snap at you. It's just…just a personal thing." Emery pulled her hair away from her neck and fastened the towel over her turtleneck, then leaned back to let Pasha wet her hair.

Pasha poured the water slowly, careful to keep Emery's clothes dry, and ran her hands through the dark strands to make sure it all got wet. Another small spark of electricity arched from her fingertips at the first touch, and the now-familiar euphoria blossomed and coursed through her. "Okay, that's good." She pressed the ends of Emery's hair in the towel to keep it from dripping. "You can sit up now."

"I really am sorry."

"We all have things we find difficult to talk about." Pasha ran her large-toothed comb through Emery's hair. "I always worry about how people will react when I tell them about my sixth sense. Some think psychic abilities belong in the same category as unicorns and leprechauns. Or that those who claim to have them are delusional."

"I have no problem believing mysterious things are at work in the universe. Miracles happen every day."

"Yup. They certainly do." Pasha picked up her scissors. "Okay. Here we go. Want just a light trim or do you trust me to do what's best for your hair?"

Emery turned and looked into her eyes. "I trust you."

She started cutting, taking more care and time than needed just to make sure she did a job Emery would be happy with. Pasha had worked at the salon as an assistant, washing hair, sweeping up, and doing blow-dries. But several of the stylists had showed her how to cut hair, and she'd since been servicing a lot of her friends. Dita wanted her short-cropped cut trimmed every couple of weeks. "So, Emery, you know my story. The most important parts, anyway." Snip. Snip. "Are you ready to tell me what precipitated such a big change in your lifestyle?"

CHAPTER TWENTY-ONE

Y ou know, I wondered why you seemed to sense more about me than anyone I've ever met," Emery said. "Your questions take me to places I try to avoid."

"I don't mean to make you uncomfortable, Emery, or have you volunteer anything you're not ready to," Pasha replied gently. "Though it often helps to talk about painful things."

Emery rarely allowed herself to think about that day in Sofia, and other events that still gave her nightmares. Doing so left her depressed and anxious. With Pasha, however, she could revisit the past. Since her recuperation, Emery had rarely wanted to get close to anyone beyond the occasional sexual liaison. But her inexplicable connection with Pasha reached beyond a mere craving for physical intimacy. She felt compelled to see where it might lead, and that could only happen if she helped Pasha understand what had made her the person she'd become. "I told you my parents were killed by a drunk driver when I was ten. I didn't tell you I was in the car, too."

"Oh, Emery." Pasha stopped and put a hand on Emery's shoulder.

The simple gesture strengthened and calmed her, as though she'd received a fast-acting drug. "We hit a big delivery truck broadside when he ran a red light. My dad couldn't see him because of a building on that corner." Emery's hands curled into fists. "The impact crushed the front of our car and killed them instantly. I was in the backseat. Both my legs were broken in several places, along with my hip and my left arm. The first police on the scene told reporters they couldn't believe anyone lived through it, but I never lost consciousness. I remember it all."

Pasha exhaled loudly. "Jesus."

"Ten years later, in college, a group of us went to a football game one afternoon," Emery said. "The wind came up during the fourth quarter and the sky grew dark, but it didn't rain, just misted." She forced herself to picture the players on the field and not the faces of her friends. "We stood on the sidelines watching the last minutes because we wanted to reach the parking lot before the big rush. Out of nowhere, a massive bolt of lightning struck the edge of the field near us." Her voice shook, so she took a few deep breaths. "Initially everything inside me seemed to boil, building pressure, like my insides were melting. I couldn't see or hear anything, or move, or talk. But, almost hyperaware, I knew what was happening with my body. My heart pounded, then stopped. Paramedics managed to start it again and I ended up in the hospital for a couple of weeks, but fully recovered. I didn't learn until several days after the accident that two friends standing next to me had died instantly."

Pasha's arms wrapped around Emery's neck from behind in a comforting embrace. Another wave of calm infused her, allowing her to push past her grief.

"About two years ago, I got on an elevator in a hotel in Sofia, Bulgaria. I'd just made a delivery to a client when that big earthquake hit. Remember? I was alone. Trapped. The cable snapped, and the elevator fell eight stories."

Pasha gasped. "Dear God."

"The impact shattered my legs and pelvis, and broke a couple of bones in my back, a few ribs, my jaw. I almost drowned in my own blood."

Pasha caressed her back.

"The doctors couldn't believe I survived. After two weeks in a coma, I woke to the news that I'd probably never walk again. It took a lot of metal pins and more than a year of healing, surgeries, and physical therapy to prove them wrong." Reliving her trio of near-death experiences taxed her more than she anticipated and suddenly left her emotionally drained and physically exhausted.

"I don't know what to say, Emery. I wish I could take away some of what you've suffered. You're a hell of a strong woman to have survived and come out whole."

Whole? She didn't feel whole. Not yet. She'd hoped by now to face the end of each day without needing a painkiller to help her sleep. To run like she used to. And her emotional deficiency was worse. No matter how amazing her latest adrenaline-rush escapade—whether from an extreme sport or passion-filled woman—she remained hollow inside. "In a situation like that, you either have to give up or believe the unbelievable. Maybe that's why I don't find it hard to accept your unusual abilities. None of us really knows our hidden strengths or talents until something happens to test us."

"I don't understand something." Pasha resumed cutting Emery's hair. "After enduring all that, how can you so cavalierly put yourself in danger?"

"Don't you get it? In all my accidents I merely followed my everyday, same-old-thing routine. I didn't do anything risky, but I nearly died anyway. *Three times*, Pasha. How long before my luck runs out? How often can anyone cheat death? I'd rather die living life to the absolute fullest—and look back with absolutely no regrets—than have another freak mishap cut me down before I pursue my dreams."

"You sound like you're expecting another accident any minute." Pasha came around in front of Emery and started to trim her bangs. "Surely you don't think you're doomed to die young, do you?"

"I'm just more aware than most that we have only limited time. One shot, and it flies by or is taken from you before you know it. I spent months in that hospital bed examining my life. I worked like a fiend to guarantee a nice retirement, wasting my healthy years. Do you know what dying people regret the most? The majority wish they'd had the courage to live a life true to themselves, not the one others expected of them."

"Is that what you did? Lived up to someone else's expectations?"

"To a certain extent. My fear of giving up a good job and comfortable home for the unknown held me back, but I also made a lot of decisions to keep my girlfriend happy."

"Is she still your girlfriend?"

"No. Not any more." Emery didn't want to elaborate and hoped Pasha wouldn't ask. She still carried a lot of guilt about Lisa and didn't want to have to deal with it along with the other difficult memories this conversation had stirred up.

"I absolutely believe you have to live a life true to yourself." Pasha stooped to assess her results so far, then stood to Emery's left to resume cutting. "But don't you think you can share your life with someone?"

"I'm just not wired to fall in love. And a one-sided relationship always hurts the other person."

Pasha put a calming hand on her shoulder again and somewhat eased the resurfacing tug of guilt. "You shouldn't kick yourself because things didn't work out, not if you told her the truth."

"What about you? Ever serious about anyone?"

"No." Snip. Snip. Snip. "I had a few relationships that lasted some months, or a couple of years at most. But never really serious. More great friends with side benefits."

"That sounds pretty good to me, but I've never been able to achieve it. The few women I've dated any real length of time, and the one I lived with, became more emotionally attached than they meant to, I guess."

"No one can control who they fall in love with, Emery."

"So they say. I wouldn't know."

Pasha ruffled her hair and surveyed her handiwork. "Done. Hope you like it." She rummaged through the cookware and produced a stainless-steel fry pan with a mirror-like interior. "Probably not the best, but..." She held it in front of Emery.

From what she could tell, the haircut looked like one of her better ones lately. How wonderful to have her bangs out of her eyes. "Thanks, Pasha. Looks great."

"Want some decaf, or some tea?" A jangling sound startled them. "That's the satellite phone." Pasha dug through her daypack and pulled out the device. "It's Pasha." She cupped her hand over her other ear to hear better and stepped away from the noisy river. "Dita? I can barely hear you." She listened for several seconds.

"Repeat that?" More listening. She frowned. "Okay. Got it. I'll pass the word. We'll be ready." She stuck the phone back into her bag. "That storm forecast for the day after tomorrow looks like a real bitch, so our three-day has become a two-day. We leave tomorrow night."

"Well, I'm not surprised. Dita warns everyone that weather can shorten or lengthen any trip. Not that big a deal to me since I've got a lot more to look forward to, but I bet the others will be disappointed."

"Hey!" Chaz shouted to them from upriver, the smiling clients trailing her.

"Welcome back!" Pasha yelled, and Emery waved.

Judging from the photos everyone eagerly shared around the campfire a bit later, Emery had missed seeing an impressive bull moose and female with her leggy calf, as well as a bald eagle, peregrine falcon, and other birdlife. But she didn't regret her choice.

She'd learned a great deal about Pasha in a very short time, things that only increased her interest. And sharing the most painful details of her life had indeed helped, as Pasha said it might. Emery felt lighter, somehow, her burden lifted. And when she crawled into her sleeping bag, she didn't take her usual pain pill. Despite the plane flight and long walk that morning, she felt better than she had in a long time.

CHAPTER TWENTY-TWO

Next day, June 6

Pasha gazed over the river valley, watching a solitary eagle catch the thermals looking for breakfast. She hadn't slept well, engrossed in replaying her conversation with Emery, and the restlessness finally pushed her from her cot at four a.m.

Emery's readiness to accept her sixth sense had encouraged her, as had her willingness to explore and understand their connection. She had displayed a lot of trust by candidly sharing the details of her hellish accidents.

Obviously Emery had considered her daredevil lifestyle carefully and seemed determined not to allow anything to interfere with her plans.

Words kept ringing in Pasha's head, how the dying say they "wish they'd had the courage to live a life true to themselves, not the one others expected of them." Was she right to try to change Emery's mind?

Restricting their relationship to friendship would probably help both of them, she decided. Emery already felt guilty about the girlfriend she'd hurt, and Pasha didn't want to give her reason for any more regrets. And if they became intimate, Pasha would have an even more difficult time telling Emery good-bye when she moved on.

She hadn't reached that decision easily, even during rational solitude. Could she uphold it when she saw Emery and the power insisted she follow her heart, not her head? All her life, she'd blindly followed whatever course the power directed, and she hesitated to defy it now when it so powerfully guided her to embrace all possibilities with Emery.

A subtle shift in the current of their connection alerted her. Emery was awake and getting ready to join her. Pasha had a fresh cup of coffee ready by the time Emery emerged from her tent.

"Good morning." Pasha held out the mug.

"Morning." When Emery reached for the coffee, their fingertips overlapped and the resulting shock made them jump. A little of the coffee spilled.

They laughed.

"Well, that sure woke me up." Emery hefted the mug. "Thanks for the coffee."

"I remembered it's your can't-do-without drink. Figured you're like me—have to have that first cup right away to feel human."

"Exactly right." Emery took a long sip and sighed. "And I gotta say, for being out here so far in the boonies, you make a damn good brew." She glanced around the campsite. "No one else up and around yet?"

"Nope. Only us." She glanced at her watch. "It's just six. Chaz set her watch alarm for seven."

Emery looked curiously at Pasha. "How'd you manage to have a cup ready and waiting for me, then?"

"I…I felt you get up and knew you'd be out soon."

Emery shook her head. "I won't pretend to understand what's happening, and sometimes I feel unnerved that a near-total stranger can *feel* where I am and what I'm doing." She smiled. "But it's rather wonderful as well."

"I'm happy you feel that way. Not like I have much control over it, that's for sure." Pasha picked up her own cup and topped it off with what remained in the French press. "Sit?"

"Sure."

They sat in adjacent camp chairs placed beside the riverbank, sipping their coffee and admiring the landscape. The sky, clear and cloudless, didn't hint about the approaching storm.

"Sleep well? Emery asked.

"I kept replaying last night in my mind."

"Me, too. I just wanted to say thanks. Talking about it did help."

"I'm glad. It had to be very painful to dig all that up again. But I'm honored you shared it with me."

"What's on tap for today?"

"Chaz and I decided last night to pack in as much as possible to try to make up for leaving early. She knows a route that'll take most of the day to cover, but you'll have a good chance to see a lot. I've already packed some bag lunches."

"And you? Will you be coming?"

Pasha shook her head. "I get to pack all the gear while you're gone and prep a fabulous final dinner."

"Damn. I forgot." Emery frowned. "I promised Geneva I'd let her fix me dinner when we get back. I almost said, since you and I'll be back unexpectedly, maybe we could do something together tomorrow."

"I'm sure Dita will keep me busy. It's okay." Pasha fought to calm the sick feeling in her stomach at the thought of Emery and Geneva together. Perhaps Emery should fulfill her sexual needs elsewhere, but frustration and loss overwhelmed her.

"At least we have another trip in a few days to look forward to."

"Yup. And more beyond that."

They turned at the sound of boots on gravel approaching from behind. Joe and Mandy apparently rose early, too. Joe hailed them. "Morning, ladies."

"Any more of that coffee?" Mandy asked when she got close enough to spot their mugs.

"Ready in just a minute." Pasha rose from her chair and looked at Emery. "I'll miss getting this kind of precious time with you until we go rafting," she said in a low voice the Fillmores wouldn't hear.

"No more than I will." The intensity in Emery's eyes ignited the embers of bliss into a bonfire of longing, so painfully sweet Pasha's breath caught in her throat.

No way on earth could she deny any possible opportunity to be close to Emery.

❖

Bettles
Next day, June 7

"The clients all raved about the trip," Dita commented as they sorted through the unused supplies, tents, cookware, and other gear, organizing everything into piles on the long tables in the office lounge. "Didn't seem to mind too much having to come back early."

"Chaz had the magic touch for finding wildlife, and giving them some of their money back helped, I'm sure." Pasha glanced out the window. Sheets of driving rain obliterated the view, the sky as dark as dusk. The drumming on the roof and jarring cracks of thunder had commenced at five a.m., driving them out of bed. "You definitely made the right call." Pasha wondered whether Emery was entirely comfortable with thunderstorms, though it had been many years since lightning had struck her. If not, certainly she could endure the storm more easily from the safety of the Den than her tent.

"They loved your cooking, especially the bisque." Dita paused. "Hey, did Toni tell you she and Ruth are staying?"

"No. Staying? What do you mean?"

"She came by last night after you went upstairs. Asked if we had any openings on your rafting trip, and that Baltimore couple canceled the day before. Apparently they had too much fun to leave and arranged to take some additional vacation time. Alyson has to head back."

"That's great. I really like them."

"Actually works out well that you got back a day early. Things have been crazy here, and I need to catch up on some of my vendor orders. You mind manning the desk today?"

"No, I expected I could be useful." Pasha didn't want to spend her day watching Emery and Geneva together. Working would make the time pass quicker.

❖

Emery stared out the window at the charcoal sky, flinching when a brilliant flash of lightning and instant-later boom of thunder broke her reverie. She drew the curtains with a trembling hand and switched on the bed lamp. Storms usually didn't bother her any more, but she felt unusually vulnerable after unearthing her long-buried memories of the day her friends died.

A good day to sit inside and read, update her journal, and rest. The nagging, residual ache in her legs, pelvis, and back had resurfaced with a vengeance during the night, and her pain meds had just started kicking in when the storm began to batter her windows. She'd slept at most only a couple of hours, because she'd been up late thinking about Pasha.

She still didn't understand why she'd found it so easy, and so comforting, to tell Pasha about her past. Or why she knew Pasha would keep everything she'd told her in strict confidence. Somehow Pasha had snuck through all her carefully constructed barriers designed to prevent people from seeing her pain or getting too close.

Pasha's extraordinary intuition no doubt made her unusually sensitive to the moods and inner turmoil of those she met and spent time with. But their mysterious and wonderful connection entailed much more than that. Did Pasha experience such intensity with everyone who triggered her sixth sense...all those she'd seen with an aura who had become her close friends? She found that hard to believe.

Or maybe, Emery mused, she just didn't *want* to believe this bond was less unique for Pasha than for her.

She still didn't understand a lot, but she certainly couldn't date both Pasha and Geneva. She didn't want to risk hurting Geneva, and her expression when Emery got back told her everything Bryson had warned her about was true. Geneva was obviously already falling for her. She had learned to run from that look.

Besides, the disparity in her attraction to Geneva and Pasha had grown too vast during the past few days to ignore. Sweet, beautiful Geneva's attributes had become less compelling, while Emery's fascination with Pasha had blossomed into a near obsession. When, precisely, had she memorized every nuance of her delicate features? She could easily recall a perfect, three-dimensional clone. In fact, she found it difficult to think very long about anything else.

She needed to talk with Geneva, *now.* They hadn't exchanged more than brief hellos when she'd returned last night, because Geneva was working in the packed Den and wasn't downstairs when Emery went to breakfast. But it was after ten now, so she should be awake.

Emery went down the hall to Geneva's room and knocked softly. "Geneva? It's Emery."

Geneva opened the door halfway. Her hair wet and wearing only her robe, she'd obviously just emerged from the shower. "Hi, Emery! What a nice surprise. Come in."

"I'll let you get dressed. Want to meet me downstairs? I'd like to talk to you."

"Sure. See you in a few."

She detoured through the sparse lunch crowd and many open tables to the bar.

"Back again." Grizz smiled, displaying shiny, pointed canines. "What can I get ya, Emery?"

"I want to try a new local brew. On tap." She studied the row of logoed spigot handles above each keg. "What do you recommend?"

"Light or dark?"

"Dark. And I've already had Pipeline."

"Hmmm." He scratched his beard. "Either Prince William's Porter or Oil Rig Oatmeal Stout."

"Let's go with the Porter." The first sip of the rich-bodied microbrew told her she'd made an excellent choice. "Wonderful. Thanks. I'm meeting Geneva. Add this to my tab?"

"You bet."

She chose a table away from any windows because the storm still raged outside. Her beer was still half full when Geneva joined her.

"So, how was the trip?" Geneva asked. "Shame it got cut short."

"Awesome. Great views in every direction, and we saw all kinds of wildlife. Caribou the first day, and yesterday Chaz took us to see Dall sheep. Lots of birds, too, and a couple of moose."

"Get some good pictures?"

Emery laughed. "I kind of went overboard. Took something like four or five hundred and got a ton of really good ones. Thank God for digital cameras with huge memory cards. I'd be broke if I still shot film."

"Wish I could have gone with you." Geneva reached across the table and put her hand on Emery's. "Want to take a walk after dinner?"

"Geneva, look…" Emery gently extricated her hand, and Geneva visibly stiffened. "You're wonderful, and I can't tell you how flattered and honored I am that you're interested in me—"

"*But*…I think I know what you're about to say." Frowning, she looked at Emery curiously. "Did I do something? Say something?"

Emery shook her head. "Please don't think it's anything you did. I just think it's best we remain friends. I like you. A lot. I really do. In another time and place, it well might have happened, even though I'm not convinced you're the type of woman who can deal well with a brief affair." She folded her hands on the table and looked squarely at Geneva. "I can't start something with you because Pasha and I had a lot of time to talk and get to know each other on the trip. I've become quite interested in her, Geneva, and want to focus my attention on her. I'm sorry. I know you two are friends, and I hope this doesn't create an awkward situation."

Geneva sat back and chewed thoughtfully on her lower lip, her eyes sad. "I can't say I'm not disappointed, Emery, or I'd be lying. But you don't need to worry about this hurting my friendship with Pasha or making things awkward. We're solid. You both have tried to consider my feelings, and I appreciate that."

"Thank you for being so understanding."

"I hope we can stay friends and maybe hang out together if Pasha's busy and you're between trips. I'm totally respectful, believe me. I won't hit on you. I think too much of both of you."

"Then I'd like that very much, too." Emery admired Geneva's grace. She'd reacted very much the same way when Emery had informed her she wanted to date both of them. And, apparently, when Bryson had ended things between them. No drama, no pouting. Just genuine good wishes for the ones who got away. "You know, Geneva, whoever does end up with you is one lucky woman."

Geneva blushed, and some of the sadness in her eyes eased. "Thank you. I'll miss your charm, among other things."

"Can I buy you lunch?" Emery asked.

"The least you can do. I'm suddenly in the mood for lobster."

CHAPTER TWENTY-THREE

Next day, June 8

Emery popped a Percocet before she headed downstairs to dinner. Thanks to the rain, she'd done virtually nothing in the last two days but sleep, read, and watch TV, but her joints and back still hadn't recovered from her hikes with Chaz and the others. Sleeping on a cot in a confining sleeping bag hadn't helped, either. Her next excursion, ten days of whitewater rafting, began day after tomorrow. Hopefully, additional rest would get her in good shape for the challenge. At least sitting in a raft should be easier on her legs than hiking.

Yesterday's pounding rain had given way to a cold, stiff wind and consistent heavy mist, so thick it soaked her hair in a few minutes. The forecast for the trip was clear and sunny, at least to start, but with unusually cool temperatures—high fifties during the day and below freezing overnight. At least that should help minimize bugs.

The miserable weather had also kept her from spending time with Pasha. She'd called the office yesterday hoping for a date after dinner, but Pasha had said rescheduling the grounded charter flights and deliveries would necessitate working through dinner and well into the evening. A follow-up call this morning had brought only slightly better news. Pasha couldn't take a break but hoped to make dinner with the group.

Emery missed her, more than she'd ever missed anyone she'd so recently met. Oh, a few women had lingered in her memory for a while, but she hadn't felt this driving desire to see them again. Certainly not with a woman she hadn't even slept with yet.

Her mind involuntarily conjured up an image of Pasha beneath her in the throes of passion, green eyes boring into hers. A shudder of arousal settled low in her abdomen. *Please be there.*

Most of the other members of ADLIB hadn't made it to dinner the night before, either, Karla stranded in a remote village and Chaz at home tending to Megan, who'd contracted a cold. So just Bryson, Geneva, and she had eaten together, and the party broke up early. She hoped more could make it tonight, especially if Pasha couldn't get away. She could use the distraction.

A little before six, she headed downstairs and found the place packed. She spotted Geneva first, filling her drink tray at the bar, then Bryson, alone in the corner booth. Emery tried to suppress her disappointment as she headed over to join her. "Hey, Bryson. Megan's still sick, I take it?"

"Getting better, but they decided to stay in again and eat some soup."

"And Karla?"

"Reached her by phone." Bryson drummed her fingers impatiently on the tabletop. "She's staying with the family of the little girl she treated, so she's fine. Weather forecast calls for fog and wind tomorrow, but I may get a window in the afternoon to go pick her up."

"You get stir-crazy when you're grounded very long, don't you?"

Bryson laughed. "Occupational hazard, I guess. No secret I live to be up there, and pretty much the case with every other bush pilot I know. Lot worse, though, when Karla's not here to keep me otherwise engaged."

Geneva headed their way, looking more harried than Emery had ever seen her. "I swear to God, if another person asks for some special order—cottage cheese instead of salad or no meat in their chili—they're going to be wearing their food home."

"That bad, huh?" Bryson asked.

"Going to be a long summer. Drinks?" Geneva pulled out her pad.

"Usual," Bryson answered.

"Coffee, please," Emery said.

"No new microbrew? I had one all picked out for you."

"Not tonight, thanks." The Percocet wasn't handling her pain very well, so Emery would probably have to take another before long. Though she didn't always adhere to the doctor's warning not to mix her pain meds with alcohol, she probably should tonight since she wanted to be in the best possible shape for her next trip.

"Be right back with those. Know what you want for dinner yet?"

"Just six now," Bryson said, after consulting her watch. She looked at Emery. "Mind waiting a while, in case Dita and Pasha can get away?"

"Sure. Fine by me."

Geneva brought their drinks and returned to bustling between tables. Emery noticed Ruth and Toni at the bar and waved, inviting them over, but they pointed to their full plates of food and declined with broad smiles.

"I bet you'll be busy the next few days making up for all the cancelled flights," Emery remarked.

"Yeah. Good thing it's light now twenty-four seven. Gives me a lot of latitude when to fly, but makes for some very long days." Bryson sipped from her bottle of Black Fang. "I was supposed to shuttle you guys up for the whitewater trip, but Skeeter's going to have to take you instead. Had to reschedule a resupply run up to some miners, and I'm the only one who knows that area real well. Tough place to land."

"Shame you won't be going. I hope you're all caught up by the time we get back, at least, so I can book another private charter in the Cub. That's truly *the* way to see Alaska."

"I'd love that. Don't often get a client who's happy to fly the way I like to." She reached for her beer again, but paused with it halfway to her lips and grinned. "Hey, look what the cat dragged in."

Emery followed her gaze and saw Pasha and Dita hanging their wet coats over the antlers at the roadhouse entrance. Her spirits lifted. When Pasha turned, their eyes met, and they both grinned like fools. This time, Pasha slid into the booth next to her, though she stopped short of touching her.

"Glad you made it," Emery said.

"Hi, Emery."

"Had to, didn't get a break all day and we're both starving." Dita slipped into the seat next to Bryson. "But can't stay long. Still rearranging the schedules."

"That's a pity," Emery said.

Geneva paused by their table, her tray full of drinks. "Hey, Pash. Dita. Drinks?"

They both ordered coffee and told her they had to eat and run, so she delayed her deliveries long enough to take their meal orders.

"Looking forward to the rafting trip?" Dita asked Emery.

"Are you kidding? Wish we could leave right now." She glanced at Pasha, who had a shy smile.

"Toni and Ruth feel the same. They stopped in today to get a map and more info on where we're going." Pasha nodded toward the bar where they sat, and they all turned to look.

Even Emery didn't suspect Pasha had deliberately diverted Bryson and Dita's attention so she could reach beneath the table to touch Emery's thigh. The resulting shock, after forty-eight hours of separation, briefly made her hair stand on end. Fortunately, she gasped in surprise so softly, probably only Pasha heard her. However, Pasha didn't giggle as subtly.

"What's so funny?" Bryson asked.

"Oh, nothing," Pasha replied. Her hand remained on Emery's thigh, and once again, Emery marveled at the strong sensation of calm and contentment that flowed into her. That giddy-happy feeling whenever they got together was becoming addictive.

Unfortunately, their food came right away, and they had only an hour together before Dita announced they should get back to the office.

"Any chance you'll get some free time tomorrow?" Emery asked Pasha in a low voice as Dita and Bryson planned an early-morning briefing on the rescheduled flights.

"Unlikely, I think." Pasha frowned. "Much as I'd like to, there's—" Her eyes widened.

"What is it? What's wrong?" Emery's worried tone alerted Dita and Bryson that something had happened, because their conversation halted and both turned to look at Pasha as well.

Pasha's face went white and she grappled for the edge of the table a millisecond before they all felt it.

The ground began to shake.

A half-dozen glasses perched too near the edges of tables crashed to the floor, and assorted cries of surprise and alarm echoed through the roadhouse. The lights blinked off, then back on.

A seed of panic took root in Emery's chest but had no time to bloom before the movement ended.

A burly guy at the next table spoke first. "What the hell?" Obviously a tourist, from his way-too-shiny boots and the BlackBerry on his hip. "Was that an earthquake?"

Bryson answered the man. "Yep. Pretty good one, too. But don't worry. They're pretty common here. We get more, and stronger ones, than any other state. A seven or better almost every year. But most of the time they're so small you never notice 'em."

Emery felt Pasha's hand on her thigh again.

"You okay?" Pasha asked.

Emery nodded. Everything had happened so fast she hadn't finished processing it. For an instant, she'd been back in that elevator, bile rising in her throat, but Pasha's comforting touch helped restore her sense of well-being.

Grizz's baritone rang through the room. "Settle down, folks. No harm done. Just watch the glass on the floor until we can sweep it up."

"I could do without any more of that," Emery said.

"Don't blame you." Bryson turned to Pasha. "Everything...all right?" she asked vaguely.

"I told Emery about my premonitions, Bryson, so you don't have to be so cagey. And I think it's over."

"How did you know about it?" Emery asked. "What did you feel?"

"I got this…this weird sensation of falling, and terror, and being enveloped in darkness."

Exactly what Emery had felt in Sofia. From the look in Pasha's eyes—a combination of confusion and recognition—she, too, had made the connection, but couldn't explain it.

"Scary moment for sure," Dita said. "And not to downplay it, but we really should get back, Pash."

"Right behind you." Before she slipped out of the booth, however, Pasha leaned over and whispered, "I'll try to call you later."

"I'd like that," Emery whispered back.

Bryson didn't linger much longer because she wanted to try to reach Karla and check on her, so Emery got back to her room by eight. Still unsettled, she turned on the TV and immersed herself in a repeat of *Doctor Zhivago*. By the end, she'd moved Russia up on her itinerary.

The late news came on, the quake topping the headlines. "A large portion of the state felt an earthquake measuring six-point-one on the Richter scale shortly after seven p.m. Pacific time, from Anchorage north to Coldfoot, and as far west as McGrath," the dour-faced, blue-suited newscaster reported. "Scientists at the U.S. Geological Survey located the quake's epicenter on the Denali Fault, between Anchorage and Fairbanks. That's the same region where the 2002 quake that measured seven-point-nine originated. Hospitals have admitted several people but there are no known fatalities from this latest tremor. Authorities report widespread power outages and numerous instances of damage to structures." The screen changed and a cute young blond reporter replaced the dour anchor. "Serena Matthews is in Fairbanks, outside a school that lost a roof. Serena?"

"Hi, Russ. I'm standing outside Hunter Elementary, where some four hundred students attend kindergarten through sixth-grade classes every day. Fortunately, the place was empty tonight when the quake hit, because the roof caved in. At least one or two nights a week, after-school events take place in the gymnasium."

Emery switched off the TV. She felt edgy and anxious, and too restless to sleep. She stared at the phone, willing Pasha to call.

It rang less than a minute later.

"I can feel your anxiety from here," Pasha said as soon as she answered.

"I was trying to get you to call me. I guess it worked."

"Reliving it all again, aren't you?" Pasha asked, her voice etched with concern.

"Some. Trying not to. Uncanny, though, you feeling what I felt...right before it hit."

"I'm sure I only got a taste of what you went through. But it was awful enough."

"I don't suppose you've finished work?"

"I'm sorry. No time soon. I wish I could be there as much as you do. I'm supposed to be working right now, but I told Dita I needed something from my room. I couldn't bear the feeling I was getting from you."

"I'm better now, just talking to you. What about tomorrow?"

"We're packing for the rafting trip. We didn't receive some of the supplies we ordered, so we have to improvise. I really hope the rest of the clients make it here from Fairbanks on schedule."

Emery personally wouldn't mind a smaller group because Pasha would have less to do. She didn't want Dita's business to suffer, though, and she could imagine the nightmare of reshuffling things at the last minute. "I know you should go, so I won't keep you. I kind of like knowing you can tune in to me. It helps."

"I'm glad, Emery. I'll miss you until I see you again."

"Me, too. And if that's not for a while, warn me next time before you touch me, will you?" She couldn't help laughing. "I nearly jumped out of my skin tonight."

Pasha laughed, too. "I promise. Sleep well, Emery. Can't wait for our trip."

"I'm sure it'll be one to remember, Pasha. Sweet dreams."

Chapter Twenty-four

Two days later, June 10

Emery woke in a buoyant mood, welcome sunlight streaming through her window. The waiting over, they could leave today. The weather had cleared enough yesterday afternoon to fly all the rafting clients into Bettles, and this morning she saw only blue sky between the Den and the distant Brooks Range. With any luck, they'd be aloft in a few short hours, headed once more into the depths of the wilderness.

Pasha and Dita had missed dinner again, but Karla and Bryson made it, and Megan had recovered enough to come in with Chaz for soup. Being with them had highlighted another day of bed rest, which helped alleviate her aches but made her antsier than ever to get back outdoors.

She'd already packed, so she showered and dressed and headed downstairs for a quick breakfast. She didn't want to be late.

To her delight, Karla came in the front door just as she stood surveying the room for company, and they sat together at the bar.

"Get any sleep?" Emery asked. Karla had almost dozed during dessert the night before, after spending two nights tossing and turning on her patient's bedroom floor.

"Like a rock, once I got back to a real bed and Bryson. Keep your fingers crossed no one disturbs my precious day off 'cause I need it."

"I can't wait to start on the raft trip. Though I'd appreciate some warmer weather."

"Bryson really wished she could take you guys. She left a half hour ago. Lots of runs today."

They made more small talk over reindeer sausage, eggs, and toast. Emery kept eyeing her watch and, at twenty minutes before seven, flagged Grizz for her bill. "See you in ten days," she told Karla before heading back to her room.

"Have a great time!"

Pasha opened the outer door to the office a few minutes before seven when she saw clients already assembling with their bags. "Good morning, ladies. I'm Pasha, one of your guides. Come on in and have a seat. Help yourself to the coffee on the counter. We'll do introductions and get started as soon as everyone gets here."

Four clients so far, no one she recognized. Only two more strangers, Toni and Ruth, and Emery. Her power sensed Emery was heading this way, but not too close yet.

Chaz and Dita were finishing up in the back, so she ducked out the side door for a moment alone to gather her thoughts. She felt crazy and jumbled this morning. Maybe by trying to focus she could decipher what the power was trying to tell her.

She'd awakened with a sense of delicious anticipation, counting the minutes until Emery arrived and they began their adventure. The power was clear then, all eager euphoria, and built all morning as her intuition sensed Emery was awake and moving around, perhaps even thinking about her. Everything helped confirm her hope that their ten days together would bring them even closer.

Not long ago, however, as she helped Dita and Chaz pack, something changed. A sense of unease bordering on dread began to compete with her elation; the power was sending off mixed signals and she couldn't figure out its message. Was it cautioning her against moving too fast with Emery? Or telling her to guard her heart wisely? She leaned against the side of the building, closed her eyes, and tried to clear her mind.

But a battle still raged between desire and doom, and she had no clearer idea of its meaning.

Pasha headed back when she felt Emery growing very near and waved when she spotted Emery entering the front door just as she came in the side. Emery waved back, all smiles, and dumped her duffel by the door before heading her way. Everyone was present and accounted for, including Skeeter, who would fly them to their remote put-in spot.

Her heartbeat accelerated as Emery drew closer, and her nerves and senses sharpened in a glorious tension of anticipation. "Hi. Missed you."

"Hey there. I thought about you a lot, too." Emery's eyes shone with excitement, and she shifted her weight from foot to foot in pent-up restlessness. "Don't dare touch you in front of all these people," she said in a low voice. "I'm afraid—"

"Can I have your attention, please?" Dita waited until the room had quieted. Most of the clients took seats, but Emery stayed where she was. "Welcome, all. I'm Dita Eidson and I'd like to introduce your guides, Chaz Herrick..." She paused while Chaz waved. "And Pasha Dunn."

Pasha smiled and held up a hand.

"And this is Mike Sweeney, your pilot." Dita put her arm over the burly, red-bearded pilot's shoulder.

"Call me Skeeter," he told the clients.

Pasha's earlier unease reasserted itself, nearly drowning out her heightened sense of blissful calm from standing beside Emery. It quickly ebbed again to a quieter presence but simmered there, festering, refusing to let her ignore it.

As Dita presented the standard briefing about bears, safety, the leave-no-trace tenets of camping, and other assorted matters, Pasha tried to match up the strange faces in the crowd with the client files. The six newcomers included four thirty-something friends from Madison, Wisconsin and an older, butch-looking dyke from Texas with a much-younger blond companion named Lucy. In full makeup, newly painted nails, and designer jeans, Lucy had a Barbie-doll look that suggested she could be a handful.

"The Cessna you'll be flying in can't carry everyone and all our gear, so Skeeter will be taking two shifts up," Dita told them. "The first will leave right away and include Chaz, Terri and Joan, Melissa and Kathy," she said, referencing the Wisconsin friends, "and Fran and Lucy, along with their personal duffels and this pile of gear." She pointed to the smaller of two heaps against one wall. "The rest of the supplies will go with Pasha, Emery, Toni, and Ruth in the second flight. That'll leave as soon as Skeeter gets back."

"I'm figuring about ninety minutes each way, maybe a little more," Skeeter said. "If everyone's ready, let's head down to the runway. If you're on the second flight, please help carry gear."

While they transferred the cargo and loaded the green-and-white Cessna, Pasha introduced herself to the clients she hadn't met. Emery, she noticed, was never far away. She helped tote tents and sleeping bags, and kept an eye on whatever Pasha did. Too close an eye, almost. That nagging feeling of disquiet had resurfaced, and she did her best to conceal it. She didn't know what it meant and didn't want to alarm anyone. Surely, she kept telling herself, her gift was telling her to proceed with caution with Emery.

Once the plane took off, Toni and Ruth headed to the Den to wait until the second departure, but Emery followed her and Dita back toward the office. Pasha hung back with her once they got to the entrance and let Dita go inside alone.

"Got a lot more to do?" Emery asked.

"No, actually. Everything's ready. I suppose I could volunteer to man the phones until we leave, but Dita's already told me she can handle it."

Emery grinned. "Super. What shall we do to pass the time?"

"Hungry?"

Emery shook her head. "Just ate, with Karla. You?"

"Nope. Had a big breakfast. Feel like walking?"

"Sure."

Pasha ducked inside for binoculars and Emery got her camera. She headed downriver along the banks of the Koyukuk, away from town. The rock-strewn beach made for slow and careful walking, but she had a destination in mind that was worth it. "Been this way yet?"

"No. Something special up ahead?"

"I'll let you be the judge."

Pasha zipped up her jacket. Despite their exertions, the strong breeze was chilling. A flash of movement from her left caught her eye and she froze. Emery, a couple of steps behind, did as well. "See it?" she whispered.

"Yes."

An Arctic fox stared at them from the edge of the trees, its bushy tail a shade lighter than the grayish-brown fur of its body. A handsome animal, not much bigger than a cat, with intelligent dark eyes and rounded, fluffy ears.

He watched them for another few seconds, but disappeared into the undergrowth of the forest behind him when Emery reached for her camera.

"That was Willy," she told Emery.

"You named him?"

"I've been seeing him around here since last summer. His mate's den is a little farther on. That's where we're headed."

"We won't be bothering her, will we?" Emery asked.

"I won't take us too close, and Willy's never seemed to mind. I come out here sometimes with a book and sit for a while, and he'll reveal himself like that for little visits. You should see his coat in the winter. Thick, and snowy white. Really gorgeous."

"Beautiful animal."

A few minutes later, she stopped beside the river and sat on a fallen log. She patted the space next to her and Emery took it. Training her binoculars on the slope of a bank farther downriver, she quickly spotted the entrance to the den. Almost as though responding to a summons, the faces of three young fox pups came into focus. They looked a lot like kittens. "Here." She handed the binoculars to Emery and pointed. "See the small hill up there? Look about halfway up, near that cluster of rocks."

Emery trained the binoculars on the hill and focused. "Wow. Babies. They're so tiny."

"How many do you see?"

"Two. How many do they have?"

"Five to ten, usually. The babies should be coming out regularly to explore any time now."

"We'll have to come back here and keep track of their progress."

"For sure."

Emery watched for another couple of minutes, then handed the binoculars back. "Thanks for bringing me here."

"Mostly selfish. I wanted to get you alone."

"The last few days, I couldn't stop thinking about you," Emery said.

"Good thoughts, I hope."

"All good. A few wickedly good."

"Wickedly good, huh? I like the sound of that."

"I still can't get over what happens when we touch. The shocks, this feeling of calm happiness I get. It's almost tangible. I swear I can feel it coming into my body right where you're touching me, until it fills me up." Emery shook her head. "Sounds crazy, doesn't it?"

"No, Emery." She could hardly have described it better herself. "Not crazy at all. I get the same sort of feeling."

"So…it's been a couple of days." Emery raised her eyebrows in question.

"Should be a pretty good one, I would think. About the same as my touching you under the table."

Emery laughed. "At least I'll be expecting it this time." She held out her hand.

Pasha took it in hers.

The jolt made them laugh. Pasha relished the explosion of bliss that set her heart fluttering in her chest. Her eyes met Emery's.

Emery's dark-brown pupils were shining and serene, her whole face lit with joy. "Have you wondered what it'll be like when we kiss?" she asked.

"I notice you said *when*, not *if*." Pasha stared at Emery's mouth, The scar bisecting one side of her curved upper lip gave her a roguish character. A badge to her survival spirit and courage.

"Oh, that's a given." Emery's hand curled tighter around hers. "I've barely been able to resist since the other night."

"You know, I considered telling you we should just remain friends."

Emery's smile faded. "Why?"

"Because, Emery, even though I know this can only be fleeting, I'm not sure how successfully I can keep from getting emotionally involved. I'm finding you way too damn irresistible. And you make me feel so…well, like *this*." She could tell from the strength of the pull between them and the look in Emery's eyes that Emery had to be feeling much of the same euphoria she floated on right now.

"And if you did get emotionally involved…" Emery searched her face. "It would hurt more when I left, if we'd been intimate?"

Pasha nodded.

"But you said you *considered* telling me we should just be friends."

"Yup. I thought about it." Pasha glanced down at their enjoined hands, epicenter of the tremors of happiness pouring into them. She envisioned kissing Emery, and more—of what it might be like to feel how the thrill of their mouths upon each other and their naked bodies entangled in passion would enhance this very tangible current. How could she ever have imagined she could resist? "I realized very quickly that I don't want to pass up this opportunity. I'll happily embrace whatever I can have with you, as long as it lasts."

"I don't want to hurt you, Pasha, or have you regret getting involved with me for any reason. But I'm happy that's your decision. It'd be awfully tough to try to keep my distance."

"Would it now?"

Emery squeezed her hand. "I didn't tell you, but I had a talk with Geneva the other night."

"You did?"

Emery nodded and stared into her eyes. "I told her I couldn't date her. That I'd become very interested in you, and that's where I wanted to focus my time and attention while I'm here."

"I see." Pasha couldn't stop grinning. *She wants me, and me alone.* "You know…when we just talked about kissing, you said you were having a hard time resisting."

Emery chuckled. "That's an understatement."

"So…exactly *why* have you been resisting?"

Emery put her hand gently against Pasha's cheek. "Because there's a time and a place for everything." She drew closer, her gaze fixed on Pasha's mouth. "Mostly, I didn't want to be interrupted."

And then Emery kissed her, a soft, sensuous kiss that began tentatively, lips brushing hers in discovery and exploration. Pasha's heartbeat accelerated as a surge of warmth coursed through her veins, her senses so painfully heightened she could hear the rhythmic whoosh-whoosh-whoosh of blood in her ears.

Emery teased her, tracing the tip of her tongue lightly along Pasha's lower lip, withdrawing slightly whenever Pasha opened her mouth in an effort to deepen the kiss. Tormenting her to new heights of delicious but maddening anticipation, until finally Emery claimed her with a deep, fierce unleashing of passion that Pasha returned with equal intensity.

Time stood still, and she almost forgot even the spectacular magnitude of their surroundings. Immersed in their kiss, body and mind and soul, the power of their connection, a heady rush, blotted everything else from her consciousness.

Minutes later they separated, both breathing hard, but remained with their faces close together, foreheads touching. In the heat of the moment, she'd ended up with Emery's arms around her waist and she with her hands laced around Emery's neck, but she didn't remember how or when it happened.

"Jesus, Pasha," Emery managed, which was more than Pasha could accomplish. "I wish I could put into words how you make me feel."

Desire fogged Pasha's brain, and her heart took a long while to calm. "At least you can form words," she finally replied. "Amazing."

They pulled back to look at each other. "I just feel this incredible sense of serenity," Emery said, "in addition, of course, to wanting you like crazy mad."

Pasha nodded. "I know just what you mean." She glanced at her watch, heartsick to discover they needed to head back, right away. "But we've got to go. Skeeter should be getting back soon."

Emery sighed. "I don't suppose we can make it happen on the trip, can we?"

"Where there's a will, there's a way." Pasha smiled. "We've got free time built in, and you'll have a two-person tent alone."

Emery got to her feet. "Then let's get going," she said, offering her hand. "The sooner we get there, the sooner I can seduce you."

Pasha put her hand in Emery's and nearly wept with joy at the strong current that soared between them as Emery's aura blazed gold.

They held hands all the way back, and just before they reached the final curve before town, Pasha pulled Emery to her and kissed her again, a short but passionate cementing of their intention to follow wherever this took them.

The bliss that had kept Pasha's head in the clouds dissipated when they reached the runway and she spotted the Cessna in the distance. Her feeling of unease returned, even more powerful now.

Chapter Twenty-five

For the first time since her accident, Emery felt like her old self. No, even better—conscious of none of the numerous pins, rods, screws, and other artificial implants that cobbled her body together and with so much energy she could scale Mount McKinley, the one Alaskan adventure she'd considered but finally rejected as beyond her capabilities.

Most amazing, though, a serene exhilaration calmed her lifelong restlessness. Even once she'd started seeing the world as she wanted, she'd experienced an underlying expectancy that remained unfulfilled. But right now, she felt absolutely content and happy.

She followed Pasha into the hangar to help carry gear as the green-and-white Cessna taxied down the runway toward them. Toni, Ruth, and Dita already stood there, and to Emery's surprise, so did Karla, off to one side. She obviously didn't intend to see them off, because her medical bag and a large first-aid kit lay at her feet and she looked serious.

As they neared, Pasha asked, "What's going on?"

"I'm hitching a ride," Karla said. "I have an emergency up in Kaktovik, a little girl with a high fever. Your put-in spot's right on the way and Skeeter's got room."

"Oh, I hope she's okay." Pasha glanced over at the others, who had already grabbed armfuls of gear from the pile by the door. "I'm getting a kind of…odd sensation, like something's wrong," she told Emery and Karla in a low voice. "Maybe that's why."

"If you're sensing it's serious, let's get going." Karla grabbed her kit and bag. "I'll come back to help you load the rest."

"Save me the seat beside you," Pasha told Emery as they started toward the plane carrying supplies.

"With pleasure," she replied. Once they'd stacked all the gear by the plane, Emery settled into the left-side seat behind Skeeter's. Toni and Ruth sat behind her, and Karla climbed into the co-pilot's seat. While they'd moved the gear, Skeeter had removed a second row of seats farther back to accommodate it.

Emery glanced out the window, anxious to get underway. Skeeter stood sucking on a cigarette as he looked over the plane's exterior, and Pasha hugged Dita good-bye. Pasha certainly had a round, well-proportioned ass and lean legs. When Pasha turned toward the plane, she caught Emery staring and smiled, but her smile was forced; she seemed worried.

Karla seemed troubled, too. She stared straight ahead out the windshield, her jaw firmly set and her brow furrowed. Toni and Ruth chatted, laughing about something and unaware of the apparent severity of Karla's medical mission.

Pasha climbed in beside her, and as Dita secured the passenger door, Skeeter took his seat in the cockpit.

"Welcome aboard, ladies. Make sure your seat belt's securely fastened, please." He turned in his seat. "You know where the doors are: the two in the rear and these two to the cockpit seats. We won't be flying high enough to need oxygen, and yes, you can use your seat cushion as a floatation device in the unlikely event we have to ditch in water. In addition to your cargo, I have a survival duffel in the back and a fire extinguisher under my seat. Questions?"

"How far to the drop-off point?" Toni asked.

"Roughly two hundred miles. It'll take us about ninety minutes." Skeeter stretched the headset over his black wool cap and started the engine. "The wind's picked up this morning, by the way, so we might go through some turbulence. I'll try to steer clear of it." After completing his preflight checklist, he turned the Cessna toward the runway and radioed the FAA station.

Emery was looking out the forward windshield over Skeeter's shoulder as they took off, so she jumped when Pasha suddenly grasped her hand, sending a jolt through her.

Pasha's expression had darkened further. She was obviously finding it difficult to conceal her concern.

Leaning over so the others wouldn't hear, Emery asked in a low voice, "Everything all right?"

"I don't know," Pasha whispered. "I don't like what I'm feeling."

"Is it the sick girl or something else?"

"I'm not sure. I don't want to alarm the others, but I usually don't get these kinds of feelings of danger or dread unless they affect me personally. And they're getting stronger by the minute."

"Do you think you should say something?" Emery whispered.

"What? That my stomach's in knots and I don't know why? I can't jeopardize the trip without good reason."

Emery glanced forward. They gained elevation as they neared the Brooks Range, and the plane shook as it soared through a level of rough air, but within seconds things smoothed out. She heard the click of shutters behind her. Toni and Ruth busily took pictures through the windows while pointing out objects of interest below to each other. Karla and Skeeter were calculating when she would arrive in Kaktovik.

"And now?" Emery asked Pasha.

Pasha shrugged. She still looked worried and didn't stop squeezing Emery's hand, but she stared out her window and said nothing more.

In no time they flew above the snow-cloaked peaks, following a wide green river valley far below. Nothing but spectacular mountains as far as she could see. Another burst of turbulence shook the plane and they dropped several feet. Pasha inhaled sharply and Ruth gasped.

Emery's pulse quickened. Given the perfectly clear sky, the threat's invisibility made it even more unnerving. Skeeter gained altitude to put greater separation between the plane and the mountains, but they remained in rough air for several more minutes before finally leveling out.

"Sorry about that," Skeeter called back. "Everyone doing okay?"

"Beginning to wish I hadn't had that reindeer stew," Ruth said. "Really feeling kind of queasy."

"You'll find airsick bags in the pocket behind my seat, Emery. Will you pass one back?" Skeeter asked.

She let go of Pasha's hand to fish one out for Ruth.

"Anything I'd give you now probably won't help much." Karla unhooked her seat belt and turned around in her seat. "We'd be getting there about the time it started working."

"I'll be okay as long as we don't go through much more of that," Ruth replied.

Karla stared out one of the left rear windows with a puzzled expression. "Skeeter, what's going on behind us?" Emery followed her gaze, as did Toni and Skeeter.

A plume of smoky haze covered a wide swath of the sky behind them, rolling toward them fairly fast. Skeeter cursed under his breath and flipped on the radio. As he spoke, he increased the throttle and the propeller roared louder. "E1329D Cessna to BTT. BTT, come back?" He listened for several seconds, then repeated the call.

As he dialed in a new frequency, Karla asked, "No one there?"

"Jim only subs for me at the FAA station when a flight's due in. He doesn't hang out there otherwise like I do. I'll try listening in on some other frequencies, see if I can locate some chatter." He went quiet and turned the dial a couple more times before he apparently hit a significant channel.

No one said anything. Emery glanced back at the haze, which seemed to be gaining on them despite their increased speed. As she straightened, the plane began to descend sharply toward the valley far below.

"That's volcanic ash," Skeeter told them. He tried to appear confident and collected, but Emery could hear the tension in his voice. "Mount Wrangell erupted just about the time we took off. Everything's grounded between there and here, and we've got to set down as fast as we can."

She looked at Pasha, who trembled all over, her face pasty white. Emery took her hand. The usual calm serenity she felt when touching Pasha had become a distraught uncertainty. Her own mouth dried.

"Are we in trouble?" Karla asked, undisguised fear in her voice as she refastened her seat belt.

Ruth retched, then vomited into her airsick bag. Emery tried to take shallow breaths as her own stomach recoiled in response to the sudden stench.

"God, sorry, everybody." Ruth moaned.

They hit the same layer of turbulence that had made her sick in the first place, and Emery gripped the edge of her seat with her free hand as the plane vibrated and bounced. Fearful of what she'd see, she reluctantly looked back again as they neared the tops of the highest mountains.

The ash, swept along by the turbulence they flew in, had almost caught them. Emery's heart began to jackhammer. "It's getting very close," she said.

"I know," Skeeter replied. "Ladies, I'll do my best to put down somewhere safely. I've landed in the backcountry hundreds of times. I just need a few hundred feet of solid, flat ground. As we get closer, you can all help me find a good prospect."

The plane dropped again, at least twenty feet this time. Karla awkwardly fumbled for one of the airsick bags, managing to open it just in time. The stench in the plane became almost unbearable, and Emery got out her own bag in readiness.

"Pass a couple more back, will you?" Toni asked. Pasha reached for one, too.

They had just descended below the highest peaks when the propeller began to labor. Skeeter cursed and adjusted his controls, but the sputtering continued for several more seconds before the engine quit completely.

The sudden dead silence filled Emery with terror. No one spoke as the rate of their descent increased.

"Mayday. Mayday. This is E1329D Cessna out of BTT." Skeeter read their current GPS location off his instruments as he tried to restart the engine. "My engine's quit because of the volcanic ash. Trying to restart, going in for a forced landing. I have six souls on board." He listened for a response before repeating the call.

The plane continued to drop. Pasha's grip on Emery's hand nearly cut off her circulation. Toni quietly prayed, and Karla stared forward in horror, gripping her overhead strap.

Emery looked over Skeeter's shoulder. He held the controls firmly with both hands, wrestling to keep the plane centered in the valley, but something was sweeping them left, toward the sheer rock cliff face of an enormous mountain.

"Son of a bitch," he said under his breath. Groaning from the strain, he took one hand off the controls long enough to try unsuccessfully to restart the engine. Their sideways momentum increased, buffeting the plane.

The ground seemed to rise toward them at alarming speed. Emery could make out more features in the landscape below, and what she saw didn't comfort her. The area looked like an enormous swamp with a river running through it, a river devoid of the sandbars she and Bryson had landed on. The waterway here was too straight and the current too strong. The banks didn't look any better.

The haze had reached and overtaken them. Emery found it harder to see; the plume muted the sun and cast a thin veil around the plane that partially obscured some of the surrounding landscape below and behind.

Skeeter tried again to restart the engine, but still failed. He called back, "I don't have much choice where to set down. I won't be able to see anything in a couple minutes. Prepare for an emergency landing. Remove any sharp objects on your body, and when I say so, put your head down and lace your fingers behind your neck. Try to relax. I know it's a tall order."

They seemed to almost level off for several seconds, as the plane caught a current of air and Skeeter worked to keep them away from the mountain. He tried repeatedly to restart the engine as they covered another mile or two and the landscape changed. In the gaps between the haze, dense forest replaced much of the swampland below on their side of the river. And the lower mountain now to their left had gentler slopes, though at this altitude, a thick layer of snow still cloaked everything.

"I'm going to try there," Skeeter pointed ahead at a fairly flat expanse of snow on a long ridge well above the tree line. "Best option we got. Hang on, everybody."

Toni's recitation of the Lord's Prayer accelerated, and Ruth joined in.

Emery looked at Pasha as she gripped her hand tighter. Pasha's eyes were wide in shock, and pure, stark horror emanated from her.

They would all die, Emery thought. Pasha sensed it. Even without that confirmation, she wasn't entirely surprised. She'd been luckier than anyone could expect in cheating death so far, and during her long recovery, she'd accepted that perhaps she would die prematurely. That realization had helped her overcome her fears and take the risks she had the last few months.

But she was afraid now, and angry. She hadn't yet done a fraction of what she wanted to, and it seemed so damn unfair to have her life snuffed out just as she'd met the most intriguing, compelling woman of her life. Most of all, she was angry that when fate came to claim her, it so often took the lives of those closest to her.

Dear God, if it's my time, so be it. But please don't take Pasha and the others.

"I'm sorry we never got the chance..." Pasha said in a shaky voice.

She held Pasha's hand between both of hers. "I know. Me, too."

"Heads down!" Skeeter commanded. "Brace for impact." He lowered the flaps and the plane slowed dramatically.

Emery risked a quick glance ahead before she got into the position. They hurtled toward a wall of white and were, at best, mere seconds from crashing.

She put her head between her legs, laced her fingers together behind her neck, and closed her eyes. Her heart pounded so hard it threatened to burst through her chest. *Our Father, who art—*

Emery catapulted forward against Skeeter's seat back when they hit, then the plane somersaulted and she flew head over heels, still strapped to her seat. Time slowed, and her senses sharpened. She tasted blood as cold air rushed in and a sharp stabbing pain as something pierced her side. Screams and curses blended with the sound of tearing metal. Then all went quiet.

Chapter Twenty-six

A nything?" Megan stopped pacing long enough to ask. Dita shook her head and frowned as she set down the satellite phone. "Nothing's working. I can't reach anyone. Just static." She got up and looked out the window. Volcanic ash obliterated the sun, making it like dusk. But it hadn't fallen heavily onto the village, yet. The wind, strong and in their favor, carried the bulk of the plume high and farther west. Still, with particles visible, everyone was staying indoors with the windows shut. Not that she planned to go anywhere anytime soon. She'd remain near the phone until she heard from everyone. She worried mainly about Skeeter's flight and Bryson's. Both pilots had been airborne when the volcano erupted, on long flights in the plume's path.

No one had communications in the surrounding area, she imagined. She'd received a handful of calls in the early stages, after Grizz phoned about a breaking news report. She'd immediately turned on the office TV and watched raw footage from the scene. The news anchor reported that the initial blast from the Mount Wrangell eruption had calmed somewhat, but the volcano continued to spew ash into a strong, fast air column from the south. A graphic replaced the video, showing the ash plume's estimated path hour by hour, Bettles located at the danger zone's edge. She hurriedly called the other Eidson offices, telling them to immediately ground all flights and warn any guides out in the field.

Despite repeated tries, Dita hadn't been able to reach Bryson on a charter freight run between Fairbanks and Anaktuvuk Pass, or Skeeter, and though she'd contacted Chaz, the connection had failed before she said three words. Since that time, she'd heard only static from the world outside. No Internet or satellite TV, either. She'd never felt more isolated and powerless.

Dita had faith that Chaz and her group of clients would fare all right, as long as the ash didn't bury them and planes could fly before too long. They had nearly half the ten-day trip supplies, and Chaz had abundant experience outdoors.

No one was better attuned to environmental changes or a better pilot in emergencies than Bryson. No doubt she'd set down somewhere to ride out the weather, well equipped with survival gear and outdoor savvy.

She worried most about the Cessna 208. Possibly Skeeter had stayed ahead of the plume and landed safely at the drop-off spot, but from the projected speed and path of the plume, she thought it unlikely. The Cessna couldn't fly at top speed with its heavy load, so the forward edge of the plume had probably intersected the plane's flight about halfway.

Studying the topographical map of the region didn't reassure her. The area where the ash cloud had likely overtaken Skeeter consisted of high mountains, swamps, a few patches of forest, and not much else for miles in every direction. A few tiny cabins dotted the map, likely old trappers' huts or seasonal hunting or fishing retreats. Few people occupied places up here year-round.

The region didn't look ideal for a forced landing, especially since the Cessna's tundra tires limited the surfaces Skeeter could put down on. Also, Skeeter didn't know this particular area nearly as well as Bryson. Bryson called the area between Fairbanks and the North Slope "my territory." Skeeter had a lot fewer years in interior Alaska and tended to stick to commercial charters that took him between the more-developed airstrips at villages. Oh, he'd racked up a lot of flights in the backcountry, too, but never in this particular area. In fact, Chaz had ridden along on the first flight because she'd been there before and excelled at reading a topo map. Skeeter's GPS would get them fairly close, but the readings up here were never ideal.

She hoped he saw the danger in plenty of time and got down safely in a good area. But she would worry like crazy until she knew for sure. She felt a deep sense of responsibility for the safety of her clients, pilots, and guides. Pasha, in particular, had become like a younger sister.

Megan had hardly stopped pacing in the last half hour, except for brief pauses at the window to look outside. Worried sick about Chaz, she had tried several times to reach that group's satellite phone. "I can't stand all this waiting, being so cut off from everything. Not knowing what's going on, who's safe and who's not."

The news blackout had to be especially difficult for Megan because of her background. During her long years in 24-hour live news, she'd had access to instant updates and extensive detail about every major world event. "All we can do is keep trying," Dita said.

She reviewed the equipment list for the rafting trip, sorting through what gear had gone with each flight to assess how well-equipped each of the two parties would be if separated. They'd deliberately divided the tents and sleeping bags, and each party had its own personal duffels. Both also had some of the food, but they'd packed the crates according to weight, not by meals, so one group might have more and better options than the other. And Chaz's gang had the bulk of the kitchen cookware, while Pasha's had most of the rafting equipment.

The second flight also had Karla along, which comforted her somewhat. Level-headed, Karla could handle many medical emergencies.

Geneva came in, carrying two paper bags of food from the Den. "Anything new?" A thin layer of grayish ash muted the shoulders and front of her jacket, normally a vivid green. She shook it off before hanging it on a peg by the door.

"No," Dita replied. "Still down. The Den?"

"The same. Everyone's trying. It's so damn frustrating." Geneva set the paper bags on the counter and started to unpack them. "I know you both said you're not hungry, but you need to eat something. We're in for a long night and need to keep our strength up."

Megan reached for a salad. "At least they all have PLBs. Once we can get flights in the air, we should be able to find them even with communications still down."

"When I talked to the other offices, I alerted our pilots outside the zone to be ready to head this way as soon as the flight ban is lifted," Dita told them. "And I'll notify authorities and ASARA as soon as I can." The Alaska Search and Rescue Association included a number of highly trained volunteer organizations and individuals.

"Resources might be stretched thin," Megan said. "No telling how many planes had to make forced landings. Or what other problems they may have to deal with because of the eruption."

Dita shrugged. "I'll call in favors, if necessary, to find them."

Chaz sorted through the pile of gear, separating what they'd brought into three piles: personal duffels, food and kitchen supplies, and tents and sleeping bags. Her clients had gathered around her in a semicircle. "We should set up camp while we wait to hear what's happening. They probably won't make it today." She grabbed their three two-man tents and handed one to each couple. She'd have to sleep under a tarp. "Find a level spot in this area and pitch your tent, then situate your personal gear. I'll set up the kitchen downriver a ways."

Skeeter's second flight was two hours overdue, and she tried hard not to panic. About the time she'd expected the Cessna to return, the sky had grown hazy, diffusing the sunlight and darkening the landscape, but not until the plume passed directly overhead, raining bits of gray-brown ash, did she realize a volcano had erupted somewhere south of them.

She couldn't reach Skeeter or Dita by satellite phone, which only increased her concern and frustration. She could only hope the plane never made it off the ground and that everyone was safely in Bettles. Obsessing about the alternative—that Skeeter'd had to ditch somewhere—would make her crazy and less effective.

For now, she could only focus her energy on keeping her clients healthy and happy. The ash itself worried her. It had already covered everything with a thin, dusty layer, which was one reason she wanted to get the tents up and sleeping bags and other gear inside. Fortunately, they had a large canopy for the kitchen area to protect those supplies as well, but if the ash continued to fall at this rate, breathing the stuff might soon present a hazard. She'd have to investigate moving their camp to a better-protected area or farther from the fallout.

As she set up their kitchen and cooking area, Chaz assessed how long their food supplies might last. Volcanic eruptions could continue for weeks; no telling how long they could be stuck here, though she didn't want to tell the clients quite yet. She'd trim the usual number of meals per day to two right away and calculate meager but adequate portions, hoping the situation resolved itself before she had to take more drastic measures.

Unfortunately all the bear-proof containers but two were with the other flight. They'd have to be especially diligent in suspending their excess food and garbage from trees each night, out of reach of grizzlies and other predators.

❖

Bryson stared at the sky once more before she ducked into her tent. She'd put her cowling and spinner covers on the Super Cub, hoping they'd keep the ash from her engine, but she'd left her wing covers at the hanger. She'd removed them from the cargo hold at winter's end to save space. What would the abrasive, acidic fallout do to her beloved brick-red plane?

She'd been flying low when she recognized the ashfall from a distance, having witnessed several previous plumes firsthand: the Mount Augustine eruption in 2006, the Crater Peak blast in 1992, and the Redoubt eruption in 1990. Setting down on a short, grassy hill within a wide river valley, she could wait for a week at most, as long as the ash didn't get too thick. Her survival duffel had everything she needed, though she'd have to severely ration her meager food supplies if she couldn't supplement them with fish, game, or edible plants. But all her efforts to communicate either by radio or satellite phone had failed. She hated being in the dark.

Bryson worried most about Chaz, Pasha, Skeeter, and the rafting clients. Skeeter would've had to ferry the group in two trips and probably wouldn't have been able to complete both journeys before the plume hit the area. Which meant he'd likely have had to set down somewhere fast, and that route didn't have many likely prospects. Who was on the second flight? Certainly Chaz or Pasha— they always put one guide with each group in such a situation—and possibly Emery, who'd become a good friend in a short time.

At least Karla was safe in Bettles, though the eruption had no doubt ruined her long-anticipated day off. She was probably in the Eidson offices right now, checking on her. She'd worry, and Bryson hated putting her through that, but with any luck, the wind would change soon and she could make it the last hundred miles home.

Chapter Twenty-seven

Cold and disoriented, Pasha awoke groggily to an eerie quiet. Her head hurt. When she tried to open her eyes, one had crusted shut. Gingerly probing the area, she realized she had a cut in her forehead, but it had already stopped bleeding.

Some of her mental fog cleared and her eyes shot open. She moved her arms and legs, assessing her mobility. Some bad bruises, but otherwise she had survived. Miraculous. But she gasped in horror as she took in her surroundings.

The front of the Cessna lay buried in snow, and the plane rested half on its left side. The windshield had shattered on the pilot's side and a coating of white powdery fluff covered everything in the cockpit, including Skeeter's hunched, unmoving figure and Karla, mostly obscured behind the co-pilot's seat.

Glancing left when a blast of cold air blew snow into her face, she saw a gaping hole in the side of the plane where Emery had sat. Her seat had vanished, the left wing torn off. "Emery!" she yelled as her stomach churned. "Emery! Answer me!" Nothing.

As she fought to unbuckle herself, she saw Toni and Ruth both coming to. Some of the cargo had escaped the tie-downs and bungee nets that secured it; duffel bags and other gear lay scattered throughout the cabin. The tail of the plane had caved in on one side.

"Toni, Ruth, you both all right?" She finally unfastened the seat belt and stood.

"Cold. And my chin hurts." Toni unbuckled her seat belt and stretched. "Bruised. But nothing's broken. When Ruth failed to respond, she bent over her. "Don't see any visible injuries. Ruth? You hear me?"

Pasha cleared away the debris that had flown toward the cockpit "Karla? Skeeter? Talk to me." Finally she got a better look at Karla.

Strapped in her seat and slumped forward, half-resting on the bent remains of the instrument panel, Karla's head bled and her left arm hung at an unnatural angle.

"Karla, can you hear me?" Pasha gently touched her shoulder, rewarded with a low groan. "Karla, it's Pasha. We've been in a crash. Move slowly. You have a bad cut on your head and your left arm's broken." Another groan, and Karla began to stir.

She turned her attention to Skeeter. He'd also been thrown forward into the control panel, and the snow around him was stained red. His section of the plane had taken the brunt of the impact. Only the left side of the windscreen had disappeared, and the instrument panel in front of him had caved in more severely. Had he courageously maneuvered to sacrifice himself so the most could live? The controls seemed embedded in his chest, his legs concealed by twisted metal, and his head turned away so she couldn't see the extent of his injuries. "Skeeter? Mike, please answer me. Please wake up." She held her breath and, with a trembling hand, pressed her fingers against his carotid artery.

His pulse, weak and thready, showed he was still alive.

"Hang in there, Skeeter. Stay with us. We'll help you soon."

"Ughnnn." Karla slowly rose to an upright position, bracing herself on the dashboard with her right arm. "What…what's happening?"

"Karla, we crashed. You broke your left arm and have a cut on your head. But I pray to God you're okay, because we need you. Skeeter's hurt bad, and Emery's not in the plane. I have to go look for her. Please try to wake up."

"Ruth's coming to," Toni said. "Go. I'm okay. I'll watch them."

"Great." She zipped up her jacket and climbed through the opening, careful not to tear her clothes on the sharp, jagged metal, and found herself in thigh-deep snow. The top several inches consisted of light powder, but from the knees down it felt compact.

Around the front and sides of the plane the snowfield looked smooth and unbroken, though turning a light brownish-gray from the ash that drifted from the sky, swirling around her in the steady breeze. Behind the Cessna lay a long, twisted trench in the snow several feet wide, with a number of holes in the snowfield on either side where loose debris had flown from the plane. Most of the left wing stuck upright out of one hole, like a billboard. Not far from it she found several other large depressions in the snow. She headed toward the nearest one as fast as possible, but the effort tired her. "Emery! Emery, can you hear me?"

When she got closer, she saw a ripped duffel bag, half its contents missing. A square piece of fuselage had created the depression beside it. As she neared the next big indentation, she spotted the top of a seat. "Emery!"

The seat lay on its right side with Emery still strapped to it, not moving. Dried blood matted the hair above her left temple, and Pasha saw more blood on the snow beneath her. She squatted and noticed the open front of Emery's coat and the blue turtleneck beneath stained crimson, She spotted a rip—no, more a clean, round, hole—in the sweater, just below Emery's rib cage.

No movement that she could see, no rise and fall of her chest. But it's a thick sweater, she tried to tell herself. You might not be able to tell. Most foreboding, though she knelt mere inches from Emery, she couldn't feel their connection.

She'd known disaster would come. The sense of doom and dread had built until it suffocated her, and that's when the cloud appeared. What could she have done? She had no idea what form it would take or when it would strike. Could she have prevented all this?

Pasha scooped away the loose snow around Emery's face. "Emery? Talk to me. Please tell me you're all right." When she gently caressed the cool skin of Emery's face, she didn't experience any shock. The power had been completely silent since the crash. Did she even have her gift anymore? Heartsick at what she thought she'd find, she pressed shaking fingers against the carotid artery in Emery's neck and held her breath.

The heartbeat pulsed beneath her fingertips, slow, but steady. *Thank God.* "Emery?" No response.

She used her pocketknife to unjam the seat-belt buckle and free Emery. She didn't dare move her until Karla examined her, but she worried about leaving her in the snow. She stripped off her heavy jacket and gently tucked it under and around Emery's head and neck, then closed her coat. Placing her face near Emery's, she tried again to rouse her. "Please, Emery. Hang in there and fight to wake up. I'm going to get help. I won't be long."

Pasha retraced her footsteps to the plane. She had an easier time pushing through the path she'd already plowed than breaking new ground, but she had soaked jeans and numb fingertips, and the wind cut through her sweatshirt.

Toni, leaning into the cockpit, turned when Pasha got back. "Did you find her?"

"She's alive, but unconscious, with a head wound and some kind of injury to her abdomen that's bled a lot. How's Karla?"

"Getting there," Karla replied.

Pasha picked her way over the bags and debris so she could see past Toni. Karla, alert and aware, had unzipped her jacket halfway and tucked her broken arm into it to keep it immobilized. With her good hand, she examined Skeeter, still out cold. "I have only superficial head wounds, I think. I'll need to set my arm. It hurts like a bitch. But we have higher priorities right now."

"What do you want us to do?" Pasha asked.

"The radio's shot. Do we have a satellite phone?"

Pasha shook her head. "It's with Chaz. Skeeter should have his in his bag. Do you know which it is?"

"No. We'll have to search. But let's get Emery and Skeeter triaged and stabilized first. Toni, see if you can lay your hands on a couple of sleeping bags and sleeping pads," Karla said. "What's it like outside, Pasha? Can you get a fire going?"

"The snow's pretty deep, and the wind's stiff. We're a long way above the tree line." Pasha glanced around. "But I saw pieces of the plane outside I could use to build a fire on and to make a windbreak, and if we break up the wood from the food crates, we'll have enough to burn for at least a while."

"Get working on that, and I'll go assess Emery." Karla worked her way out of the cramped cockpit, holding her left arm. "See my medical bag anywhere?"

"Back here." Ruth held up the black valise and Toni passed it forward.

"You all right?" Karla asked.

"Cuts and bruises, mostly," Ruth replied. "My knee's swollen, but I can bend it a little."

"You and Toni should add some layers and check yourselves. I'll see to your cuts in a bit." Karla glanced over at Pasha. "And you need to get out of those wet jeans and find a coat. We don't need for you to get hypothermic."

"I won't argue. Follow the path I cut and it'll lead you right to Emery." While Karla headed outside and Toni and Ruth got to work in the back, Pasha dug through her duffel and hurriedly changed. Her kayaking dry suit would provide the best protection from the elements, so she put that on over silk long underwear and added a thick sweater and waterproof windbreaker as well. A ball cap and her neoprene rafting gloves completed her ensemble and made her much more comfortable.

She emptied two of the food crates and carried them outside, along with a box of waterproof matches. Karla hunched over Emery, who looked still nonresponsive. She headed toward them. "How is she?"

Karla frowned. "She's lost a lot of blood and her temp is down a couple of degrees. We need to get her warm in a hurry and take care of this puncture wound. Start a fire. I'm going back for the first-aid kit."

Pasha leaned over Emery. "Stay with me, Emery. We'll get you warm very soon." She spent a few minutes laboriously scooping snow away from a large area next to Emery, using a flat piece of metal as a shovel. Then she laid out another, larger piece in the depression to build the fire on and broke up the food crates into small pieces. She returned to the plane just as Karla emerged with her red first-aid kit.

"Skeeter's temperature is dropping fast," Karla said. "I wish we could figure out a way to either warm the cabin or take him outside by the fire."

"I'll try to think of something," Pasha said. "I came in to find some tinder. I should have the fire going in a minute."

"How's this?" Toni held up a paperback she'd brought along.

"Perfect. Thanks."

"Grab a sleeping bag and pad for Emery, and some water," Karla shouted to Pasha as she left. "I had a quart bottle with me, up by my seat."

Pasha struggled to maneuver the large portion of wing into a windbreak that protected both the fire pit and Emery before she lit the fire. Then she laid out the sleeping pad and bag beside it and, under Karla's direction, gently moved Emery onto it. Karla had stabilized Emery's neck with a plastic brace.

"Why isn't she coming to?" Pasha asked.

"I'm not sure." Karla opened the medical kit. "She took a good hit to her head that bears watching. Might be a concussion, even a skull fracture, though I didn't feel any open breaks. We need to take care of her side right now, and I'll need your help, Pash. Can't do much one-handed." She fished out a pair of scissors. "Cut away her clothes around the wound so I can get a better look."

Pasha did as instructed. It did look like a puncture wound. The bleeding around the neat round hole had diminished, but not stopped.

Karla rinsed the wound with water. "The bleeding probably flushed out most any debris or dirt." She handed a sterile pack of large gauze pads and tape to Pasha. "I'll put on some antibiotic ointment and you can dress it. We'll need to change this frequently and keep an eye out for infection."

They had almost finished dressing the wound when Toni joined them. "How's she doing?"

"Got the bleeding stopped. Now we wait." Karla zipped the sleeping bag around Emery.

"I've been thinking about what you said, about getting the pilot out here," Toni said. "I think I have a solution."

"You do?" Pasha fed a few more pieces of wood to the fire.

"Come see what you think."

They returned to the plane where Ruth sat in the co-pilot's seat, monitoring Skeeter. "He's coming around, I think," she told them.

Karla examined him, while Toni led Pasha to the back. "We cobbled together a kind of stretcher that should work. But it'll take all of us."

Toni's handiwork impressed Pasha. She'd disassembled two of the take-apart oars and bound them together with seat belts. The loops of the belts encased one of the sleeping pads. It looked sturdy enough to support Skeeter's weight. "Great job, Toni. Let's carry it up near the front."

"Looks like his legs might be pinned," Karla said. "Does he carry a crowbar? Bryson has one."

"I saw a toolbox in the back, under the bungee net." Toni headed toward it and returned carrying a standard-sized crowbar. "Let me," she said. "Just tell me what to do."

"You probably do have the advantage," Pasha said. "See if you can get some leverage there," she pointed to a section of the twisted metal by Skeeter's knees, "and bend it back so we can slide his legs out."

Toni put her back into it and let out a grunt of exertion. The steel began to bend. She repositioned herself and bent it farther until they could slide him from the seat and onto the makeshift stretcher.

It took all four of them to carry him out to the fire, which had nearly gone out by the time they got him settled. Pasha quickly built it up again. Skeeter groaned a few times as they carried him and opened his eyes for the first time as Karla assessed his injuries.

"What's going on?" he mumbled.

"We crashed, Skeeter," Karla told him. "Try not to move around. Can you tell me what hurts?"

"Mmm. Face," he answered. "Left leg." His nose looked broken, and he had several minor cuts and lacerations on his face, and a big gash across his forehead. His leg, below the knee, was soaked in blood. "And chest. Hurts to breathe."

"You probably have some broken ribs," Karla told him. "And maybe internal injuries. Lie quiet."

"Cold." His lips were bluish, his skin pale.

Pasha went back into the plane for a sleeping bag and broke apart another crate to build up the fire. Karla was examining Skeeter's leg when she returned. It had a deep laceration along the shin, but she managed to stop the bleeding and dress the wound with Toni's help. Once she finished, they zipped him into the sleeping bag and Karla tended the cuts on his face.

When she'd done all she could, Karla rose and surveyed the landscape. They were high on the mountain, probably at nine thousand feet or better, with no sign of civilization as far as they could see. "Skeeter, do you have a sat phone in your duffel?"

"Yeah." He was still kind of groggy, but growing more alert by the moment. "Big green bag with the L.L.Bean logo."

"I'll find it." Toni headed back toward the plane.

"Ruth, would you mind checking out here?" Pasha asked. "Some of the gear got tossed into the snow—you can see the indentations. Would you round up what you can?"

"No problem." Ruth limped toward the nearest depression.

"How bad are they?" Pasha asked Karla in a low voice once Ruth was out of earshot.

"They need to be in a hospital, but I can't believe any type of rescue aircraft will be able to reach us any time soon. Any idea where we are?"

"Roughly. I recall seeing a few cabins along the route, but that's all. I have no idea how close we are to any of them or what they might be like." She studied the mountain they were on. "And it's a long way down to the valley. I can't imagine how we could get them down there."

"For now, anyway, we're better off staying put," Karla said, "and concentrating on keeping everyone alive until they reach us."

"Agreed. I'll start sorting through the supplies and see what we have. I'm concerned about how cold it'll get tonight. We don't have enough burnable material to keep the fire going very long. We're better off staying in the plane, I think, than in tents. We can take out the seats and make room in the back for us all, try to insulate it as well as possible, and keep a close eye on these two."

"That's a good plan," Karla said. "While you're doing that, I'll try the sat phone and get Toni to help me set my arm."

Pasha spent the next hour making the plane as snug and comfortable as possible. Toni and Ruth collected all the gear and she sorted through it, laying aside everything that would help them survive. They had three two-man tents, a sleeping bag and sleeping pad for each of them, two rafts, a good supply of food and extra clothes, and a number of survival items from Skeeter's duffel: a wool blanket, PLB, satellite phone, mirror, small butane stove with two canisters of fuel, candles, a saw, axe, and gun. They lacked firewood and kitchenware. They had only one large pot to cook and melt water in, so they'd have to improvise.

She activated the PLB and gave the satellite phone and cooking pot to Toni. "Fill this with clean, white snow, and set it by the fire. Then keep feeding it. We're going to need water. And come tell me right away if Karla manages to reach anyone."

"You got it."

Now that she knew what they had to work with, she and Ruth removed the passenger seats to make more room, then spread out one of the deflated rafts along the floor of the plane. On top of this they spread the sleeping pads and stuffing cut from the plane's seats, until they had a relatively cushioned, flat surface big enough to hold all of them lying side by side. Duffel bags filled with extra clothes would serve as their pillows.

"Not too bad," she told Ruth as they surveyed their handiwork. "We can use the other raft to block the opening once we all get in here. It's plenty big enough."

"How cold will it get?" Ruth asked.

"They were forecasting lows around freezing for the next few days. But it'll be colder than that at this elevation, especially in the wind. We'll have to try to seal every crack we can."

"When do you think someone will come for us?"

"Hard to say. I imagine all flights, even rescue missions, will stay grounded until the skies clear. We'll make do until they get here. We're very lucky to have Karla along."

She started to say they should go check on the others when the power abruptly switched on, heightening her senses and sending the familiar tension of anticipation coursing through her body. Pasha knew what it meant.

Emery had finally awakened.

CHAPTER TWENTY-EIGHT

Emery drifted from a placid dream into a nightmare of pain. Her head throbbed and she shivered. So damn cold.

"Emery, can you hear me?" Karla's voice, very near.

She opened her eyes and tried to focus. White. She lay in snow.

"Emery? Do you know where you are?"

She turned her head toward the voice, wincing at the pain. Karla hunched over her, her arm in a sling, her face marked with cuts and lacerations, and blood staining the front of her coat.

In an instant, Emery flew back to the moment of the crash. Another brush with death, and she'd beat it yet again. "Yes." She tried to move, but as soon as she tried to sit up, her head throbbed worse.

"Lie still. You took a good blow." Karla laid a hand gently on her shoulder to keep her prone. "You probably have a concussion, at the very least."

Pasha. Pasha had been next to her on the plane but wasn't here now. Emery shivered, from fear this time. "Pasha all right?"

"She's fine. Everyone survived."

"Help coming?" Her mouth and throat felt incredibly dry. She had to struggle to speak.

"Communications are down," Karla replied. "We'll keep trying, but the crash should have triggered the Emergency Locator Transmitter in the plane and Skeeter has a PLB. They'll find us, even if we don't get through, but we may have a wait. I doubt anything can fly in this ash."

"Emery!" Pasha's voice, from a distance.

She tried to turn in that direction, but the pain in her head and Karla's quick hand on her shoulder stopped her.

"Please, lie still, Emery," Karla said gently. "Pasha's coming. She'll be right here."

And a moment later, she was. Pasha knelt in front of her and placed a hand on Emery's cheek. She felt a slight shock, then a surge of healing warmth against her skin. "Welcome back. You had me worried. How you feeling?"

"Head hurts. Thirsty."

"Can she have some water?"

"A few sips," Karla replied. "Toni, could you put some from the pot into my water bottle?"

"Coming right up."

Emery couldn't see Toni, but she sounded close. Her limited range of view enabled her to see only snow, Pasha, Karla, and a portion of the plane's wing, which jutted up in the snow a few feet away.

"Careful now. Not too much, and try to move as little as possible," Karla said as Pasha put the mouth of an aluminum water bottle to her lips. The warm water helped allay her thirst.

"You really all right?" she asked Pasha.

"I'm fine, Emery. I'm worried about you, though, so no moving around, okay?"

"Whatever you say." It was easy to agree. Emery felt like a truck had run over her. In addition to her throbbing head, her whole body ached. And as her mind cleared, she realized her side felt especially tender. "My side?"

"Something punctured you," Karla said. "I think it missed your vital organs, but you lost a lot of blood. You'll be weak for a while."

Emery mulled over what they'd told her and what she remembered before the crash. "Pasha...you sensed it, didn't you?"

Pasha's eyes looked dark with worry and regret. "Yup, but I didn't know what it meant. I'm sorry. Maybe if I'd said something..."

"Don't beat yourself up," Karla said. "We're all alive, and we're going to keep everyone safe until help arrives."

Emery agreed. "What she said."

The remark made Pasha smile, though her eyes remained troubled. "What can I do to make you more comfortable?"

"I'm so cold."

"You were out here for a while in the snow before I found you. I'll build up the fire some more." Pasha rose and disappeared from her limited field of vision. Not long after, she heard the sound of wood splitting and felt a surge of warmth against the back of her neck.

"Better. Thanks."

Pasha squatted and gently rearranged the soft padding under Emery's head. "You rest. I'll fix us all something to eat. Something nice and warm to make you feel better."

"Don't be gone long."

Pasha stroked her cheek, the simple gesture warming her and making her feel safer than even the fire. "I'll be right out here with you. Just need to get the food."

Emery did feel warmer soon, but as she became more comfortable, she also became incredibly drowsy.

"Emery?"

She opened her eyes to find Pasha sitting cross-legged beside her, holding a tin can whose label read Fresh Packed Niblet Corn.

Pasha smiled when she saw Emery staring at it. "We don't have any dishes or utensils," she explained. "This is soup." She motioned to someone out of view. "We're going to help you sit up just enough to drink this. Move very slowly. We have a duffel bag for you to lean against."

Pasha supported one shoulder and someone gripped the other. She turned her head and saw Toni, but the effort triggered another burst of pain behind her eyes. She allowed them to assist her into a half-reclined position, which enabled her for the first time to get a good look at her surroundings. Toni, Ruth, and Karla had gathered around a big pot near the fire, sipping soup out of an odd assortment of containers—another tin can, a collapsible plastic cup, and the water bottle she'd drunk from.

Skeeter lay on the other side of the fire, propped up like she was, most of his body encased in a sleeping bag. His face was badly swollen and laced with cuts and abrasions, but he seemed alert as he sipped from a red plastic lid of some kind.

Beyond them all, the plane lay tilted to one side with a deep trench behind it. With the tail dented in, the nose buried in snow, and a gaping hole surrounded by twisted metal right where she'd sat, it seemed miraculous that any of them had survived, especially her.

"Here. Drink this." Pasha held the can near her lips.

"I can do it." She pulled her right hand out of the sleeping bag and took the tin. The aroma of garlic overpowered the smell of wood smoke from the fire as she sipped. Chicken soup, and not the store-bought stuff, but homemade, with thick egg noodles, corn, carrots, and peas. She welcomed the warm, fragrant liquid like a medicinal tonic. "Delicious. Thank you."

"Our meals won't be quite as elaborate as I planned," Pasha said. "The other group got a lot of the supplies, and we need to conserve what we have until we know when help is coming."

"Sounds like you guys have it all handled. Sorry I'm not in shape to help."

"Just get better. That's your assignment. How's your head?" Pasha asked.

"Hurts like hell." Emery looked up at Karla. "I have some Percocet. All right if I take some?"

"No. I'm sorry. Percocet would mask any signs of altered consciousness, and the acetaminophen in it can cause bleeding in the brain. You shouldn't have any painkillers until doctors can run tests." Karla put her mouth near Emery's ear so the others wouldn't overhear. "Do you have any medical conditions I should be aware of?"

"No. I just have the pills because sometimes old injuries come back to haunt me when I overdo it."

Karla kept her voice low. "I'm not presuming or judging anything, Emery, but I know Percocet is addictive. Please resist any urge to take some right now, no matter what the pain. Tell me if it gets unbearable. Promise?"

"You have my word."

"I won't even ask for pain pills if you let me have a cigarette," Skeeter called from the other side of the fire.

Karla stood and gave him a disapproving look. "I'd rather you didn't, Mike, for obvious reasons. The blow to your chest may have compromised your lungs, and smoking also decreases the ability of wounds to heal."

"I'm breathing okay," Skeeter said. "Yeah, I probably have a couple of broken ribs 'cause it hurts if I suck in too deep. But just a few drags, huh? Come on, I'm a big boy."

"A *few*. Against my better judgment."

Skeeter smiled like he'd just won the lottery. "Someone please get my pack for me? It's in the side pocket of my door."

Toni volunteered. "I'll go. I need another sweater, anyway. Feels like it's getting colder."

"The wind is picking up." Pasha glanced at her watch. "It's already seven. Once the rest of the fire burns down, we should get everyone into the plane and seal it as tight as we can."

Emery tugged the cuff of Pasha's jeans. "Got any more soup?"

"You bet."

Pasha picked up the pot with a makeshift towel-potholder and refilled Emery's can. After topping off everyone else's with the remaining soup, she refilled the pot with clean snow and set it back by the fire. "Make sure you all stay plenty hydrated. I'll make a big pot of herbal tea to have in the plane, if everybody agrees."

Emery would rather have coffee, but a diuretic probably wasn't the best choice given their situation and her loss of blood. "Sounds good," she replied with the others.

An hour later, all six lay shoulder to shoulder in their sleeping bags in the plane, lined up like sardines in a tin. To lie as flat as possible with the cabin's weird tilt, they rested their heads on duffel bags on the floor and propped their feet up along the left side of the plane. They had based their precise sleeping arrangement on several factors. Karla was farthest in the back so she wouldn't have anyone on the side with her broken arm. Skeeter, and then Emery, came next, so she could keep an eye on them both. As Emery hoped, Pasha slipped in beside her, then came Ruth, and finally Toni, who needed the widest portion of the plane. Unfortunately, she was nearest the hole, but Pasha had effectively sealed out the bitter wind with a raft and some duct tape from Skeeter's toolbox. And because she had the most vulnerable position, Toni used the wool blanket Skeeter carried to supplement her sleeping bag.

Under protest, Emery had convinced Karla her neck was fine and she didn't need the stiff brace. Removing it had made her a lot more comfortable. The padding beneath her insulated her pretty well from the cold metal, and Pasha had helped her change from her ripped and bloody turtleneck into fleece and a heavy sweater, so she was relatively warm despite temperatures near freezing. The hot soup and the tea they were all drinking had put everyone in an optimistic mood, although they still hadn't gotten anything on the satellite phone but static.

The situation wouldn't be so bad except for the pounding in her head, which had worsened when they moved her.

"Anything we can do to shorten our stay here?" Ruth asked.

"I've been thinking about that," Pasha replied. "I plan to walk farther up the ridge tomorrow to see if I can get a signal there. It'll also give me a different perspective so maybe I can discover a way down to the valley. Not that I'm advocating we do anything but stick with the plane. I just want to consider every option if this eruption continues and we start running out of resources. I'd like to have more wood than we have, for starters."

"Could burn the tires," Skeeter said. "Smoke's pretty toxic but they make a good signal fire. They're buried, though, aren't they?"

"Looks like it," Pasha said. "Unless they snapped off and are hidden in that big trench somewhere."

"I can look tomorrow," Toni offered. "I'd like to help some way."

Ruth chimed in. "I would, too. Not much good at bending, though, with my knee like this."

They told stories and played word games to keep themselves occupied until all but Pasha and Emery began to drift off. One by one, they retreated deep into their fluffy, mummy sleeping bags, closing the hoods around their faces until only their mouths and noses were exposed. Emery doubted anyone could overhear their conversation, but they still spoke in low whispers.

"It scared the hell out of me when I came to, saw the hole, and you gone," Pasha said.

"Probably about how I felt when I woke up and you weren't there." Emery shifted position to try to get more comfortable. They all had to lie very close together to fit into the cleared space, and it was the best way to keep warm, but she tended to move around a lot in bed and found the arrangement uncomfortably confining. "You know, you might want to reconsider spending a lot of time with me, since I seem fated to have one brush with death after another."

"I'd say just the opposite. You seem to have an inordinate amount of good luck, to keep escaping like you do. Maybe it rubbed off on us all, and that's why everyone survived."

Emery chuckled. "I guess that's one way to look at it. In other words, you're a half-full-glass kind of woman, and I'm a half-empty?"

"There are always two ways to look at things," Pasha said. "And I do usually try to stay optimistic and hope for the best, instead of worrying about the worst-case scenario."

"They do say opposites attract."

"Emery, if I felt any more attracted to you, we'd be in a lot of trouble."

Despite her raging headache, she welcomed their flirtatious banter as a pleasant distraction. "Oh? That so? What kind of trouble?"

"Give me a few hours alone with you once you've mended and I'll elaborate."

"Definite rain check, okay?" Emery shifted again, snuggling closer to Pasha. "I'm happy that seeing some of my worst scars hasn't turned you off." She'd been concerned, but Pasha had seen her tracheotomy scar and the ones on her upper torso when she'd helped her change clothes and hadn't flinched.

"Hardly," Pasha whispered. "We all have scars, Emery. Some visible, some not. Yours testify to all you've endured."

"I wouldn't have survived this one without you and Karla. I'm very grateful."

"I'm pretty sure you'd have done the same for either of us. How's your head?"

Emery rubbed her temple. "Horrible, honestly. Got a lot worse when you moved me in here. I don't know how I'll be able to sleep."

"What can I do?"

"How about you tell me a story? Something I don't know about you. And maybe you can cuddle up a little closer?"

"Come here." Pasha opened her arm and Emery inched nearer, until she lay on her good side with her head nestled into the crook of Pasha's shoulder. Pasha slowly caressed her back, and though she could barely detect her hand with all their layers, their proximity alone made her feel better. The sense of serenity and happiness that sprang from their touch and connection began to ease her headache almost immediately, as well as any pain meds might have.

"How about if I tell you about the first time I had a premonition?" Pasha whispered.

"Yes, please." Emery closed her eyes and melted into Pasha's embrace.

Pasha put her mouth next to Emery's ear. "I was six, riding in the car with my mother. She kept going on and on about something, I don't even remember what, but all of a sudden her voice began to fade. Weird, like someone had turned down the volume, you know? I could see her talking like usual, but I could barely hear her. I should have been worried, but I wasn't." Pasha's dulcet low voice soothed Emery nearly as much as her touch. "It just made my other senses more acute, and I knew instinctively I needed to pay closer attention to what I was seeing and feeling. Ahead of us a few blocks was a big intersection, and when I looked at it, I got this strange but very powerful sick feeling in my stomach. I just knew danger was there, so I hollered, 'Stop, Mommy! Stop!' She pulled over to the curb and started to ask me why I'd yelled, but I just pointed to the intersection. We both watched as a big propane truck collided with a taxi. The explosion melted everything around, and we were just out of range."

The story fascinated Emery, but their embrace and Pasha's lulling whispered tone made for a potent sleeping pill. She drifted off, cozy and content, her headache completely gone.

CHAPTER TWENTY-NINE

Next day, June 11

Pasha awoke to find Emery still nestled against her side. Everyone else was asleep as well, despite Skeeter's buzz-saw snoring and temperatures so cold she could see her breath. She didn't have a reason to get up yet. They had little to do but wait until help arrived, and it made no sense to start breakfast before everyone started moving because they needed to conserve what little fuel they had. So she lay there searching for ways to improve their situation and maximize their resources. Every now and then, however, despite her best intentions, her mind drifted to Emery and their growing connection.

She'd accepted the undeniability of their attraction days ago, and the impossibility of a long-term commitment. But not until the accident and her terror at the prospect of losing her had the depth of how much she had fallen for Emery really hit her.

The thought of Emery's departure devastated her. Pasha already couldn't imagine how she could deal with it, and once they had sex the pain of their separation would be even more acute, yet she wanted as much intimacy as possible once Emery healed and they were safe.

In that sense, she began to understand Emery's current adrenaline-rush lifestyle, her desire to walk the razor's edge. When a consuming need drove you, risks became afterthoughts.

Emery stirred.

"You awake?" Pasha whispered.

"Mmm. Sorta. I really need to pee but can't stand to get out of this sleeping bag."

"How's your headache?"

"Gone. Completely. I actually feel pretty good, a lot better than last night."

"That's wonderful. But you should rest as much as you can today."

"Exactly right." Karla's voice drifted over as she sat up. "It's a very good sign that your headache's gone, Emery, but I don't want you to move around too much."

"I can see I'm outnumbered," she replied.

The others began to rouse, so Pasha kissed Emery's forehead then gently extricated herself from their embrace to slip from her sleeping bag. "I'll start some coffee and rustle up some breakfast. Be a lot warmer for you all to stay put."

"No arguments here. I never get breakfast in bed," Ruth joked.

Pasha set up the stove on a piece of metal just outside the plane, which acted as an effective windbreak. As the water boiled for coffee, she stared at the sky. The haze seemed as thick as when they'd gone to bed, and during the hours they'd slept, the fine brown-gray dust from the plume had further muted the landscape's colors. The vivid green of the valley below had turned to a pasty olive. She tried the satellite phone again and wasn't surprised to hear only static.

The improvised raft-door that covered the opening in the plane drew back and Emery emerged, Toni right behind her.

"Me first. I'll be quick," Toni announced before ducking around the plane to their designated latrine area with a roll of toilet paper.

"I can't believe how much better I feel than last night." Emery gazed over the valley below.

The difference amazed Pasha. Emery didn't look so pale, she seemed to move around without pain, and her eyes shone, alert. "I'm so glad. But don't do anything today except come out here for pit stops. Right?"

"Yes, ma'am." Emery grinned. "Long as you keep me company as much as possible."

"I'll do my best."

After she'd served them all coffee and wild-blueberry pancakes they ate with their hands, Pasha caught Karla outside the plane when she went for her own bathroom break. "I'm going to hike up the ridge a ways and try the satellite phone again. Get a look at what's around us. I should be back within three or four hours. How's Skeeter?"

"He's holding his own, so far," Karla replied. "I'm worried about infection developing in his leg wound, though. I'd like to get him out of here before that has a chance to happen."

"Emery looks a lot better."

"Remarkably so, I'd say. But given the blow she took to the head, a subdural hematoma could definitely develop, so we need to keep her quiet until she can get to a hospital for tests."

"I'll leave you to watch them both." Pasha zipped up her heavy coat and put the hood on. Stained with Emery's blood, it painfully reminded her of the danger she still faced. "Wish me luck."

"Be careful."

Pasha set off toward the top of the ridge, carrying a six-foot length of thin metal tubing—a wing strut that had snapped off the plane. It made an effective probe to discern any hidden crevasses or overhangs in the snow. The depth of the snow and her meticulous care in testing the under layer before every step slowed her forward progress. She also had to pause to catch her breath if she exerted herself too much, and the higher she got, the more dangerous the ridge became, with sharp drop-offs on either side.

She tried the satellite phone again. Still no luck, so she pushed forward until her legs began to protest the strain of struggling against the thigh-high drifts. Resting, she stared out over the valley. She could see from here better than from the plane, but still not enough to find any reasonably safe way off the mountain. She pushed on.

Bryson emerged from her tent and stared into the cloudless sky, still hazy with ash. She doubted she might get out today but was still disappointed. She tried her satellite phone. Static.

After a breakfast of oatmeal and coffee, she spent nearly an hour clearing the ash off her plane. Still only nine a.m. She'd go crazy just sitting and waiting, so she packed her daypack with water, a couple of PowerBars, matches, the phone, flares, and a signaling mirror, and headed off toward the foothills of a nearby mountain.

The farther she got from the riverbank, the boggier the terrain became. Sodden patches of thawed permafrost that could trap an errant step as easily as quicksand surrounded uneven hummocks of fairly solid earth. She spent most of the morning reaching the base of the mountain. She'd chosen this particular peak because of its potentially scalable façade and its low height. Its steep rise, covered with scree—gravel-like rock debris that would be treacherous to climb—beat the nearby alternatives, all with sheer rock cliffs.

Gaining elevation to improve her chances of successfully making a call was worth the risk. She started climbing.

For every yard she gained, she slipped back a foot or two. Partway up the slope, she lost her footing and slid several feet on her knees. The sharp scree cut into the fabric of her pants like razor blades, shredding the material. "Damn it!" The bloody lacerations covering her knees stung like hell. She used some of her water to wash out the dust and debris, but she'd left her first-aid kit in the plane.

She rested only a couple of minutes before continuing her climb.

Four hours later, she hauled herself onto a narrow ledge about three-quarters of the way up the mountain. She could go no farther. She'd consumed her water, PowerBars, and energy reserves, and she couldn't cover the remaining distance without climbing gear. Rocky scree gave way to a sheer ice wall.

Bryson pulled out her satellite phone and tried again to reach Dita. More static. She debated the wisdom of remaining here for a while to try again. She didn't have to worry about darkness falling and obscuring her way back, and she didn't have much else to do, but as soon as she'd stopped moving, the steady breeze chilled her.

She pulled up the hood on her coat and hunkered down to wait.

❖

Bettles

Dita unplugged the coffee pot and threw a blanket over Megan, who'd finally conked out on the couch in the back after staying up all night and most of the day trying to reach Chaz. She hadn't been able to reach Bryson, Pasha, or the outside world either.

Geneva was putting on her coat when she returned to the outer office. "Time for my shift. Let me know right away if you get through, huh?"

Dita nodded. "You gonna be okay? You look plumb tuckered out."

"Gee, thanks, Mom." Geneva smiled tiredly. "I'll try to catch a nap after work, then head back over to relieve you if we haven't heard anything. You should try to rest, too."

"I will."

As thoroughly exhausted as she was, however, Dita wouldn't rest until she'd heard from all her people. She tried her satellite phone every few minutes and her computer every half hour. She'd muted the TV so she could see the instant a picture replaced the words *satellite signal lost.*

At seven p.m., Megan emerged from the back room with tousled hair and two mugs of coffee. "Bet you can use this." She handed one to Dita. "I take it you haven't heard anything or you would've waked me."

"Nothing." Dita took off her glasses and rubbed her eyes.

The bell above the door sounded and Geneva rushed in, still wearing her waitress apron under her jacket. "Tourist just got a call through on his satellite phone." She sounded out of breath. "He got cut off, but his wife in Seattle has been watching the news 'cause she's worried about him. She says they just reported that the eruption has slowed and a front is moving in tonight that'll cause a shift in the wind pattern. That's all. He couldn't get the call back, but I thought you should know. Maybe it's clearing up."

"Thanks, Geneva." Dita started to reach for the satellite phone, but Megan already held it.

"Please? I'll be fast." Megan pled with her eyes, and Dita knew how frantically she wanted to find out about Chaz, so she nodded.

"Nothing," Megan reported after three attempts to connect. She handed the phone to Dita.

She tried Skeeter's number first, encouraged by a break in the static, but heard no ringing and no response. She nearly jumped out of her skin when the phone rang a millisecond after she disconnected. "Eidson Eco-Tours. Dita."

She had to hold the phone a couple of inches from her ear because of the static but thought she heard a voice cut in and out, so she forced herself to remain patient. "Hello? Bad connection. Repeat, please."

More static, then the voice again, clearer this time. Clear enough for her to recognize Bryson and the words *forced landing, but all right* before it faded again to unintelligible noise. "Bryson? Got part of that. Where are you?"

"...valley, hundred miles north, near—" Bryson replied, before static cut off the rest.

"Bryson? Repeat." The quality of the connection was awful, but Dita didn't dare hang up to try again.

More static, then, "...Karla there?"

Dita gripped the phone harder and debated whether to tell Bryson that Karla was missing along with the rafting party. Bryson would just worry, but she couldn't lie to such a good friend. "Karla isn't here. She hitched a ride with Skeeter and Pasha to a medical run. We haven't been able to reach them. They're missing."

Amidst still more static, she made out the word *repeat,* so she recited the message two more times.

When she listened again, she thought she might have lost the connection, but finally heard the words *area? What time did*—before Bryson's voice cut out again.

Dita wasn't certain, but it sounded like she was trying to determine where the plane ditched based on the flight's departure time. And Bryson could best calculate that. She knew the route, she knew the Cessna, and she'd been in roughly the same area when the plume forced all aircraft from the sky. "They left at ten thirty," she replied. No response, only more static. "Did you hear me, Bryson? They left here at ten thirty yesterday morning."

She had no idea whether Bryson heard her. The line went dead. She tried to get it back several times, but came up empty. She had the same result trying to reach Chaz, Skeeter, or any of the other Eidson Eco-Tours offices.

"At least we know Bryson's safe," Megan said. "The ash probably isn't too bad up there, then, right?"

"Apparently bad enough to keep Bryson grounded," Dita replied. "But maybe Skeeter set down okay, too." She walked over to the window and stared at the sky. The haze seemed to have cleared somewhat, but she couldn't tell with the sun so low in the sky. Could be wishful thinking. "At least Bryson knows what's going on and is closer to them than we are. If the ash keeps us from getting a fix on their location through their PLB or the plane's emergency transmitter, she's our best option for getting to them."

Chapter Thirty

"What time is it now?" Emery's watch had broken in the crash, and she hated to have to keep asking the others for updates. According to Karla, Pasha had expected to be gone three or four hours, but lunch, such as it was, had come and gone. Still no sign of her.

"Half past three," Toni said. "She left more than six hours ago. Shouldn't one of us go after her? I'm willing."

"No," Karla replied. "Not yet. She knows what she's doing, and she'd kill me if I let you put yourself in danger. If she's not back by five, we'll talk about it."

"I'm the only one who can go, Karla," Toni said. "And you know it. You can't, with your broken arm and having to see to Skeeter and Emery, and Ruth wouldn't get very far with her swollen knee. Besides, it's a lot easier for me to plow through this stuff than you shorties."

Karla smiled. "If we ever organize a debating team, I'll make you captain, Toni. You make a compelling argument. But the answer is still no. For now." She had hunched over Skeeter, and her smile faded as she unwrapped the dressing on his leg to look at his wound. "You can help me over here, however. Will you bring the first-aid kit?"

"Look bad?" Skeeter asked.

"I'm not crazy about how you're healing." When Toni handed Karla the kit, she fished through it for a thermometer and put it beneath Skeeter's tongue. "Could be early signs of infection, which isn't unexpected. I want to see if you have a fever."

"And if I do?"

"I'll start you on antibiotics, though I'd rather not give you anything with your head wounds. Are you allergic to anything?"

"No."

"Listen! Hear that?" Ruth asked.

Everyone became very still. Then Emery heard it, too. A very distant *Hey! Anybody home?* Pasha. Her relief almost made her dizzy.

Toni swept back the makeshift door flap and peered out. "I see her," she told the others. "She looks okay." Then, louder, she called, "Hey, Pasha! You had us worried sick."

A couple of minutes later, Pasha came in, shaking loose snow from her coat. "So you all missed me, did you?"

Though she tried to appear cheerful, Emery could see by the way she moved that Pasha was near collapse and more worried than she let on. "Sit." Emery patted Pasha's sleeping bag. "You've got to be exhausted."

"Just for a minute and then I'll start dinner. You all must be starving. I'm sorry I was gone so long." Pasha sat beside Emery and shed her hat, gloves, and boots, then replaced her wet wool socks with dry ones.

"We had granola bars and dried fruit," Emery told her. "We managed fine."

"I can cook dinner," Ruth said, "if you tell me what you planned to fix and show me how to use the stove."

"Not necessary, Ruth, but thanks." Pasha looked around at them. "I wish I had better news, but I couldn't get a signal. And I didn't see any sign of civilization from up there, or a good way to get off this mountain."

No one said anything for a few seconds.

"I don't want you to be discouraged," Pasha said, staring out at the somber faces. "I'll go the other way along this ridge tomorrow and try again. Besides, if you know anything about the weather up here, you know it changes all the time. When the wind shifts direction they can send someone for us. I intend to work on making us more visible from the air tomorrow as well."

"You're the resident encyclopedia, Toni," Ruth said. "What do you know about Alaskan volcanoes?"

"Hmm. Well, let's see. Alaska has more than ten percent of all the world's volcanoes. And the largest eruption of the twentieth century happened here, at Novarupta, in 1912. Way, way bigger than that eruption in Iceland a couple years ago that shut down air traffic all over."

"I had a ticket to London the day that happened," Emery said. "It took ten days before I could fly."

"Anybody know how long eruptions usually last?" Ruth asked.

"Anywhere from a few hours to years. Kilauea in Hawaii has been active for twenty-five years, at least," Toni said. "The average, unfortunately, lasts about seven weeks. But like Pasha said, the weather and wind direction change up here all the time. I bet we're out of here pretty quick."

"Did you say seven *weeks*?" Karla asked. Emery saw her glance first at Skeeter, then at her, worry in her eyes.

Emery had felt much better than expected this morning, but a couple of hours ago, her headache had begun to creep back. And she'd glimpsed Skeeter's leg when Karla checked it. The angry red wound didn't look good.

Toni turned to Pasha. "How long will our food last?"

"We can stretch it to three weeks, maybe four," Pasha said. "I'm more concerned about fuel. We need to melt snow for water, and we have only two small canisters of butane and a little more wood. That's one reason I'm scouting. If I can find a way down to the tree line, at least I can bring back more fuel if we're stranded here very long."

"Then I suggest we not cook tonight," Karla said. "We still have enough water left from this morning, and we need to eat the fresh stuff."

"Probably wise," Pasha said. "How does everybody feel about cheese sandwiches?"

No one complained about the simple fare. In fact, as in everything they'd faced so far, the group remained supportive of Pasha and Karla's decisions. And they all put on brave and optimistic fronts, though everyone had to be thinking about a seven-week eruption. How fortunate to be stuck with such fine, decent individuals.

By eight p.m., they'd made their pit stops and had snuggled back into their sardine-can sleeping arrangement. Toni's ability to recall so much of what she'd ever read impressed them so much they played a few rounds of a new game they created, called "inane but fascinating trivia I know," which successfully lightened the mood.

Ruth: "A bay scallop has dozens of eyes and they're all blue."

Skeeter: "Turtles can breathe through their asses."

Karla: "The words *listen* and *silent* have the same letters, and so do *Santa* and *Satan*."

Toni: "Virginia Woolf wrote her books standing up."

Pasha: "For four years, the U.S. had a state called Franklin, after Benjamin Franklin. It was never admitted to the union and was later incorporated into Tennessee and North Carolina."

Emery: "In Spanish, the word *esposa* means both *wives* and *handcuffs*."

They came up with enough trivia to stay amused for a couple of hours. Then, as before, Emery and Pasha stayed awake after all the others drifted off.

"Want to curl up next to me again?" Pasha whispered. She opened her arm invitingly, and Emery quickly accepted, nestling her head once more into the crook of Pasha's shoulder.

Emery's now-familiar sense of euphoria from their touching enveloped her once again. Her lips mere inches from Pasha's ear, she whispered, "I can't believe I woke up in this same position this morning. Usually I thrash around all night and end up on the other side of the bed with the sheets tangled around me."

"Must have been pretty tired, then."

"I guess. This is nice." Her sexual liaisons, even with Lisa, had rarely included cuddling. She often didn't even spend the night when she hooked up with a stranger. When women tried to fall asleep in her arms or spoon with her, she felt confined and restless. But she would very much miss curling up like this beside Pasha.

"Very nice," Pasha said. "How are you feeling, by the way?"

"I woke up feeling great, but my headache came back this afternoon. Not as bad as yesterday, though."

"And your side?"

"Tender. This cold isn't doing my aching joints any favors, either. I wish I could take some of my pain meds."

"As soon as we get you to a hospital for some tests," Pasha said, "I'm sure they'll be able to give you something to make you more comfortable."

"Where's the nearest hospital?"

"Fairbanks, I'm afraid." Pasha stroked Emery's back. She turned her head slightly and said softly into Emery's ear, "I hope they don't keep you long. I want to be alone with you."

"Me, too." Although surely everyone was asleep and deep in their sleeping bags, they spoke in the barest of whispers, especially when discussing anything personal. The more personal the message, in fact, the more intimate the delivery. Both she and Pasha would put their lips beside the other's ear and almost mouth the words. Pasha's soft exhalations against her skin had begun to drive her a little crazy, despite her headache. "You can probably guess how I feel about hospitals, and I don't want anything to interfere with the rest of my trips. I wonder if this volcano will disrupt more of them."

"Just have to wait and see, I guess. What will you do if the eruption continues and Dita cancels the trips? Leave Alaska and head to your next destination?"

Leave Alaska? Emery supposed she should have considered what she would do, but she hadn't even thought about it until Pasha brought it up. She'd barely arrived and only gotten a taste of all she'd planned to do here. How disappointing if she had to miss the rafting, backpacking, fly-fishing, kayaking, and high-glacier dogsledding adventures she'd signed up for, not to mention more private charters with Bryson.

But she'd most regret losing her time with Pasha. The shift in her priorities startled her. She had focused solely on her far-flung itinerary the last couple of years. It had motivated her to push far beyond what the doctors predicted she was capable of, and provided the impetus for her every decision and choice in the last several months. In short, her journey had become her entire reason to live. But at least for now, no adventure, monument, or exotic locale could begin to compete with Pasha.

"Emery? Did you fall asleep?"

"No. Just thinking. I'm not sure what I'll do. I hope it won't come to that because I'm not ready to leave."

Pasha hugged her closer. "I'm glad. You know, this whole experience, and the uncertainty it's cast on the future, has only made me more aware how precious every moment I can spend with you is."

"I feel the same, Pasha."

"Hoped you'd say that. How about a real date, then, once we're out of here and you're well? I can cook us a nice dinner in my apartment. Candles. Wine. Soft music."

"And then?"

"And then…" Pasha whispered seductively into her ear, "I intend to exhaust you so thoroughly and completely it may take you days to recover."

Emery chuckled. "Well, you've certainly given me something much nicer to think about than our current predicament. But it's cruel of you, too, to put those images into my head when we can't do anything about them."

"Only fair we suffer together. I've had those images in my head almost from the minute you got here."

Bryson forced herself not to hurry too much as she descended the scree slope and focused on returning safely to her tent. She could almost ski down the slope on her boots, but she risked accelerating out of control. Large rocks sticking up from the scree could kill her if she fell headfirst.

The news that Karla was aboard the missing Cessna had turned her boring wait into a nightmare. Her world revolved around Karla, and if anything happened...

She lost her footing and slid thirty feet, pinwheeling her arms and grabbing at the scree to slow herself. By the time she stopped, her hands and ass were as badly abraded as her knees, and she had no water left to rinse out the sharp, gritty material that made them sting like someone had poured salt into them.

Traversing the rest of the scree field and negotiating her way back through the swampy hummocks took another two-and-a-half hours. She didn't arrive at her riverside campsite until after midnight, her mouth so dry she could barely swallow. She gulped the second water bottle she'd left in the plane and leaned against the Cub to study the sky.

As much as Bryson itched to search for the Cessna, it would be suicidal to try to take off with so much particulate material in the air, even if her engine did start. She needed to eat, replenish her water, catch a few hours' sleep, and hope conditions improved enough to start early in the morning.

She stripped off her torn jeans at the river and washed as much of the scree as possible from her abrasions, then hurriedly applied antibiotic ointment and pulled on a clean pair of sweats. Shaking from the cold, she built a small fire to warm herself and boil some river water.

Once she'd refilled both bottles, she dumped dried beans and rice into the rest of the water in the pot and ate the concoction in the Cub. She hadn't seen any grizzlies, but she kept food away from her tent and washed the pot a good distance downstream.

She crawled into her sleeping bag at almost two a.m. Thoroughly spent, she worried too much about Karla to get any beneficial sleep.

CHAPTER THIRTY-ONE

Next day, June 12

Pasha turned off the butane to the stove after deciding the oatmeal was palatable. She carried the pot back into the plane, where the rest still cozily snuggled into their sleeping bags drinking hot herbal tea.

"What's it look like out there?" Toni asked. The frost-crusted plane windows made it impossible to see the status of the ashfall.

"Seems clearer than yesterday, but I still couldn't reach anyone on the sat phone." Pasha served them their breakfast, topping off the barely cooked oatmeal with dried fruit, brown sugar, and a splash of soy milk. "Hey, I meant to tell you, great job finding one of the tires yesterday. And pretty nifty job making these." She held up one of the six wooden spoons Toni had carved with her jackknife from a slat off a food crate.

"Wish I could do more," Toni replied.

"I can use your help after breakfast. If we can find a way to tap enough fuel from the tank to ignite the tire, it'll make a good signal fire. We can also take a couple of our tents and lay them over the top of the fuselage. The orange will be a lot easier to spot from the air than what we've got now."

"Sounds like a plan."

"How are you doing this morning?" Pasha asked Skeeter as she handed him his portion.

"Jonesing for a cig, but hanging in there."

Karla laid her hand on his forehead. "I think your fever's up. I want to get a look at your leg when you're done eating. Ruth, you up to helping me?"

"Sure. Blood doesn't bother me. My kids were always getting banged up riding their bikes or skateboards and climbing trees."

"I feel top notch this morning," Emery said. "Sure I can't do something?"

"Yes. Rest," Karla said. "No matter how you feel, you have to stay prone as much as possible."

Emery gave her a thumbs-up but didn't look too happy about it. Pasha imagined after spending so many months confined to a hospital bed, she found it more difficult than most to remain inactive very long. But thankfully Emery had awakened without a headache and her puncture wound showed no sign of infection.

She and Toni spread the tents over the top of the plane and secured them with bits of wire and duct tape, which took a good hour and a half. Then they placed the tire on a piece of metal away from the plane and managed to siphon enough aviation fuel into one of the bear-proof containers to set the rubber afire if they heard an approaching aircraft.

Emery emerged for a bathroom break as they finished.

"I'm going to take off a layer or two," Toni said before heading back inside. "All this work has heated me up."

Emery and Pasha stood side by side, gazing out over the valley.

"You know, I know we're in this dire predicament, but I still appreciate this view. I just can't get over how *big* everything is here," Emery remarked. "And how primitive. Unchanged for thousands of years. I almost expect to see a mastodon or saber-toothed tiger."

"On one of Chaz's trips a client found a snail fossil more than three-hundred-million-years old."

"Can you keep 'em?" Emery asked.

"Plants and invertebrate fossils, yes, if you collect them on public lands. But, by law, you're supposed to leave any vertebrate fossils or native artifacts where they lie unless you have a special permit. The North Slope is the best place to go fossil hunting. Maybe you can get Bryson to take you up there."

"That'd be way cool."

"I'm glad you're feeling better."

"I know this will sound kind of crazy," Emery said, turning to face her. "But I'm really beginning to think that your...special abilities are responsible. It's not a coincidence that two nights in a row, my raging headache begins to subside as soon as I cuddle up next to you and only comes back when we're separated for hours. The sense of happiness and calm I get from your touch apparently has healing qualities."

"For real?"

Emery nodded. "Even back in Bettles, my old injuries bothered me a lot less if we were in close contact."

"I certainly hope you're right," Pasha said. "I wouldn't mind that at all." She caressed Emery's cheek. "You should have several doses a day."

Emery grinned. "I won't mind filling that prescription."

"Regardless of how you're feeling, you shouldn't stay out here too long. And I should get going if I plan to explore the other side of the ridge and be back in time for dinner." Pasha almost laughed out loud at Emery's childish pout of disappointment. "Scoot. Do your business, and get back inside. I mean it. Or no cuddling for you tonight."

"Although I'm pretty sure that's an empty threat, I won't argue. The sooner you get going, the sooner you get back."

Pasha retrieved her long probing pole and started away from the plane, but she hadn't made it twenty feet before Karla's voice stopped her. "Hey, wait a sec!"

"What's up?"

"Skeeter remembered he had a map of the area, and Toni found it under the snow in the cockpit. Thought it might help you figure out where we are." Karla handed her the topographic chart, wet but still legible.

Pasha tucked it into her coat pocket. "Thanks."

"The infection in Skeeter's leg is worse, despite the antibiotics," Karla said, "and his fever's up to a hundred and one. I hope to hell we can get out of here soon."

"You and me both. Wish me luck."

"Be careful. And Pash? You're doing a great job keeping it all together and looking out for us. Dita will be very proud."

Pasha set off down the ridge. Her still-fatigued muscles and the need to test the integrity of the snow every few feet made forward progress excruciatingly slow. Every half hour or so she stopped to rest and try the satellite phone.

When she came to a sharp downward slope, she hesitated. The snowfield here radically differed from the rest of the vast area she'd explored. An avalanche had collapsed the overhang on the left side of the ridge, exposing clear rock. It would be extremely dangerous to venture any farther.

Pasha got out Skeeter's map and tried to match the geographical features she could see with the symbols and colored lines of elevation. Finally, she spotted the area where everything seemed to fit. If she was right, she would find a cabin in this valley about a mile farther north, and the contour lines showed her the best possible way to get there.

If she could get past this dangerous area, she'd come to what looked to be the gentlest slope to the valley. She might not be able to negotiate a path all the way down, but it was the best possibility she'd seen so far.

She debated whether to risk going forward or return to the plane, and decided not to leave the others for such a risky and potentially futile endeavor.

Before she headed back, she once more dialed the office number. Encouraged by intermittent breaks in the static, she kept trying but could never make a connection.

Chaz stared dejectedly at the chaos of plastic wrappers and pieces of foil at the tree's base. Something had eaten the food. She'd done her best to hang it out of reach, but they had only thin nylon rope and the short growing season here stunted the spruce trees. More likely a black bear than a grizzly, because they climbed better.

And at least it hadn't molested their campsite—no one had heard a thing. But the nocturnal visitor had devoured everything she hadn't been able to fit into their two bear-proof containers, which amounted to the bulk of their supplies.

They should keep a fire going all night in case the bear decided to come back, but she'd leave the wood gathering to the clients, who so far had endured their predicament with a minimum of complaint. She'd have her plate full setting snares in the woods and trying to catch some fish.

Megan must be worried sick by now.

She hadn't had any luck reaching Dita or anyone else. But the wind, coming from the north this morning, seemed to help dissipate the ash cloud, at least at lower altitudes. The first encouraging development since they'd arrived.

Bryson slept longer than she'd meant to, but when she awoke she found the sky had cleared enough, at least at the lower elevations, to risk getting back into the air. She hurriedly packed her stuff and removed her engine covering.

She held her breath as she hit the ignition switch. When the Super Cub's engine roared to life, Bryson cheered aloud and thumped the windshield with her fist. "That's it, baby. Nice and smooth."

The cowling and spinner covers had done their job. The propeller purred like a kitten on steroids. She went through her preflight checklist much quicker than normal and was in the air a short time later, her map spread out on the co-pilot's seat. *Hang on, Karla. I'm coming.*

Fortunately she had enough fuel to be out for a while, after topping off her tanks from three ten-gallon containers she carried when on long runs.

She flew as low as she dared, nearly clipping the treetops, because she could see the haze now only in the upper elevations, above five thousand feet or so. She had to take a circuitous route to where she thought the plane might have ditched, following river valleys and avoiding the higher mountain passes where she might encounter the ash.

When she finally bisected Skeeter's route, her fuel gauge still read more than half full and she had a couple of hours of search time before she'd have to head back to Bettles. She tried her radio for the umpteenth time. "A2024B Piper to BTT. Anyone there? Over." She listened. Nothing. "Repeat, A2024B Piper to BTT. Come in, BTT. Over." She tried several other frequencies but couldn't reach Bettles or anyone else.

Slowing her speed, she scanned the wide river valley a thousand feet below, searching for the green-and-white Cessna. *Where are you, Karla?* Mile after mile of forest and swamp passed by, with no sign that any human being had ever been this way. *Please, dear God, let her be all right. Show me where she is.*

Her fuel gauge kept dropping as she neared the place where the rafting trip should have commenced. Not seeing the plane almost encouraged her; perhaps Skeeter had arrived safely after all.

Finally, in the distance, she spotted the campsite, and her heart fell when she saw no plane there and only three tents. As she neared, two women sitting by the fire jumped up and began waving frantically in her direction. Four others came out of the tents and did the same. She wagged her wing tips to acknowledge that she'd seen them, then banked left for the best approach to the gravel-bar runway. As she set down, Chaz bolted out of the woods and ran to meet her.

"Am I glad to see you," Chaz yelled as the propeller died and Bryson stepped from the cockpit. They embraced as the six clients headed their way. "We haven't been able to get through to anyone on the satellite phone. What the hell's going on?"

"I take it you haven't heard from the second flight?" Bryson asked.

"No. They never got here. I was hoping they didn't take off."

Bryson shook her head. "I talked to Dita briefly last night. Had to ditch about a hundred miles from here. The Cessna's missing and no one's heard from them. I followed the route but didn't spot the plane." Struggling to keep her voice from breaking, she added, "Karla's on board."

Chaz gripped her shoulder. "Jesus, Bryson."

"If anything's happened to her—"

"Don't go there. Skeeter's a good pilot. Maybe he just veered off the planned route for some reason. Tried to go around the ash."

"Maybe. Look, I've got to get back up there," she said in a low voice as the six clients neared. "Everyone here okay?"

"We lost most of our food to a bear last night, but we're fine otherwise."

"Hey! When is help coming?" one of the clients asked.

"I'm not sure," Bryson told her. "I'm searching for the rest of your party. I wish I could take one or two of you out, but I need to save what little room I have in case someone's injured. I'll get back to Bettles later today and inform them of your situation. Wind's changed, and the ash seems to be confined to the higher elevations, so some flights may already be in the air. Just sit tight." She turned to Chaz. "Wish I could help you out on the food, but I'm just about tapped out. I only have my emergency supplies."

"I'll make do. Go." Chaz gave her another hug and led the clients away from the plane. "Good luck, and Godspeed," she shouted as Bryson restarted the engine.

Bryson lifted off and retraced her path, heading back toward Bettles but at a higher elevation. It was risky to flirt so close to the ash plume, but she had to eliminate all possibilities. If Skeeter hadn't been able to land safely in the valley, the plane might be somewhere in the mountains.

She tried not to picture the wreckage of her father's plane, but the image was as firmly implanted in her mind as when she'd spotted it from this same cockpit seven years earlier. *Not again, God. Please. Not again.*

CHAPTER THIRTY-TWO

Bettles

"The ash plume from the Mount Wrangell eruption has created havoc over the south-central part of the state, grounding all air traffic from Cook Inlet to Glacier Bay, and reaching as far north as Denali National Park," the newscaster reported. "That's bad news for residents of Anchorage, who are being advised to remain indoors with their windows closed. Sam Feeney filed this report a short time ago."

Video of empty streets in downtown Anchorage, barely visible through the thick fog of ash, appeared on the screen as a male voice detailed the school closings, grocery-store panic buying, flight cancellations, and other repercussions of the change in the wind direction. The reporter, who looked barely out of his teens, delivered the last portion of his story from beneath a hooded jacket covered with ash. "Officials within the Alaska Rescue Coordination Center here at Fort Richardson are spearheading efforts to locate a dozen small aircraft and numerous individuals who have been missing in the sparsely populated interior and northern regions since the eruption—the first areas impacted by the ash. The AKRCC is tracking several PLBs—Personal Locator Beacons—activated in the backcountry, along with two aircraft Emergency Locator Transmitters, which emit signals automatically if a plane crashes. Unfortunately, the ash interfered with many of those signals, making it difficult to calculate their exact positions. And most of the state's rescue resources are based in Anchorage, so the coast guard and other entities have had to call upon their auxiliary stations in the north for help."

Dita turned down the volume when the next report appeared, a feature story about residents of Anchorage coping with the ash. She, Megan, and Geneva hadn't moved from their chairs since the TV signal had reappeared in the outer office an hour earlier, though Dita and Megan kept passing the phone between them trying to reestablish contact with the rafting parties and Bryson. "I wish we knew if one of the two plane signals is from the Cessna."

Calls were still sporadic, but improving. She'd managed to get through to the AKRCC to report that she had three missing parties: two adventure groups and a charter pilot, all of whom had PLBs. She gave them Chaz's location and details of Skeeter and Bryson's flight plans, and asked them to keep her informed of developments. They told her fifteen PLBs had been activated since the eruption, and two small planes had apparently crashed, triggering their emergency transmitters. They planned to dispatch helicopters and search planes from the North Slope Borough.

Dita had then contacted three seasoned bush pilots in her Kotzebue and Winterwolf offices, well outside the danger zone, and asked them to get in the air to help search. She couldn't do much else now except wait and keep trying to establish contact with her parties in the backcountry.

"Why don't you try to get some rest," Megan said. "You've hardly slept. I'll keep trying and let you know immediately if I hear anything."

"I'm staying, too," Geneva said. "Grizz gave me the day off. So no arguments. We've got it covered."

Exhausted, Dita didn't protest. "I'll lie down in the back if you swear not to let me sleep more than an hour or so. I want to follow up with the other offices and see if they've found anything."

"Promise." Megan took the phone from her and shoved her gently toward the lounge.

Dita collapsed on the couch, and exhaustion finally won the battle with worry. She fell asleep almost at once.

❖

Bryson leveled off at five thousand feet, just below the visible layer of ash, keenly alert to any minor fluctuation in her single-prop engine's familiar cadence. She flew down the middle of the river valley at her lowest cruising speed, scanning the mountains' cliff faces. Any time she spotted anything slightly suspicious, she circled the area and flew closer, until she knew it couldn't be the Cessna. Every now and then, she tried to raise someone on the radio but still couldn't make contact.

Karla had to be all right. They had just holed up somewhere and she had to find them. A sudden change in the weather had stranded her more times than she could count, and, like all bush pilots, she took it in stride. But Karla already hated flying in small planes. Though part of her job, she'd never gotten used to it and felt only reasonably comfortable when Bryson piloted. She'd probably never want to set foot in one again.

Bryson focused on the mountains on either side, peering at every shadow or color change on the steep façades. Every now and then, she looked up and assessed the ash plume. This time she saw a stream of black within the haze. *Smoke.* Her heartbeat accelerated along with the whirr of the prop as she hit the throttle, heading toward the source.

Above her, probably around the nine-thousand-foot level, she reckoned, on the ridge of a mountain a half mile ahead. She inched higher. Six thousand feet. Seven. Eight. *Did the engine sound different?* Bryson knew every nuance in its tone and could detect the prop labor slightly.

Peering up through the haze, she spotted four tiny figures at the smoke's source, which must be from a burning tire. One of them held up a large piece of orange fabric and the rest waved their arms and jumped up and down. Still too far away to recognize, the one with the fabric had to be Toni because of the height difference.

She clutched the controls tighter, ignoring her painfully lacerated palms, as she crept up to eight-thousand, five-hundred feet. The engine unmistakably labored now, but she had to know if Karla was there. She grappled for her binoculars and nearly wept with joy when she saw her, smiling and waving. With one arm, Bryson realized, her other in a sling. Toni stood next to her, then Emery and Ruth. She quickly swept the area around them with her binoculars and saw the tail of the plane, sticking up at an angle, the rest obscured because she flew below it. What about Pasha and Skeeter?

The plane had plowed nose-first into the ridge, and Pasha would probably have taken the co-pilot's seat. Were they both dead? Injured?

Bryson waggled her wing tips to acknowledge she'd seen them, then circled to make another pass. The engine sounded rough, but still functioned all right. As she straightened, she tried to raise them on her Eidson-issued satellite phone. Dita had given every pilot and lead guide one and programmed everyone's numbers on speed dial.

She hit the button for Skeeter's number and, after several seconds' delay, heard ringing. She expected one of the four, maybe Karla, even, to answer, so was shocked when Pasha picked up.

"Bryson! Thank God!"

"I don't see you. Are you hurt?"

"I'm fine. I'm way down the ridge from the plane, to the south. I can see you. I'm heading back."

"Where's Skeeter?"

"In the plane. He has a bad leg infection. We need to evacuate him right away."

"Lot of ash up here. Not sure if I land whether I'll be able to take off again. Engine's running rough."

"Nowhere for you to land, anyway," Pasha said. "We need a helicopter."

"Is Karla all right? Looks like she has a broken arm."

"She does, but she's okay. Taking good care of the rest of us."

"Gotta head back, my fuel's low. I'll get a chopper here soon. And Pash?"

"Yup?"

"Tell Karla I love her, will you?"

"You bet, Bryson. Get home safe. We're relying on you."

She waggled her wings at the foursome one more time before descending to a safer altitude. The engine still had a worrisome knock but seemed marginally better. She pushed the throttle forward and headed to Bettles at top speed.

❖

Pasha raced back to the plane and arrived not long after Bryson's call to find Toni and Ruth still celebrating upwind of the still-burning tire.

"Did you see the plane?" Toni hugged Pasha fiercely. "She saw us! That was Bryson!"

"I know." Pasha grinned. "We talked on the satellite phone. She's going back to Bettles to arrange for a helicopter to come get us."

"Do you know when?" Ruth asked.

"No. It may not be right away—it's still dangerous to fly this high, apparently. But she knows Skeeter needs to be evacuated and exactly where we are." She patted Toni on the back. "Great job getting the fire going."

"We were so discouraged," Toni said. "We heard the plane when it came through going north and ran out here, but she had already passed, flying really low. By the time I got it going good, she'd disappeared. We'd given up hope and thought we'd wasted the tire. Thank God she tried again."

"I'm going in to tell the others and then start dinner. We can safely use some of our fuel for a really special meal. We've got good reason to celebrate."

Emery, Karla, and Skeeter sat laughing about something when she pulled back the flap and joined them.

"You're back!" Emery's relief was obvious.

"I knew if anybody found us, it'd be Bryson." Karla jumped up and hugged Pasha with her good arm.

Pasha teased her. "I have a message from her, as a matter of fact."

"You do? You talked to her?"

"She raised me on the sat phone. She's headed back to Bettles to arrange for a helicopter. It may be a while, because of the ash, but she'll do whatever it takes soon because of Skeeter." Pasha leaned closer to Karla and added in a low voice, "She wanted me to tell you she loves you."

Karla smiled broadly as a faint flush of pink colored her cheeks. "Thanks. I needed that."

Pasha headed toward the food supplies and began to sort through them. "Hope you're hungry. I'm going to whip up a feast."

They devoured her pasta with enthusiasm, buoyed to an almost giddy fever. They talked about the first things they would do when they returned and made pacts to keep in touch. Toni and Ruth, undeterred, both said they'd be back one day to complete their aborted rafting trip.

Pasha went outside to try the satellite phone again after dinner but couldn't reach Dita. Ready to go back in, she felt the power tell her Emery was headed her way, so she stayed there, looking out over the valley.

"Great dinner." Emery held out her hand, and Pasha took it.

"Thanks." At nearly nine p.m. the sun was low in the horizon, casting the landscape with the golden hue found only in the land of the midnight sun. "Doesn't look like anyone's coming today. Can you stand another night here?"

"Next to you? I'll suffer through it," Emery said. "Although I'd much rather be back in Bettles, taking you up on that dinner-candle-music-and-more scenario."

"That's for when a doctor pronounces you completely well, Emery."

"I'm fine."

Pasha knew better. She'd learned how to read the nuances of Emery's expressions and could tell something was wrong. She glared at her with open skepticism.

"All right, so I have a bit of a headache again," Emery admitted. "And I'm a bit achy. But I'd bet you good money I'll feel right as rain tomorrow after another night next to you."

"I hope so. We'll see," Pasha said.

Once they'd all made their requisite bathroom visits and climbed back into the plane, Pasha sealed the entrance with duct tape for what she hoped was the last time and crawled into her sleeping bag beside Emery. In high spirits, no one wanted to turn in early tonight.

Pasha actually fell asleep before any of them, succumbing to her need for rest. She awoke briefly much later, when Emery roused her enough to nestle protectively against her shoulder.

As she drifted off again, lulled by Emery's soft breath against her neck, she tried to memorize the way their bodies fit so perfectly. From now on, she'd loathe sleeping alone.

CHAPTER THIRTY-THREE

Bryson had never been so relieved to see the familiar runway strip at Bettles. Her engine had failed twice on the journey back. She'd managed to restart the Cub both times but had been flying so low because of the ash she'd almost crashed, too. She'd have to completely overhaul the engine before she'd dare venture up again.

She got clearance to land and set down, parked the Cub beside the hangar, and ran to the Eidson Eco-Tours office, bursting through the door to find Dita and Megan hunched over the computer.

"Bryson!" Dita rushed over and hugged her, with Megan close behind.

"I found them," Bryson said. "Everyone's okay in both parties, but the Cessna crashed—high up, on a snowy ridge—and Skeeter needs to be evacuated right away."

"What about Chaz?" Megan asked anxiously.

Bryson nodded. "Chaz is fine. I stopped there first. A bear got most of their food, but they're okay for now. Found the plane quite a ways south of there but couldn't get up to it because of the ash, and couldn't land anyway. Reached Pasha on the sat phone, and she told me Skeeter has a leg wound with a bad infection. Karla has a broken arm. But they're all alive and hanging in there."

"Thank the Lord." Dita unfolded a topographic map of the area. "I've been in touch with the AKRCC. Rescue flights out of

Anchorage are grounded, so they're using helicopters from the north and west. Where exactly did you find them?"

Bryson studied the map. "Here." She pointed. "At about nine thousand feet. The ash extends down to about eight thousand but seemed to be clearing."

Dita immediately got on the phone and updated the rescue center. When she hung up, she told them, "They think they can get a chopper there in the morning, provided the fallout has cleared enough. May be another couple of days before they get to Chaz's crew."

"If you can locate a plane for me, I can go get them," Bryson said.

"I've got three pilots in the air from our other offices," Dita told her. "One's in a seven-passenger Beaver. I'll try to raise him."

After several tries, Dita got through and told the pilot to immediately divert to Bettles. "John's good," she said after she hung up, "but I'd rather send you, since you're so much more familiar with the area."

"What'd you do to your hands?" Megan asked, apparently noticing the abrasions on her palms when she stripped off her jacket.

"Oh, right." Bryson had nearly forgotten about her injuries. "Got a little banged up on a scree field."

"John won't be here for a couple of hours," Dita said. "Why don't you run over to the clinic in Evansville and have someone take care of that?"

"Probably wise." Bryson knew how quickly infections could develop, and she hadn't been able to clean her wounds in the river very well. "Be back in a while. I've got my phone. Call me if anything new develops."

"Will do." Dita hugged her. "I'm so proud of you for finding them, Bryson. I thought I'd lose my mind."

"You and me both," Megan said.

Bryson shrugged off the praise. "When you told me Karla was on the plane, I almost had a heart attack. I don't know what I'd do if anything happened to her. She's everything to me."

❖

Next day, June 13

"Shouldn't be long now." Pasha marveled at how much the skies had cleared overnight. A steady wind had blown away the haze, and though they still couldn't raise anyone on the satellite phone, Bryson would deliver on her promise to get a helicopter to them at the earliest opportunity.

She and Emery kept watch, ready to light their signal fire as soon as they detected an approaching aircraft. Because of the acoustics in the high mountains, they could usually hear the low buzz of a prop long before a plane or helicopter appeared.

This fire wouldn't be as visible as their previous one, or as long-lasting. They'd stacked up everything that could possibly burn, but it didn't amount to much and wouldn't produce the thick black smoke the tire had. Her signal mirror would provide backup to alert rescuers to their exact position.

The others were all in the plane, packing their necessities and readying to leave. Pasha had told them they'd likely have to leave their duffels and most of the gear behind to fit in the same chopper. No one complained, not that she'd expected any resistance. She felt lucky to have been stranded with such down-to-earth, brave individuals. All of them said they were just happy to be getting out of there.

"I hope we don't overload the chopper after that breakfast," Emery said. "I think you should get a cooking medal for coming up with that one."

"Glad you liked it." When she'd seen the familiar azure-blue skies, Pasha decided to use whatever food and fuel she wanted, since they couldn't take any non-essential items anyway. She had treated them to coffee and a savory one-pot hash comprised of potatoes, onions, powdered eggs, reindeer sausage, cheddar cheese, and herbs—an improvised concoction that drew rave reviews.

Pasha couldn't remember feeling so many conflicting emotions: joy and relief that they'd probably leave today, but sadness that she and Emery would have to separate, with a very uncertain future. Who knew how long Emery might be hospitalized and what the status of their future trips might be?

She turned to study Emery's face in profile—cheeks pink from the cold, dark hair blown back by the wind. Even with her cuts and bruises, she was striking. "You are so incredibly beautiful."

Emery glanced her way, seeming surprised. "Why, thank you, though I feel anything but, since I've never needed a shower more. What brought that on?"

Pasha gripped the front of Emery's jacket and pulled her close, then kissed her soundly. "I'm already missing you, that's all," she said when they parted.

"I'm not thrilled about being separated, either," Emery replied, wrapping her arms around Pasha's waist. "And not just because your power seems to be the best medicine on the planet." She gazed intently into Pasha's eyes. "But it's only temporary. As soon as I can, I'll be on the first plane back to Bettles. And even if Dita cancels every single trip, I'm not going anywhere any time soon. I need significantly more alone time with you."

Pasha's eyes grew moist. "For real?"

"Absolutely." Emery kissed her forehead. "I'm counting the minutes until I can take you up on our date."

"I hope—" Pasha froze. "Listen."

They both turned toward the faint, intermittent sound from the north. Definitely manmade. "Get the others!" she told Emery as she hurried to the signal fire and lit it.

By the time the helicopter came into view, they all stood outside, waving colored jackets and anything else they could find to draw attention to themselves—all but Skeeter, who'd been helped from the plane and lay on a sleeping bag on the snow. Pasha signaled with the mirror, apparently not needing to. The red-and-white chopper headed directly toward them, then circled above, its huge prop blowing up snow and ash as the pilot searched for a place to land.

"We need to evacuate you one at a time with a litter," a voice boomed through a bullhorn from the open side door. "Everyone step back, please. We're sending someone down." A crewmember dressed in an orange jumpsuit descended in the metal rescue basket.

Pasha and Karla headed toward him as he unstrapped himself and gave the pilot a thumbs-up.

"You guys are very lucky," he said, glancing over at the plane. "What do we have in terms of injuries?"

"I'm an RN. I have a broken arm, but Mike's worst off." Karla pointed to Skeeter. "He's got a serious leg infection, probable rib fractures, broken nose, possible concussion. Emery..." she pointed again, "says she's feeling better, but she needs to be examined for possible brain injury. She took a bad blow to the head and has a puncture wound in her abdomen. Ruth, there, wrenched her knee and should be x-rayed."

"We've got room for all of you," he said. "Bet you're more than ready to leave."

"You got that right," Pasha said.

It took more than an hour to load them all into the chopper. As they pulled away, Pasha looked down at the crash site and marveled anew that they'd all escaped alive.

"Bettles is on the way," the pilot called back to them. "We'll stop off to deliver the two uninjured before proceeding. We've called ahead and your people will meet you. We need the room because we have two more to evacuate en route to Fairbanks."

"I can't go with Ruth to the hospital?" Toni asked Pasha.

She shook her head. "Apparently not. I'd like to go, too. Maybe we can get Bryson to fly us down."

Emery, seated beside her, took her hand. "Nice if you can. I know it'd help get me out of there faster."

"This eruption keeping you guys busy?" Karla asked one of the rescue crew.

"Nonstop," he replied. "Nothing's getting out of Anchorage. A lot of planes were up when the plume came through and had to ditch."

"Any casualties?" Pasha asked.

The man nodded solemnly. "Our last run. Seven killed when a Cessna like yours hit the side of a mountain. Bodies unrecoverable."

He looked at their ragged group and smiled. "Wish you could've heard the cheer that went up in here when we spotted all of you out there waving. So many times, especially in winter, we don't get there in time."

"Did you pick up our ELT?" Skeeter asked.

He shook his head. "Signals have been bad with all this ash. Somebody name Dita called last night with your exact location."

"Bryson made it back, then," Pasha told the others. "I knew she would."

"We're almost there," the pilot announced. "Get ready. I'll touch down just long enough to drop you off."

"Take good care of yourself," Pasha told Emery as she clasped her hand in both of hers, "until I see you again."

"Count on it. I have a very important date." Emery looked into her eyes with such longing and regret, Pasha almost wept. The current of their connection surged with an intensity she felt in every pore of her being. Emery felt it too; she could see it in her expression.

Letting go of her was one of the hardest things Pasha had ever done.

Dita, Megan, and Geneva stood waiting at the edge of the runway and ran toward Pasha and Toni as soon as the helicopter lifted off again.

Geneva and Megan reached them first, nearly bowling them over in a group bear hug that Dita joined seconds later.

"We were so worried. Thank the Lord," Dita said. "You sure you're all right? How are the rest?"

"We're fine. Karla's worried about Skeeter's leg, and Emery may have a concussion, but I think they'll be okay." Pasha turned to Toni. "You were invaluable up there, Toni. I can't thank you enough."

"Certainly got a bit more adventure than I bargained for." Toni grinned. "Boy, do we have a story to tell, huh?"

"I bet you do," Megan said.

"We want to hear all about it," Geneva put in.

"I know you both probably want to shower, eat, and rest," Dita told them. "Grizz knows you're back early, Toni, and has a room waiting. When you're ready, come by the office. Of course I'll give you a full refund, plus credit for a future trip on me, if what happened hasn't completely scared you off."

"Not at all. Ruth and I already talked about coming back next year." Toni looked at Pasha. "But I was hoping we might get to Fairbanks today?"

"Me, too. Where's Bryson?" Pasha asked. She spotted the red Super Cub parked by the Eidson hangar.

"She's picking up Chaz's group," Dita replied. "I got in another plane for her. Not sure when they'll be back. They'll have to pack all their gear and everything."

"Great they'll be getting in today," Pasha said. "But I guess we're not going anywhere."

"You two need to rest," Geneva said.

"I second that," Dita said. "I plan to ground Bryson, too. I wasn't thrilled about her going on this run, but she insisted."

"In that case, I guess I'll go back to the Den." Toni stretched. "A hot shower sounds like heaven."

"I'll walk you back," Geneva said, and the two of them started off toward the roadhouse.

"I'm going to wait in the hangar out of the wind, until Chaz gets in." Megan gave Pasha another hug. "So glad you're back safe, Pash."

"Me, too. See you soon." She and Dita started toward the office.

"You're headed straight to bed, young lady." Dita wrapped one arm around Pasha's shoulder as they walked. "I don't want to see you until dinner, at the earliest. Unless you need me for something, of course."

"Any idea what all this means in terms of the rest of the summer? Future trips?" Pasha asked as they paused at the base of the stairs leading up to her apartment.

"Not yet. The volcano's still active, we're down a plane, and we've lost a fair amount of gear. I've already cancelled the next two trips, though I'm having trouble reaching some of the clients. I should have a better idea in a couple of weeks. Now go. Get some rest."

"You promise to call if you hear anything from the hospital?"

"You know I will."

Pasha soaked in a hot bath for a half hour, relishing the small comfort of being truly warm for the first time in days. The danger had passed, and with any luck, Emery would be here before she knew it, sharing this tub with her. *I'm not going anywhere any time soon. I need significantly more alone time with you,* Emery had promised.

She climbed into bed, daydreaming about their private reunion, and quickly fell asleep.

CHAPTER THIRTY-FOUR

Four days later, June 17

"Oh, my God, I'm in love," Geneva said as she delivered coffee and desserts to the corner booth. "Did you see her? The brunette at the bar?"

Dita, Karla, Megan, and Pasha all turned to look at the stunner.

"Who is she?" Pasha asked.

"Connie, from Texas. Gay, single, and moving up here to work at the rangers' station. Gotta go."

They all laughed as the music resumed.

Pasha found the Bettles Band, a ragtag group of local talent, in rare form tonight. Too bad about the nearly empty roadhouse. Normally this time of year, tourists packed the place. But the continued ashfall, along with the trip cancellations, had turned the village into a near ghost town. Toni had departed two days ago, when Ruth got out of the hospital, to join her on their flight back home, and the rest of the rafting clients had left, too.

In addition to the usual band members—Bryson on drums, Grizz on bass, Ellie on piano, and Lars Rasmussen on alto sax—Chaz sat in with her concertina, so they played a lot of jazz and Cajun zydeco.

"I've never heard Chaz play," Dita remarked. "She's really, really good."

"You've no idea," Megan replied, then giggled. "She has a lot of talents."

"I'd match Bryson against her any day in that department." Karla wedged a chopstick into the space between her cast and skin. "Damn but this thing itches like crazy."

Dita, Karla, and Megan had fun watching and listening to the group, but Pasha wouldn't be truly happy until Emery was out of the hospital and back in Bettles.

She'd had to spend so much time notifying clients and reworking schedules she hadn't made it to Fairbanks to see her, but she'd called every morning before work and every evening before she retired. This morning, Emery told her they wanted to keep her for observation for another couple of days, and Skeeter would have to stay even longer. Doctors had finally got his infection under control and he'd suffer no permanent damage, but the leg was healing slowly.

Pasha missed her connection with Emery with a gnawing hunger that grew exponentially each day. All of the blissful euphoria accompanying their touch had dissipated. Visiting with her friends distracted her from her misery and she tried to stay upbeat, but her mind kept drifting back to Emery.

In the middle of the band's second set, Pasha began to feel the power simmering. Was she imagining it? Before long, however, its current raged.

Almost involuntarily, she kept glancing toward the door, expecting Emery to materialize. What folly. Emery was in Fairbanks. Maybe her power had a different motive.

"Pash? Everything all right?" Karla asked. "You seem preoccupied."

"It's nothing. Really."

Dita studied her with an unreadable expression. "It's getting late. I'm sure you're just tired. Why don't you go home?"

She glanced at the clock. "Late? It's not even eight thirty yet. I'm not sleepy at all." She felt wired and restless because of the inexplicable power surge.

"You've been through a lot. Trust me." Dita slipped out of the booth. "Come on. I'm taking you home."

"But I'm not—"

"No arguments. Get your butt out here."

"As your resident medical professional, I concur with Dita," Karla said. "Go home, and go to bed. That's an order."

"What's up with you both?" Pasha asked. "Are you high or something? I *said* I'm fine."

"Dang but you're stubborn." Dita frowned. "Do I have to threaten to fire you?"

Megan started giggling, and both Dita and Karla immediately glared at her.

"What in the *hell*'s going on?" Pasha demanded.

"Should we tell her?" Karla asked.

"She'd kill us," Dita said.

"She'll kill us worse if she has to wait much longer." Megan giggled again.

Finally, she got a clue. "Emery's here?" Her voice emerged as an excited squeak, and they all roared with laughter.

Pasha flew out the door and ran home, taking the steps to her apartment two at a time. She tried the door—unlocked. Dita had an extra key. With the power so strong, Emery had to be inside.

She took a few deep breaths to calm her raging heart and turned the knob. The living room blazed with candlelight, and soft music emanated from her speakers. Sara Bareilles, the same album she'd been listening to, and singing along with, the first time she met Emery face-to-face a lifetime ago.

"Are you going to come in, or just stand there all night?"

Pasha turned in the direction of Emery's voice as she stepped forward and closed the door.

Emery stood in the doorway of her bedroom, watching her with a bemused expression. Her aura shone gold.

"You lied to me," Pasha said with no trace of rebuke.

"I wanted to surprise you, though I figured you'd know when I got in. Kind of hard to hide from your power." As Emery slowly closed the distance between them, the bemused look in her eyes became molten heat. "I've missed you like crazy."

Pasha flew into her arms, triggering a full-body shock of voltage that made them jump, then laugh as they hugged each other tight. And then they kissed, deep and passionate kisses conveying the depth of their desire. When they broke apart to breathe, she had to lean on Emery for support.

"Seems like I've wanted you forever. I haven't been able to think of anything else," Emery said. "Those days in the hospital just crawled."

"I've been running nonstop, but I thought about you just as much."

"By the way, I told Dita everything you did for us, and she happily obliged me with a small favor," Emery said. "You have the day off tomorrow to stay in bed with me."

"Mmm. I like the sound of that." Pasha drew back from their embrace to look up at her. "Are you well enough?"

"Clean bill of health. The doctors were amazed, actually, at how quickly I've healed. They just kept me as a precaution." Emery kissed her again. "Nothing's stopping us now, Pasha. We have all the time in the world."

As Emery put her arm around Pasha and led her into the bedroom, Pasha felt a pang of bittersweet longing. They didn't have all the time in the world. Emery was still only a temporary fixture in her life and would move on. If not next week or next month, certainly too soon.

She wouldn't, however, let that realization mar the happiness of this moment.

Emery had placed candles around the bedroom as well and set a bottle of wine in an ice bucket on her dresser beside two goblets. Though Pasha had made the bed before she'd left, Emery had folded back the sheets invitingly.

"Nervous?" she asked as she took Pasha into her arms beside the bed.

"Excited, not nervous. Well, maybe a little. You?"

"I'm nervous about my scars. There's a lot you haven't seen."

"Emery, Emery, Emery." She made the kind of tsk-tsk sound a parent makes with a naughty child. "I thought we'd talked about that." Very slowly, she reached beneath Emery's turtleneck, caressing her abdomen and sides as she pulled the garment up and over her head. Then she gently kissed the scar at Emery's throat. "These are part of who you are. You don't have anything to be nervous about."

She ran her fingers lightly over the thin pale lines that marred the smooth skin of her abdomen as she openly admired Emery's breasts, framed by a lace-edged, crème, satin bra barely covering her nipples. "God, you're beautiful." Her fingers found a slight roughness, and when she glanced down, she marveled at how well the puncture wound had healed—now just a faint red mark about the size of a dime.

"You have any idea what you're doing to me?" Emery asked, her voice husky with desire.

"I have an idea of what I'd *like* to do to you, but it involves far less clothes for both of us." Pasha started to unbuckle Emery's belt, but Emery stopped her.

"Me first."

Pasha acceded with a smile. As Emery removed her boots, socks, jeans, top, and finally bra and panties, the growing ardor in her eyes warmed Pasha.

"Amazing." Emery's loud, ragged breathing was audible.

"My turn." Pasha unfastened Emery's jeans and slowly unzipped the fly seductively, then playfully pushed Emery down onto the bed. After she removed Emery's boots and socks, she grasped the cuffs of the jeans and tugged.

Emery lifted her hips to allow the jeans to slide off and away to reveal thick scars badly marring her lean, softly muscled legs in several places. Emery watched her expectantly and whispered, "What are you thinking?"

"Only that I wish I could have been there for you through all this." Pasha caressed the scars lightly as she climbed up onto the bed, hovering over Emery on her hands and knees. "I couldn't be more turned on right now, Emery, if that's what *you're* thinking."

The niggling doubt in Emery's eyes evaporated, leaving only intense arousal. She pulled Pasha down on top of her and captured her mouth with her own, probing deeply with her tongue. Pasha kissed her fiercely as Emery's thigh slipped between her legs and rocked against her.

Pasha's heartbeat accelerated and her mind slipped into a fog, overcome with the sensations pouring through her body, both from arousal and the current of their connection. Her senses, especially her sense of touch, were so painfully heightened she was afraid she would come too soon.

With a groan, she pulled away, breathing hard, her chest pounding. "Get these off," she demanded, pulling at Emery's lace panties.

Emery sat up and obligingly shed her bra and panties, then they crawled beneath the sheets and Emery covered Pasha with her body.

"Do you feel it?" Emery asked, her face inches from Pasha's as they gazed into each other's eyes. "It's incredible, but I can't describe it. Your power's doing this, isn't it? Heightening everything a hundredfold."

"I feel it, Emery. But it's not just the power. I've never felt like this with anyone else. It's my power combined with your energy or something. It's *us*, not just me."

"I can't get enough of it." Emery kissed her again and their naked bodies melted together.

Every inch of Pasha's flesh that touched Emery's came alive, the nerve endings singing with joy and arousal. She could feel herself grow wet as Emery deepened the kiss and began to rock against her, their legs entwined. The pressure for release built until it was unbearable. She broke the kiss. "Please, Emery, I'm so wet. Touch me."

"I know. I can feel how close you are." Emery kissed her neck, nipping softly on the delicate skin. She shifted her body and moved lower with more kisses until her mouth closed over Pasha's left nipple and sucked.

A bolt of pleasure tore through Pasha and her muscles went rigid, her back arching off the bed as she moaned. She gripped the sheets when Emery moved to give equal attention to her right nipple, so close to climax she needed only a bit more stimulation to push her over.

Emery seemed to sense that, too, because she continued moving down Pasha's body until she reached the juncture of her thighs. She inhaled deeply as she looked up at Pasha, her pupils huge. "I love how you smell. How you feel. How you move." She claimed Pasha with her mouth, teasing her with her tongue. "And how you taste."

Pasha thrilled at the exquisite agony of trying to prolong her pleasure, but she was powerless against the magic of Emery's tongue. She cried out as she crested and collapsed back against the bed, reeling from the magnitude of her orgasm.

Emery crawled back up the bed and curled protectively around her until Pasha's heart calmed and her breathing slowed to near normal. "Intense, huh?"

"You could feel that?" Pasha asked.

"Sense, more than feel. I can't explain it."

"I think," Pasha said as she rolled Emery on to her back, "that we should just enjoy it."

"I'm all for that," Emery said, grinning up at her.

Pasha put her mouth beside Emery's ear. "Tell me what you want," she whispered seductively.

"Everything you do is wonderful. Every touch, every word, every nuance of the way you move. I'm so pent-up right now from feeling you come that it won't take much."

"No?" Pasha kissed Emery below her ear, then at the base of her throat, circling the prominent scar with the tip of her tongue. "Never rush the sweetest things in life, Emery. Savor them." She worked Emery higher with delicate kisses and nips, exploring her body with her mouth. Collarbone. Magnificent breasts. Flat abdomen. When she reached a scar, she moved over it lightly with her tongue, often eliciting a groan of pleasure from Emery.

She took her time with her teasing touches until Emery's muscles grew taut and the power told her orgasm was imminent. Parting Emery's legs, she delivered her with fevered strokes of her tongue, her arms clasped around Emery's thighs.

They curled together, Pasha snuggling into the crook of Emery's shoulder in a reverse of their positions in the plane. Beneath her cheek, she could feel the strong pounding of Emery's heart begin to calm. Neither spoke for several minutes.

Emery broke the quiet. "Could I stay here with you? Move out of the Den, I mean?"

"I meant to ask you to, but wasn't sure you'd want to."

"Silly girl. Who wouldn't want this?"

Who wouldn't indeed? Pasha thought. This was heaven on earth. She never wanted to move. But Emery would, one day. Probably one day soon. Living together until then would make their parting all the more impossible. Her eyes grew moist and she blinked to keep from crying.

"Pasha? What's wrong?"

"Nothing."

"Tell me."

"I don't want to ruin this moment."

"You can't. Impossible. Tell me."

Pasha caressed Emery's stomach. "I'll miss you, that's all… when you leave here and go off bungee-jumping and God knows what else on the other side of the planet. I know it's stupid to think about such things right now. I should be fully in the moment, not worrying about the future."

Regardless of what Emery might do or think about what she said, Pasha had to speak from her heart. She rose on one elbow and looked down at Emery. "I've believed, from the first moment I saw you, Emery, we're destined to be together. Not just for a few weeks, or months, but always. Getting to know you only strengthened my belief. And now, after making love? I'm so hopelessly in love with you I can't bear the thought of being apart from you."

Emery pulled Pasha close and hugged her fiercely, Pasha's words reverberating through her mind, soul, and body. The current shooting through her was even more powerful than her orgasm, making her boneless with joy and filling the hollow emptiness with her since birth.

Being in love felt like this? She marveled. Suddenly all those stupid love songs made sense, and all her illusions about herself drifted away.

Her epiphany in the hospital during her long recovery—to change her life, chase her dreams—seemed minor league compared to the revelation that she loved Pasha so completely she couldn't fathom life without her.

"When I checked out of the hospital in Sofia," Emery said, "the doctors told me I'd never be a hundred percent. They said I'd defied all odds just by walking and would have to rely on painkillers the rest of my life just to do normal things. I didn't believe them, not until months passed and nothing changed. I'd plateaued in my healing, but I didn't want to admit it." She lightly stroked Pasha's back. "Then I met you, my little miracle worker. You don't have to convince me we belong together. When I'm with you, I forget all the pain. Not just the physical kind, either, but the emotional kind—the pain of knowing I'm different from everybody else, incapable of love."

"What are you saying?" Pasha asked.

"I can't be without you. And I'm so glad to finally know what it's like to fall in love. I'm crazy about you, Pasha. Surely you know that?"

Pasha answered with a passionate kiss, the prelude to another round of passion that lasted well into the night.

Hours later, Emery dozed briefly, and when she awoke, the other side of the bed was empty. "Pasha?"

"In the kitchen. You hungry?"

"Starved."

"Midnight snack coming right up."

Emery's idea of a late-night snack was potato chips, maybe, or a bowl of ice cream. Pasha's was a gourmet omelet with bacon, herbs, and aged Gouda cheese, served on a tray with fresh-squeezed orange juice and some of the Den's homemade sourdough toast.

"So, any idea where we go from here?" Pasha asked as they fed each other playfully.

"I've been thinking about that," Emery said. "Here's my idea. We stay here through the high season—say, April or May through October, right?"

Pasha nodded.

"November to March, we travel. Together. Do all the things on my itinerary. Well, except maybe for the bungee jumping and cliff diving and a couple of other things too ambitious for my battered body. Which, by the way, is feeling ever so splendid right now."

"I'd love to, but—"

"But?"

"Dita would give me the time off. We don't have much to do over the winter and will have a part-timer beginning soon, anyway. But I can't afford it, Emery. I mean, I have some savings, sure. But airfare these days—"

"I guess I forgot to tell you I have something like six-million frequent-flier miles," Emery said. "Which will keep us in first-class tickets for a long, long time. And you'd be surprised how cheap you can see the world if you're willing to settle for a clean bed instead of a four-star hotel, and have a baguette and brie for lunch instead of steak. So, you game?"

Pasha pounced on her with a kiss.

"Whoa!" Emery juggled the tray to keep the juice from spilling. "Don't be wasting this omelet. I take it that's a yes?"

"An absolutely, positively ecstatic yes." Pasha took another forkful of omelet and held it up toward Emery's mouth. "I can't wait to see where we're—" Suddenly, she blanched white and dropped the fork, her mouth a large circle.

"What is it? What's wrong?"

With shaking hands, Pasha wordlessly got a mirror from her bedside table. "You want more evidence we belong together?" She held it up in front of Emery's face.

The scar beside Emery's lip had vanished.

EPILOGUE

Sofia, Bulgaria
Eight months later, February 2012

"Give me your hand?" Emery said as the taxi started away from the curb.

"We can turn around. You don't have to do this." Pasha had sensed Emery's unease and trepidation building as soon as they got off the flight from Moscow, but it began to calm with her touch.

"No. This…" Emery squeezed her hand. "Is all I need."

Pasha had been surprised when Emery said she wanted to stop in Sofia on the way to their Kenyan safari. She rarely talked about her accident. And when she did, she always had nightmares that could only be assuaged by spooning closely. The experience clearly still haunted her.

In the three months they'd been traveling since the trip season ended, they'd visited twenty-four countries on four continents, stayed in countless hotels, and seen more of the world's wonders than Pasha had imagined she'd encounter in her lifetime. Each and every place had been a treasure, the joy of discovery redoubled by sharing it with Emery, her soul mate and the world's best traveling companion. She had no idea Emery had studied so many languages until she saw her in action, and Emery always seemed to know where to find the perfect romantic restaurant or quaint café, no matter where they went.

But Emery had never gotten on an elevator. Not once. Sometimes they really had to go out of their way to avoid them. The upside was they had learned to travel extremely light, shedding clothes when they needed to and replacing them with new. And taking all those stairs had given Pasha legs of steel and a stamina she'd never known.

Emery had said, "I need to do this. I never thought I'd be able to. But I think I can, if you're with me. I need the closure. It's the only thing I'm afraid of…aside from losing you."

And Pasha sensed she was ready, despite the simmering undercurrent of terror emanating from Emery's hand. The healing power of their connection had transformed her in ways neither of them could have imagined. She hadn't taken a single pain pill since the first night they'd made love. She didn't walk up the stairs. She ran. And, most astounding, the scars had faded from her body, even the round, rough one at the base of her throat, which had taken the longest.

"We're nearly there," Emery said as they passed over yellow-cobblestone streets, the tires of the taxi making a soft thump-thump-thump that sounded like Emery's racing heart.

Pasha put her arm around Emery's shoulder, closed her eyes, and pushed her power into her lover.

It had become more focused, more intense, as if Emery's energy fed it. Pasha had begun to learn how to use it to see things more clearly, to sense when they might be in danger, and to direct its healing warmth into Emery when she needed it.

"Thanks, love," Emery whispered.

The taxi stopped in front of an upscale hotel, the Arena di Serdica, as snow began to fall.

Emery pulled out some levs and paid the driver. "Wait, please. We won't be long."

He nodded in understanding.

Emery got out curbside and extended her hand. Pasha slid over the seat and took it.

They stood in front for a full minute, holding hands, with Emery staring up at the top floor.

The anxiety emanating from Emery had abated significantly from her focused power infusion, and it calmed further while they stood there, until it became a fragment of its former self.

"Let's go." Emery tightened her grip on Pasha's hand and led her purposefully into the building, through the lobby past a confused-looking concierge, and straight to the elevator, where she punched the Up button.

The door opened immediately. The car was empty.

Emery hesitated, then looked at Pasha. "No bad vibes?"

"All good, babe. I'm right here."

They got in, and Emery pushed the button for the eighth floor, the highest one.

Classical music wafted around them as they rode silently to the top.

The door opened.

Emery pushed the Lobby button.

The door closed and they descended, got off, and returned to the cab.

Halfway back to the airport, Emery smiled and turned to her. "Ready to go see some lions?"

The End

About the Author

Award-winning author Kim Baldwin has been a writer for three decades, following up twenty years as an executive in network news with a second vocation penning lesbian fiction. She has published six other solo novels with Bold Strokes Books, in addition to *High Impact*: the intrigue/romances *Flight Risk* and *Hunter's Pursuit* and the romances *Force of Nature, Whitewater Rendezvous, Breaking the Ice,* and *Focus of Desire.* She has also published four books in the Elite Operatives Series in collaboration with Xenia Alexiou: *Lethal Affairs, Thief of Always, Missing Lynx,* and *Dying to Live.* The fifth book in the seven-book series, *Demons are Forever,* is forthcoming March 2012.

Kim has also narrated an audiobook version of *Breaking the Ice,* and her works have been translated into Russian, Dutch, and Spanish.

In addition to her full-length work, Kim has contributed short stories to six BSB anthologies: *Stolen Moments: Erotic Interludes 2, Lessons in Love: Erotic Interludes 3, Extreme Passions: Erotic Interludes 4, Road Games: Erotic Interludes 5, Romantic Interludes 1: Discovery,* and *Romantic Interludes 2: Secrets.* She lives in the north woods of Michigan, but takes to the road with her laptop and camera whenever possible. Her Web site is www.kimbaldwin.com and she can be reached at baldwinkim@gmail.com.

Books Available From Bold Strokes Books

High Impact by Kim Baldwin. Thrill seeker Emery Lawson and Adventure Outfitter Pasha Dunn learn you can never truly appreciate what's important and what you're capable of until faced with a sudden and stark reminder of your own mortality. (978-1-60282-580-2)

Snowbound by Cari Hunter. "The policewoman got shot and she's bleeding everywhere. Get someone here in one hour or I'm going to put her out of her misery." It's an ultimatum that will forever change the lives of police officer Sam Lucas and Dr. Kate Myles. (978-1-60282-581-9)

Rescue Me by Julie Cannon. Tyler Logan reluctantly agrees to pose as the girlfriend of her in-the-closet gay BFF at his company's annual retreat, but she didn't count on falling for Kristin, the boss's wife. (978-1-60282-582-6)

Murder in the Irish Channel by Greg Herren. Chanse MacLeod investigates the disappearance of a female activist fighting the Archdiocese of New Orleans and a powerful real estate syndicate. (978-1-60282-584-0)

Franky Gets Real by Mel Bossa. A four day getaway. Five childhood friends. Five shattering confessions…and a forgotten love unearthed. (978-1-60282-585-7)

Riding the Rails: Locomotive Lust and Carnal Cabooses edited by Jerry Wheeler. Some of the hottest writers of gay erotica spin tales of Riding the Rails. (978-1-60282-586-4)

Sheltering Dunes by Radclyffe. The seventh in the award-winning Provincetown Tales. The pasts, presents, and futures of three women collide in a single moment that will alter all their lives forever. (978-1-60282-573-4)

Holy Rollers by Rob Byrnes. Partners in life and crime, Grant Lambert and Chase LaMarca assemble a team of gay and lesbian criminals to steal millions from a right-wing mega-church, but the gang's plans are complicated by an "ex-gay" conference, the FBI, and a corrupt reverend with his own plans for the cash. (978-1-60282-578-9)

History's Passion: Stories of Sex Before Stonewall, edited by Richard Labonté. Four acclaimed erotic authors re-imagine the past...Welcome to the hidden queer history of men loving men not so very long—and centuries—ago. (978-1-60282-576-5)

Lucky Loser by Yolanda Wallace. Top tennis pros Sinjin Smythe and Laure Fortescue reach Wimbledon desperate to claim tennis's crown jewel, but will their feelings for each other get in the way? (978-1-60282-575-8)

Mystery of The Tempest: A Fisher Key Adventure by Sam Cameron. Twin brothers Denny and Steven Anderson love helping people and fighting crime alongside their sheriff dad on sun-drenched Fisher Key, Florida, but Denny doesn't dare tell anyone he's gay, and Steven has secrets of his own to keep. (978-1-60282-579-6)

Better Off Red: Vampire Sorority Sisters Book 1 by Rebekah Weatherspoon. Every sorority has its secrets, and college freshman Ginger Carmichael soon discovers that her pledge is more than a bond of sisterhood—it's a lifelong pact to serve six bloodthirsty demons with a lot more than nutritional needs. (978-1-60282-574-1)

Detours by Jeffrey Ricker. Joel Patterson is heading to Maine for his mother's funeral, and his high school friend Lincoln has invited himself along on the ride—and into Joel's bed—but when the ghost of Joel's mother joins the trip, the route is likely to be anything but straight. (978-1-60282-577-2)

Three Days by L.T. Marie. In a town like Vegas where anything can happen, Shawn and Dakota find that the stakes are love at all costs, and it's a gamble neither can afford to lose. (978-1-60282-569-7)

Swimming to Chicago by David-Matthew Barnes. As the lives of the adults around them unravel, high school students Alex and Robby form an unbreakable bond, vowing to do anything to stay together—even if it means leaving everything behind. (978-1-60282-572-7)

Hostage Moon by AJ Quinn. Hunter Roswell thought she had left her past behind, until a serial killer begins stalking her. Can FBI profiler Sara Wilder help her find her connection to the killer before he strikes on blood moon? (978-1-60282-568-0)

Erotica Exotica: Tales of Sex, Magic, and the Supernatural, edited by Richard Labonté. Today's top gay erotica authors offer sexual thrills and perverse arousal, spooky chills, and magical orgasms in these stories exploring arcane mystery, supernatural seduction, and sex that haunts in a manner both weird and wondrous. (978-1-60282-570-3)

Blue by Russ Gregory. Matt and Thatcher find themselves in the crosshairs of a psychotic killer stalking gay men in the streets of Austin, and only a 103-year-old nursing home resident holds the key to solving the murders—but can she give up her secrets in time to save them? (978-1-60282-571-0)

Balance of Forces: Toujours Ici by Ali Vali. Immortal Kendal Richoux's life began during the reign of Egypt's only female pharaoh, and history has taught her the dangers of getting too close to anyone who hasn't harnessed the power of time, but as she prepares for the most important battle of her long life, can she resist her attraction to Piper Marmande? (978-1-60282-567-3)

Wings: Subversive Gay Angel Erotica, edited by Todd Gregory. A collection of powerfully written tales of passion and desire centered on the aching beauty of angels. (978-1-60282-565-9)

Contemporary Gay Romances by Felice Picano. These works of short fiction from legendary novelist and memoirist Felice Picano are as different from any standard "romances" as you can get, but they will linger in the mind and memory. (978-1-60282-639-7)

Pirate's Fortune: Supreme Constellations Book Four by Gun Brooke. Set against the backdrop of war, captured mercenary Weiss Kyakh is persuaded to work undercover with bio-android Madisyn Pimm, which foils her plans to escape, but kindles unexpected love. (978-1-60282-563-5)

Sex and Skateboards by Ashley Bartlett. Sex and skateboards and surfing on the California coast. What more could anyone want? Alden McKenna thinks that's all she needs, until she meets Weston Duvall. (978-1-60282-562-8)

Waiting in the Wings by Melissa Brayden. Jenna has spent her whole life training for the stage, but the one thing she didn't prepare for was Adrienne. Is she ready to sacrifice what she's worked so hard for in exchange for a shot at something much deeper? (978-1-60282-561-1)

Suite Nineteen by Mel Bossa. Psychic Ben Lebeau moves into Shilts Manor, where he meets seductive Lennox Van Kemp and his clan of Métis—guardians of a spiritual conspiracy dating back to Christ. But are Ben's psychic abilities strong enough to save him? (978-1-60282-564-2)

Speaking Out: LGBTQ Youth Stand Up, edited by Steve Berman. Inspiring stories written for and about LGBTQ teens of overcoming adversity (against intolerance and homophobia) and experiencing life after "coming out." (978-1-60282-566-6)

Forbidden Passions by MJ Williamz. Passion burns hotter when it's forbidden, and the fire between Katie Prentiss and Corrine Staples in antebellum Louisiana is raging out of control. (978-1-60282-641-0)

Harmony by Karis Walsh. When Brook Stanton meets a beautiful musician who threatens the security of her conventional, predetermined future, will she take a chance on finding the harmony only love creates? (978-1-60282-237-5)